A Knight to Remember

Brid

Press

Other Books by Bridget Essex

The Longing
Date Knight
A Dark and Stormy Knight
Just One Knight
Forever and a Knight
Cry Wolf
Love Spell: Tales of Love and Desire
Beauty and the Wolf
Under Her Spell
The Protector
Raised by Wolves
Meeting Eternity (The Sullivan Vampires, Vol. 1)
Trusting Eternity (The Sullivan Vampires, Vol. 2)
Wolf Pack
The Guardian Angel
Holiday Wolf Pack
Don't Say Goodbye
Wolf Town
Dark Angel
Big, Bad Wolf
The Vampire Next Door (with Natalie Vivien)

Erotica

Wild
Come Home, I Need You

About the Author

My name is Bridget Essex, and I write love stories. Many are about werewolves, vampires and lady knights; but always, they're about two strong, courageous women who fall deeply in love with one another, living love stories that transcend time. I'm married to the love of my life, author Natalie Vivien.

I'm best known for my Knight Legends series, stories about women knights, real world hi-jinks and love stories that are out of this world. My Sullivan Vampire novellas are a popular series lauded as "TWILIGHT for women who love women," and I have several other series and stand-alone novellas, and I'm always putting out something new.

Together with my beautiful wife, we live in a little fairy tale cottage in Pittsburgh, and take care of several furry children who we love with all our hearts. ♥

Find out more about my work at
www.LesbianRomance.org and
http://BridgetEssex.Wordpress.com

A Knight to Remember
Copyright © 2014 Bridget Essex - All Rights Reserved
Published by Rose and Star Press
First edition, July 2014

ISBN-13: 978-1977958792
ISBN-10: 1977958796

A Knight to Remember

DEDICATION

For my own lady knight in shining armor — who, instead of a sword, wields a pen. I love you and every adventure we've shared together. Here's to countless more.

And this book is especially dedicated to Mrs. P. Thank you for always handing me a stack of books and for listening. Without your humbling kindness, I would never have become a writer. You changed my life for the good, and I'm grateful.

Chapter 1: The Beginning of the End

Everyone but me loves a Renaissance Festival.
I mean, how can I not, right? At the Ren Faire, you can get gigantic turkey legs on sticks, watch "wenches" wrestling in the mud while yelling medieval insults at each other and see gigantic, gorgeous horses bedecked in colorful armor carrying jousting knights (who also yell medieval insults at each other, but are usually a little less covered in mud). I mean, I know this might not sound like everyone's cup of tea, but it was certainly mine.

I *used* to look forward to July more than any other time of the year, because July was when the Knights of Valor Festival would pull up in its creaking, rusted train cars and set up in a little local dog park on the edge of Boston for a few weeks in July and the beginning of August. I'd get all dressed in traditional wench wear (which basically means that my chest was *almost* entirely visible in my daringly low cut white "wench blouse"), spend all of my money on overpriced fried food and hand-made artisanal soap, yell "huzzah!" approximately eighty thousand times, and generally be the happiest person in the world.

But this was all before Nicole. Or "BN," as Carly loves to put it.

I sigh as we pull into the parking lot that has been set up on the very edge of the dog park. Before us spreads out the chaotic brightly colored tents of the festival. I can already see one of the large horses—bedecked in purple and gold ribbons dangling from his halter—being shoed by a traditional blacksmith behind one of the largest tents, and the scent of turkey legs is already pumping in through the car vents. Somewhere distantly, I can hear lute music. All of this should spell happiness. But my best friend Carly puts the car into park, switches off the ignition, and savagely rips the cap off of her lipstick and starts to apply it.

Carly silently applying lipstick means that Carly is angry. Carly pretty much *never* does anything silently.

"You know…" I begin, licking my lips. I clear my throat. "You know, it might actually be fun today," I tell Carly, who's still glowering at her reflection in the rearview mirror. She snaps the cap back on her "Vixen-Red" lipstick and stares at me with one perfectly manicured eyebrow raised.

"Right. Because it's been just *so much fun* the past four years," she snorts, pushing up her visor with a roll of her eyes that's so hard, the force of her sarcasm practically melts the steering wheel.

"Carly…you don't have to come with us," I murmur, scrunching down in the passenger seat, shoulders hunched forward as my tiny bit of hope gets squashed. I know she doesn't mean for it to hurt, but it does. I mean, I wish it wasn't like this, too, but…

"Hey. *Hey*," sighs Carly, glancing sidelong at me. "Look—you're my best friend in this entire universe, and several parallel dimensions, okay?" She holds my gaze for a long moment as she reaches across the space between us and squeezes my hand tightly. "I would march with you to hell and back if it's where you wanted to go on summer vacation." Her eyes narrow. "But I'm *also* allowed to think that your girlfriend is an *asshole* if, you know, *she actually is.*" Carly pulls down the visor again and stabs another bobby pin through her tight red curls and slightly-drooping flower crown.

"I mean, *asshole*'s a little harsh," I begin, but then there's a sharp rap at my window.

And speak of the devil...there's Nicole.

When Nicole told me, a few nights ago, that Carly and I should go to the festival together, and she'd meet us there on her way home from work, I'd had my doubts she was even going to show up at all. I mean, I think it's safe to say that the Renaissance Festival isn't exactly her scene. But no—I was wrong. She's *here.*

As I stare up at her through the window, at her bright blue eyes that stare deeply into mine for half a heartbeat, I wonder if this means I've been wrong about other things. She *tried* this time. That counts for something.

But my girlfriend, the girlfriend I've been with for four years, doesn't exactly look happy to see me. Yes, her gaze flicks to mine for that heartbeat, but then those piercing eyes are trained back onto her cell phone. Nicole's standing outside of the car in her blue power suit with the crisp creases in the legs, soft black briefcase dangling from her bright red fingertips, smart phone in the process of becoming glued to her ear already. And she's frowning deeply, her full lips curling down at the corners. She turns away from me, speaking sharply into the phone.

I hold tightly to my door handle, take a deep breath and open it. No matter what, at least she's *here,* right?

"Asshole," Carly repeats quietly to me, and then we're both out of the car, standing on the grass of the "parking lot."

Nicole doesn't even look up at me, hasn't greeted me, hasn't even grunted in acknowledgment that I'm here. We haven't gotten a chance to ask each other how work was, because we don't really do that anymore. And I know—my day at the library wasn't all that exciting, really, but still. I did survive another day cataloging the gigantic endowment left by Mrs. Herschel. The most exciting thing that happened was my eating a peanut butter and jelly sandwich that I'd left in the library lunchroom for two weeks and then found miraculously when I moved the discarded magazines off the table. The sandwich was still tasty, and I didn't die from food poisoning. And if Nicole could unglue the smart phone from her ear for a moment, wipe off the purely disgusted look she has on her face when she glances at the row of people dressed to the nines in period garb, already making their way into the festival, I could tell her that story about my sandwich. Or at least tell her "hello."

But she doesn't unglue the smart phone from her ear. She doesn't look my way as she sneers into her phone.

She doesn't want to be here. It's obvious. So painfully obvious.

I realize, my gut clenching, tension rushing through me already, that I honestly wish she hadn't come at all.

"David says he'll be here shortly," says Carly, glancing down at the phone in her hand when it makes its bicycle bell sound to alert her to his text message. When she says the name "David," her voice goes all gooey, like she's been eating cotton candy, and I grin sidelong at her, folding my arms in front of me and leaning against the side of her badly rusted Ford Escort. I'm glad Carly has David. They're good people, and he's a good guy, and she really deserves a good guy.

And hey, at least two people in our group of four are going to have a good time today.

I sneak a glance at Nicole. She's turned completely away from us now, brandishing her hand as she shakes her head sharply, practically seething into the phone.

Awkward silence crushes us in place for five minutes as Nicole works on her phone, continuing to mutter short, sharp phrases into it until I shift uncomfortably against the car and clear my throat. Nicole holds up a finger, her other hand furiously pressing at the screen of the smart phone as she ends another call.

"This is important..." she mutters, and then puts it up to her ear, walking away down the line of cars. She *still* hasn't looked at me. "Jeff?" she says crisply into the smart phone as she raises her chin, her eyes flashing. "Yes, this is Nicole Harken..." She stalks quickly away from us, down the staggered line of cars parked on the grass.

"Okay, seriously, Holly—why are you two still together?" asks Carly then in frustration. Her extremely curly red hair is blowing in a slight wind, her eyes are narrowed as she stares at me, and even though I really, *really* didn't want to have this conversation (again) today, I'm struck by how dramatic she looks. The wind is actually blowing through her hair quite briskly, like she's on the set of a fantasy movie and about to go into battle...and not asking me painful personal questions. I clear my throat, shift my weight against her car and purposefully look away, my mouth suddenly dry. But she doesn't let up. *"Holly..."* Carly murmurs, stepping forward, looping one of her arms through mine tightly. *"You could be so happy.* I promise you, have I ever steered you wrong?"

I glance up at her, already feeling the lump in my throat as I swallow again. I just wanted to have a nice evening at the Renaissance Festival. I breathe out. "Well," I say, trying to crack a joke, "there was that one time in college—"

"Okay, *whatever,* we were in college. Stop bringing up the Bunny Disaster, would you?" she chuckles, but then pins me in her gaze again. "C'mon, Holly, serious time, okay? I've seen you happy. I've seen you with ladies that are *really* good for you, and I can tell you, as your best friend and person who's had a lot of experience seeing you through your highs and lows, Nicole is a definite, *definite* low. You're not a good match, and it needs to end. I mean, you *want* it to end, so why are you dragging this out? Just dump her. She doesn't care about you. We've been over this a thousand times—" she groans.

I disengage Carly's arm from mine quickly (and with a hope that Nicole actually *didn't* hear us) as Nicole turns and stalks back toward Carly's car, phone smoothly tucked into her suit pocket. "Hello," she finally tells me, but the word is cut off and curt, and she merely nods her head to Carly, and then smiles a little at me, though it's strained. She looks around, her long fingers nervously patting the suit pocket where she just, seconds before, deposited her phone, like she can hardly function without that device in her hand. "Anyway, ladies, where's David? I can only stay here maybe a half hour, hour tops—there's an account that I have to—"

"Look, *Nicole*, it costs fifteen bucks to get in," says Carly, voice sharp as she curls her shoulders forward toward Nicole, her hackles obviously rising. "You're just going to waste fifteen bucks on a half hour? Holly's been looking forward to this for—"

"Carly, stop," I mutter, voice quiet. Nicole's eyebrows are both up, and she stands with her feet apart, high heels beginning to sink into the turf beneath them, so that she sort of bends backwards, trying to maintain her balance.

"Look, this wasn't the best day for me. I had to clear my schedule when I had *no time* to do so, and my assistant Mikaylah is working double-time," says Nicole, words just as sharp as Carly's. "I'm closing a new account that's taken me *months*, and—"

"Well, this happens to be your *girlfriend's* favorite day of the *year*. Or it *was*," Carly hisses, and I gulp down air and am about to interject (or possibly fling myself between them) when I see David walking down the row of cars toward us, waving his empty flagon in the air (I see he brought the one with the axe on the side. David, in fact, has several flagons) with a very happy grin.

And, just like that, the spell is broken. Carly's not paying attention to Nicole anymore—she's running toward David with an equally happy grin on her face. Relief rushes through me.

God, things have been so tense lately. Tense between Nicole and me…tense between Carly and Nicole. I run a hand through my hair and swallow as we begin to walk after them.

"Half an hour," Nicole mutters to me as David

falls in line with Carly, and I fall in line with her as we make our way toward the brightly painted ticket turret. I reach across the space between us to take Nicole's hand, but she snatches it away as her pocket vibrates, and then she slides her hand into the pocket, and that damnable phone is in her grasp again. She's got her jaw set as she leans away from me, and it looks like she's permanently glued that phone to her ear.

Carly's wrong. Nicole's not an asshole. I know I'm her girlfriend, I'm kind of biased—who really wants to think their partner is an asshole? But I promise you: she isn't. She's just preoccupied and very, very busy, and that doesn't make her an asshole. But it makes me wish...

Well. Wish for what exactly? Nicole and I have been together four years. In the beginning? God, in the beginning, we were *great* together. There was a point about three years ago that I really thought that Nicole was the woman I'd spend the rest of my life with.

So our relationship didn't start out like this...hardly ever talking anymore, me being pushed to the back burner so that she could grow her business. Over time, we sort of fell out of the new love romance. You know the kind—the sappy, warm, sexy wonderfulness that people say never lasts when you get into a new relationship and that other person is literally all you can think about.

But I'd like to be thought of at least *sometimes*.

Sometimes, I wish I could fix it—use some sort of magic potion that would make all of the responsibilities at her start-up company sort of dissolve into a pile of goo I could mop up and dispose of. But I know I can't. In the beginning, our relationship was really important to both of us. But then Nicole stopped remembering things like dates we were supposed to go on, showing up at my house when she said she would, skipping dinners that we were supposed to make for each other. She kept blaming these absences and forgetfulness on her company, but all of the signs were there, staring me right in the face. It was obvious that she wasn't invested in us anymore. And it's been obvious for awhile.

I know we have to break up, and I think Nicole knows it, too.

We're just putting off the inevitable.

Four years? That's a long time. A long time and a pretty big relationship investment. And, frankly, a great big percentage of your heart, after all.

Right now, we're still together because it's comfortable. There's so much of her stuff at my place, and so much of my stuff at her place, and it's just so damn messy. Everything's *so* damn messy.

I shake myself out of my melancholy (or, at the very least, try to), as we approach the ticket turret. I pay for both Nicole and I when it's our turn in line, the "wench" behind the counter leaning forward and winking at me as she hands me my change, because she winks at *everyone*. I *know* she's paid to wink at everyone, but I still make a sidelong glance quickly to Nicole to see if she even noticed. But nope. Still chatting away on her cell phone as I slip her ticket into her hand. She crumples it and slides it into her pocket, mouthing to me "five seconds" as she turns away and stalks quickly into the festival, moving apart from us.

Carly shoots daggers at Nicole, reaching back and looping her arm through mine as she tugs me forward. "Okay," she smiles encouragingly at me.

"What do we want to do first?" she asks, as we walk into the festival.

I take a deep breath, inhaling the scent of horse (we're close to the jousting "arena"), leather and frying turkey legs that permeates the air. Incense is lingering in the air because we're close to the lady who hand rolls incense and makes her own soap. I let my thoughts settle, try to calm my heart, soften the little bolt of pain that keeps twisting when I hear Nicole's voice rise above the "huzzahs!" behind us, talking about accounts and dollar figures and how sorry she is that it's so difficult to hear her because she was "roped into this thing" she "couldn't get out of."

She actually says that.

The pain cuts me sharply. I think she thinks she's far enough back that I can't hear her, or that there's too much chaos for me to make out her words. But I hear them anyway.

"Let's just go to the first show," I mutter to Carly, glancing down at the festival program the wench handed to me, blinking back a tear. I clear my throat. "It's the Chivalry and Romance 101 show..." I begin, my voice catching. Oh, God, no. Actually, this is a *terrible* idea, but Carly's already got her hands at the small of my back, and is pushing me through the crowd towards the closest stage. The guy on the low, rough platform of boards is dressed up to look like Mr. Bean if Mr. Bean was dressed to look like Shakespeare, all ruffles at the cuffs and a starched and stiff Elizabethan collar that moves with him as he turns smartly on the stage, one hand raised, thick brows raised, too, as if he's waving to the queen. He grins grandly at us as we sit on the log bench closest to the stage, the only seat left free.

God, this is such a *terrible* idea.

"My fine ladies…and gentlemen…" he says, flinging his hands back in true Ren Faire dramatics fashion, the sleeves of his too-white shirt dancing in the evening breeze. "Who doesn't love *love?* I promise you—you are here to learn from the best of the best!" He pauses for effect as he waggles his hips and chuckles a little, making the rest of the audience laugh with him. It's an obvious joke, but then you go for the obvious jokes at the Renaissance festival. He continues: "You, ladies, if you wish to woo your gentlemen, and you— fine gentlemen, if you wish to woo your ladies…it is time that you learn from a *master* of romance, the *sultan* of sexuality, the *lord* of laying! I will teach you the art of romance like Casanova himself would teach it. It! Is! Time!"

Nicole comes trotting over, smart phone in her hand and not against her ear (which is a good sign), but a grimace on her face and a slight shake of the head, which I already know means that I'm getting less than the aforementioned and *promised* half hour. "I'm sorry," she whispers in my ear quickly as she crouches down beside me, "I've got to go—"

"I would like a volunteer!" calls the man on stage.

And this is where it all begins to go very, very wrong.

Carly's hand shoots up like it's always been there, pointed straight to the sky, and—of course— since we're in the front row, the actor dances over to our side of the stage with a wide grin. "Do we have a volunteer?" he practically purrs, and Carly shakes her head, grinning too.

"She volunteers!" Carly all but sings out,

pointing to Nicole.

Nicole opens and shuts her mouth ready to protest quickly, but it's a pretty packed audience on these little log benches, and the actor is already down among us, with his hand at her elbow, steering her up and toward the stage before she has a chance to say a word. I already know she's not going to back out at this point (and they made it onto the stage pretty darn quickly) because she doesn't want to make a fool of herself.

If you've never been to a Renaissance Festival before, "I would like a volunteer" is code for "I need a butt for my jokes and a good sport to do my comedy shtick on."

I feel sick—or maybe it's just because of the nerves that I feel sick. Or maybe it's the complete dread that instantly fills me that's giving me this terrible sick feeling. Carly, seated beside me and grinning like a cat, seems oblivious to the fact that things have just gone terribly, terribly wrong. Or, maybe, she wants to see Nicole squirm.

"And you are, the fair lady…" says the actor, handing Nicole a small hand-held microphone. Nicole sighs out, leaning back on her heels for a long minute before she mutters into it:

"Nicole."

"And who here is your fair gentleman?" asks the actor, peering out into the crowd.

"I'm a lesbian," says Nicole flatly into the microphone, her brow raised like she's daring him to make an issue of it, and the actor—to his credit—falters for only half a second.

"Ah, wonderful! Who here is your fair *lady*, then, my apologies?"

I'm angry at Carly. I should be. It was a dirty, rotten thing she did, but I know she's miffed at Nicole for upsetting me. But it's *not really Nicole's fault*. We're not right for each other, and we both know it. But still, even after all that, there was a small part of my heart—really, *really* small, but still there—that hoped that when Nicole went up on that stage, and when the actor took her through the whole hokey act, that when she looked at me…I don't know. That there'd be at least *something* there. Maybe one of her little grins. Maybe a softening of her face. Maybe even a smile. Something to prove that there was still a connection between us. That there was still something in our relationship that could be salvaged.

Yes, I wanted *something*, I realize, as she gazes at me with complete apathy, her mouth turning down at the corners into a frown as she points to me.

I wanted something.

And it wasn't there.

I don't remember what the actor says. I don't remember what Nicole says, mumbling into the microphone as quickly as she can to get out of this, and then trotting down off the stage steps amid the smattering of polite, chilly applause because, as the actor says, she was such a "good sport." She takes another call on her phone, slipping it out of her pocket and turning away from me, without even a single glance in my direction as she leaves the festival.

It was a beautiful day: full sun, the perfect temperature (not too hot, but warm enough for t-shirts). The weather guy predicted it to be one of the most beautiful sunsets we've seen in weeks tonight. But as Nicole leaves the faire, the soft gray clouds that had seemed so non-threatening begin to build along the horizon, turning darker as the sun descends. And it starts to rain.

Standing in the downpour as Carly waits for her gigantic turkey leg on a stick, I draw my shawl about me, feel the cold drops plink down on my neck as I stare at the mud.

It's then that I know I have to end it.

Chapter 2: It's in a Book

"Please don't be mad, Holly..." says Carly as she puts the car into park. I sit back in my seat, stare out the front window at the wall of water on the windshield. It's a proper storm out now, complete with rolling thunder and jagged bolts of lightning and enough water to drown anyone who dares step outside. The rush of rain on the top of the car sounds like Niagara Falls. I stare out at the storm, and I let out a long sigh.

"Holly," Carly begins again and shakes her head. "C'mon, please, seriously. I was just trying to help..."

I bite my lip, my eyes narrowing as I stare out the windshield at the streetlamp in front of my house. As I watch it, the light flickers and goes out.

"Well, you didn't help," I mutter, shaking a little under my soaked skirt and blouse and shawl. The rain had been so much colder than a summer shower had any right to be. "And the worst part of it, Carly?" I raise my hand as she starts up, and—to her credit—Carly stops trying to interject. "I wasn't certain before," I whisper then. "But I am now. It's over. Nicole and I...we've got to break up."

I'm so stupid. *So stupid.* I promised myself I wouldn't cry, and I'm totally going to catch my death now, because suddenly I'm sitting in Carly's freezing car in my soaking clothes, sobbing my heart out, and because I'm crying so hard, my immune system is going to be lowered, and I'm going to catch the plague.

Or something.

"Oh, honey," says Carly, and—awkward in the confined space—she turns, somehow, and reaches for me, and hugs me tightly as I sob, twisted at a completely unnatural angle, onto her comforting, sandalwood-scented shoulder.

I'm sure Carly's *happy* about this, but—to her credit—she's not visibly over-the-moon about the fact that I'm breaking up with Nicole. She doesn't say anything, actually, only squeezes me tightly until I pull back a little, fishing a useless damp tissue out of my very damp purse.

"This is so stupid…" I mutter, breathing out as a sob begins to rise in my throat again. "I mean, I knew it was going to end. That we had to end it. It's hardly news to me, you know? I just…" I turn to look at Carly, shrug helplessly. "I just thought she was the one, you know? In the beginning…she tried so hard. *Really* hard, Carly. Remember the time she had a rainbow bouquet of roses delivered to the library with a card asking me out to Pride? Or that time I was really sick, and she drove all over Boston to every single video rental place to find me a copy of *Rebecca* because I loved it so much? God, she was so thoughtful." I stare down at the damp tissue in my hands, the tissue I was beginning to shred. "All of this was before stupid Advanatech, of course," I whisper the name of Nicole's start-up company and rub at my face with the tissue, trying—and failing—to rid myself of a few shed tears.

Nicole and I had come up with that name together. Advanatech. A start up business is a really difficult enterprise to involve yourself in, and I'd tried to always be the supportive girlfriend, understanding of her constant date cancellations and her increasing shortness toward me. It was stressful to open a start-up, and I'd tried so hard to be considerate. Maybe I'd been too considerate.

"I think she *really* loved me, Carly," I whisper to her, taking a deep, ragged breath. "And I really loved her. And I had these stupid fantasies, you know? About us getting married. They were *really* stupid, because Nicole doesn't even *believe* in getting married, but the point is…" I bite my lip, squeezing my eyes shut. I know I'm a blubbering idiot, but I need to say it, need to put it out into the world, if only for a heartbeat. "The point is, that I thought I was with the woman I was going to spend the rest of my life with. And I was very wrong. And that's very hard."

Carly takes a deep breath and sighs out. The rain drumming on the roof of the car is a constant *shush* of sound, and if I keep my eyes tightly closed, it seems like the only thing that's real. It helps, for half a heartbeat, to ignore the pain in my heart. But the pain is too insistent to be ignored for more than a few seconds, really, and rushes back when I open my eyes and stare out the blurry windshield. Blurry because of the rain pouring down it, but also blurry from my unshed tears.

"This is going to be okay, Holly," says Carly then, voice resolute. Firm. Gentle. "You and Nicole weren't right for each other, and that's okay." It's the nicest she's talked about Nicole in months. I glance at her. Carly's mouth is so small, pressed into a thin line as she nods to me. "I'm serious. When you break up with her, you'll see—life will go on, get better. You guys *weren't* meant for each other. And there's another woman out there for you, Holly. The right one."

"That might be a little too soon," I tell her. "And anyway, that's ridiculous." I shake my head. "Carly, *look* at me," I mutter, feeling the waves of sadness begin to rise again. I tick down my fingers. "The Knights of Valor Festival is my favorite day of the year. I collect unicorn figurines. I'm more obsessed with books than I am with people—" I splutter.

Carly shakes her head, laughing. "I promise you, there are many other ladies out in this big, vast world who love books as much as you do. And hey, you're a librarian! Librarians are super desirable— they're hot! I mean, they make porn about librarians!"

That statement comes from so far out of left field that she actually gets a surprised chuckle out of me before I stare at her, trying not to smile. I don't know how she does it, but Carly's always been the one who, on my very worst days, was always capable of getting at least a smile out of me.

"Okay, *seriously?*" I ask, still chuckling. "How do *you* know they make porn about librarians, and *are you even listening to me?*"

"*Holly,*" says Carly, reaching out and pressing her palms against the sides of my face, squeezing my cheeks together. She used to do this in college, too, when I began to freak out about finals. "*Shush,*" she growls, brow raised, when I begin to shake my head. "Look, I know what I'm talking about, okay? And I'm telling you right now: you're beautiful, and funny, and generous, and really fucking awesome, and while it's true that not everyone thinks unicorns are as cool as they were in the eighties, *that's not going to keep the right girl from falling in love with you*, so would you *cut the shit* and break up with Nicole, and make space in your life for the right woman?" She glances sidelong at me. "You know your mother would want you to be happy."

My heart skips a beat, and I clutch the car door handle, feel myself pale. "Don't," I whisper. "Not tonight."

She lets go of my face, slumps back in her seat. "I'm sorry," she whispers.

I bite back tears. Nod. I know she is.

Then she breathes out, flings her hands in the air. "Okay! But, Holly! You could be *happy*. Are you really going to do this? You're not going to back out, right?"

I take a few deep breaths and listen to the rain dancing on the roof of the car. I sigh out, shake my head, feeling myself deflate.

I felt so sure, before. But when I think about *actually* doing it, actually telling Nicole that I don't think we're right for each other, all I can see is the time when Nicole wrote me that love letter and had it delivered in a dozen roses, and…

"You're not going to do it." Carly leans forward and bangs her head gently against her steering wheel, eliciting little beeps from the horn. "Oh, my God, you're not going to do it."

"Carly, it's not that easy…" I begin, but I stop, breathe out, hold my purse tightly against my stomach. The earlier levity is gone as if it never existed, and in that moment, I feel so defeated and small and sad. "I've got to go," I mutter, and open the car door to the deluge.

"Hey," says Carly, and I glance back at her, one foot out in the mess of the night. "I love you, okay?" she tells me fiercely. "And I'm really sorry. About earlier. I never should have volunteered Nicole. It was stupid," she says, and I gulp down more tears and a sob, and I nod as she starts the car. I can't speak in that moment, there's too much emotion running through me.

"I'll call you tomorrow!" she shouts after me as I slam the door shut, and holding my purse over my head, I run across the sidewalk, and up my front steps, squelching under the overhang as I fumble with my key ring with frozen fingers. Carly pulls away from the curb and beeps her usual, cheerful rhythm of farewell, but it gets swallowed by a crack of thunder overhead so loud that it makes my teeth rattle.

The front door opens as I manage to finally get the key into the lock, and I stumble into the darkness of my lavender-scented hallway. I shut the door behind me, sighing and leaning against it, shaking in the dark (I forgot to turn my AC unit off that morning) before I flip on the light switch, toss my keys and purse in the blue ceramic bowl on the little hall table and hang up my dripping shawl on the hook.

Shelley rounds the corner at a dead run, her white and gold mane flying out behind her, her long nose aimed like a missile, just as I begin to walk (squishing) down the hallway. She skids to a halt by running into me, and I manage to smile down at one of my favorite people in the world. Er, fur-people.

"Hey, sweet girl," I tell her, rubbing behind her soft-as-silk gold ears and crouching down beside her, and then like a total dope, I wrap my arms around my poor dog's fluffy neck, and I start to weep into her shoulder. Shelley, of course, thinks this is the! Funnest! Game! and begins to nose at me and paw at me with a small, deep "woof."

That's her signal that she's really glad I made it home and all, but she has business to attend to. I take a deep, ragged breath, stagger to my feet and wander toward the back door to let her out. There's another ear-numbing crash of thunder that follows a streak of lightning, making the branches of the tree out back lengthen in shadows against the wooden fence. I pull the sliding glass door back and Shelley goes tearing out, and as I watch her, I realize how exhausted I am. How deeply tired, a bone-deep tired.

Shelley's as drenched as I am when I let her back in, and we both end up in the bathroom amidst a lot of towels (and the laundry was already in dire need of doing, drat it). I towel off her golden-brown coat, and she rewards me with licking my face a lot, her big, joyful doggie smile so bright, that she's radiating pure joy. Her long, usually-silky ears are still damp, so she keeps shaking her head and then falling on me because she's off balance, the tiled floor is slippery, and her paws are wet. Every time she lands on me, she gives me another lick in apology.

Nicole barely tolerates Shelley. As I hold my dog's head in my hands, kissing her long, beak-like nose and telling her how much I love her (because that's simply what you do when you're around Shelley—this is the dog every pet store employee, groomer, vet and person-who-walks-their-dog-in-dog-parks within a fifty mile radius knows by *name and favorite treat*), I wonder if the reason that I ignored all of the signs that I should break up with Nicole because it was just easier not to see them. Which is, I realize, as I stand and slip into my bathrobe, a *really terrible excuse* to stay with someone.

Anyone. Even Nicole, the woman I thought, for a long while, was the one I was meant to be with forever.

I know what I need, just like Shelley does, as I fill her bowl of food with fresh kibble. She munches happily as I turn the tea kettle's burner on, pulling the box of chamomile tea from the cupboard and setting it next to my favorite mug (Bubble, bubble, toil and trouble! is printed in a really cheesy font around a cauldron that bears the name "Cat, Cow and Cauldron." It's a long story. Yes, the word "cow" is sort-of intentional.) and my honey bear. I go back into the bathroom that now smells like wet dog (and, to be fair, wet human) and start the water running for the bath, and then I'm headed to my bedroom and my glorious "to be read" pile.

Everyone has a "to be read" pile, and depending on how obsessed the person is with books, the stack (or shelf. Or shelves. Or entire bookshelves) vary in size. But when you're a librarian? Your "to be read" pile is the stuff of legends. I have books stacked all along the west wall in my bedroom in varying columns, some that go taller than my head. If I squint, the different sized columns look like a city skyline, made entirely of hardcover and paperback books. I stand and look at it now, my hands on my hips as I listen to the tear of thunder that arches through the sky again, and—in the kitchen—the insistent and cheerful whistle of my teakettle.

And I ignore my "to be read" stacks entirely, and cross the room to my bedside table. The porcelain unicorn on my lamp looks up at me dolefully as I switch it on and kneel down to fish under my bed, the hiding place of my favorite comfort reads.

My fingers grasp a familiar and well-worn volume, and I sigh with relief as I bring it out into the light.

It's an old blue hardcover, worn and threadbare on the corners and spine, and printed there in dull, gold letters are the words *The Knight of the Rose*. I hold it to my chest now, and rise, feeling the familiar skip of my heartbeat that I get whenever I pick up this book. I've picked it up a thousand times—maybe ten thousand times—but it's always the same feeling, that little pit-a-pat of my heart that tells me I'm holding a treasure.

And it *is* a treasure. This is the book that I've turned to in times of sadness, of happiness, of joy and sorrow. This is my comfort book, my *heart* book. And I need it again tonight as I wander back into the kitchen, and—unthinking and unseeing—pour the hot water over my two teabags of chamomile (it was such a rotten day, I need my calming tea at double strength). I take my mug into the bathroom, toss a handful of lavender bath salt into the tub, and let the robe fall to the ground. The water's too hot for a lobster, but I get in anyway, sink down, gritting my teeth and let the boiling liquid cover me. After a lot of pin-pricking discomfort, I sigh happily and lean back in the tub, my flesh now medium-rare and able to withstand the heat.

Then I reach over the tub's side, towel off my hands on my fluffy blue robe, and I pick up the book.

And then I crack it open. Again. The steam curls the bottom pages, just like it has several hundred times before.

I don't even need to read the first line (or, really, paragraph), but my eyes move over the worn words I know by heart, and my lips move along to them, the sadness corralled in my heart, for a moment, out of sight and mind as I slip into the story.

Once, there was a brave young girl, who wanted—more

than anything—to be a knight. She wished to don the strange, bright armor that her older brothers wore, she wished to wield a shining sword like her older brothers did, and she wished—more than anything—to leave her sad, small town and journey the world and have adventures.

"But you can't, because you're a girl," her brothers, all knights, taunted her.

This girl's name was Miranda, and this is how her story began: with a wish, and a will.

I remember, as I always do, when I read the first page, the first time that I read it. I was fifteen, standing in the first row of shelves at my school's library, having just come from the bathroom where I'd tried really very hard with makeup and a lot of cold water, to make it look like I hadn't been crying. These hadn't been a few sad salty tears I'd shed. I'd been sobbing in the bathroom stall, heart-aching, gut-wrenching sobs, for twenty minutes. I had, of course, failed miserably to mask my red, blotchy face and puffy eyes.

I came out in high school. In the nineties. It was not a pretty picture by any stretch of the imagination. I wanted to be out and proud when, really, not that many people were out in high school then, and the ones who were lead terrible, miserable lives full of homophobia. I don't know what I was thinking, but I really believed it'd be okay. Yes, even then, I was pretty idealistic. I'd had this idea that coming out would make my life *better*, not worse. That, if I came out, I might even be able to find the girl of my dreams and have some sort of wonderful teen romance. But my coming out didn't result in anything more than non-stop bullying that made my life a perfect replica of hell.

That day, like most days of my teen years, I was imagining my life as being lived anywhere but there, in that stupid little town with all of its stupid, little, narrow-minded people.

In short, I needed escape like I'd never needed it before.

And, somehow, I'd wandered into the fantasy section of the library.

"Hey," said Miss T, our school librarian, as she wandered by and happened to take note of me crumpling my face into a tissue. "Are you all right, dear?"

"No," I told her truthfully. It was a small school. She knew what I was, and why I'd been crying. But—strangely unlike the other teachers—she came up to me and offered me another tissue without flinching, staring down the row of books with a thoughtful turn of her head and its super-perm.

"You know," she said, tapping a finger to her mauve lips, "I have a book I think might interest you. If you'd like a recommendation."

"Sure," I muttered, and like some sort of magical creature, she darted forward and pulled down a slight volume with a worn, blue cover from the nearest shelf. Emblazoned on the book's spine were the words *The Knight of the Rose*.

"Everyone needs a heroine like them," she said with a smile, handing me the book. "Tell me what you think of it."

I'd had no idea, that weird, distant afternoon, what she was talking about. But I took the book home, because she'd given it to me. And I read it.

So, *The Knight of the Rose*? It's about a girl named Miranda who becomes a knight, who has a bunch of really wonderful adventures…who falls in love with a princess, and marries her at the end of the book.

A girl knight. Marries a princess. And is the heroine of the book.

Everyone *does* need a heroine like them. I'd never realized how much, until I read that story. And it saved my life. It changed me, in a way that only books can. It gave me a sense of strength, of place in the world, because I was no longer "Holly the homo" (as charmingly unoriginal as it was), what they chanted at me in the hallways of my stupid little school. I was just me. Just Holly. And I could do or be *anything*, because there was a story about *someone like me*. And hey, the heroine of *that* story had done pretty all right for herself. So maybe I could, too.

I turn the page now, sinking deeper in the water as I take a sip of tea. It burns the roof of my mouth, but I don't even notice as I dive into the words again. The steam from the bathtub crinkles the already-crinkled pages further as my breathing becomes soft and even, as my muscles relax, as I feel the warmth of the water and the story and the tea cradle me and take me to someplace else, someplace better, just like they always have.

Here's the secret: in the beginning, when I first read this book, I thought I wanted to *be* Miranda. Go off on countless adventures, be able to ride any magnificent steed, woo any lovely lady. But I don't want that anymore. If I was going to be perfectly honest with myself (and, really, when am I ever honest with myself?), I know the truth: I wish Miranda was real, so that I could fall in love with her.

Growing up, I had to be the strong one. I had to be, and I'm glad I was. But I've always been the aggressor in every relationship, and I've always been the one who went after the girl and after the woman, and I've always been the one to hold it together. But when I read these lines, this story, see how dashing Miranda is, how she builds this beautiful character of chivalry and honor and romance and devotion, I feel parts of myself beginning to crumble.

I want that, I know, as I close the book because the words are becoming too blurry. I set the hardcover on the edge of the sink and slip down, down into the water again, letting a single tear shed down my cheek.

I want that.

And I honestly don't think I'm ever going to get it.

I have the tendency to fall for *exactly* the wrong woman. Carly could tell you that I have really terrible taste in the romance category. Yes, I want the kind of love that's written into a book, a woman sweeping me off my feet, fully devoted to me, thoughtful, considerate, kind. But instead of a woman who exemplifies those things coming after me, I don't wait to see if it will happen. I end up going after the woman I feel might be what I want, but who never ends up being that way.

I don't wait, I don't have much patience when it comes to dating, but secretly, I want to be gone after. But I'm never in the right place or the right time for someone who makes my heart flutter *and* wants me, too. The one time that a woman aggressively pursued me was this lady who worked at the local coffee shop, who had a husband and a kid. I honestly believe that I just have really, *really* terrible luck in the love department. I mean, have you ever heard of anyone else this unlucky? Someone who gets impatient waiting for someone to come along, so pursues all the wrong women?

Through the open bathroom door, I see another white-hot blast of lightning, and I begin to count until the thunder, but I don't even whisper the word "one" before the deafening explosion of sound makes the walls of the house shake. From out in the hall, I can hear Shelley whimpering and then she comes dashing into the bathroom as the lights flicker. I reach out with a wet hand, pet behind her ears as she plaintively puts her long nose on the side of the tub, staring up at me with wide eyes, her long, feathery tail wagging limply.

"It's okay, baby...it's just the storm..." I whisper to her as the lights flicker again. "You're okay, baby, you're okay..." I murmur, and she lies down beside the tub, flattening her head between her paws, and staring up at me morosely with big brown eyes.

I glance up as the power flickers, as the lights begin to dim. For half a heartbeat, they come back brightly.

But then they go out.

"Well, crap," I mutter, reaching over the edge of the tub and patting the bathroom floor as I search for the soft, plush fabric of my bathrobe. My fingers connect with soft plush and long dog hair. Shelley's lying on my robe. I tug at the corner of the robe trying to gently dislodge her off of it, and I've almost gotten her off of it when I stop, because *every hair on my body* stands to attention in that instant.

Shit, is the house going to be struck by lightning? I scrabble out of the bath—I'm sure being in the tub isn't the brightest idea if lightning is about to hit the house—and I shrug into the robe with shaking hands, crouching down onto the tile floor and hold Shelley tightly, feeling her heart beat much too quickly beneath my fingers. She feels it, too. Maybe the house *is* going to be struck by lightning. But wouldn't it already have happened by now?

And then I hear it.

My first thought is that it's a scream. But not really. It couldn't be, because I've *never* heard a sound like that before. It's like a cross between a bellow, and a growl, and a scream all at once, and it's got to be an animal—no human could make that noise—but I can't imagine what *kind* of animal it could be that could sound so…so enormous, so angry…so terrifying. The scream makes the floor shake beneath my knees, makes the jar I keep my q-tips in on the glass shelf in the bathroom rattle loudly and move toward the shelf's edge.

Every hair is still to attention as I struggle to rise, my hands shaking as I try to knot the robe's belt at my waist. The sound comes again, deafening, roaring, ending in a deep, guttural yowl that is pure horror, that goes on for a solid *minute*, a sound that will live in my nightmares forever. I stumble down the stairs. It's an animal, it *must* be. And it's right outside.

In my backyard.

I stand in my living room, drawing my robe closer about me as I shake, dripping on the floor. I stare out into the backyard. The rain comes down in buckets—it's impossible to see anything beyond the water-washed sliding glass door—and every hair I possess is *still* at attention, and my skin's crawling as I peer out into the darkness, try to see.

A flash of lightning arches across the sky so brightly that it looks like day for half a heartbeat.

There's something out there.
Some*one*.

Chapter 3: Virago

I make my way across the room to the sliding glass door and stand, open mouthed and staring into the abysmal darkness of the out-of-doors. I thought I saw...

Nope. Absolutely not. I could not have *possibly* seen what I thought I saw. I blink, swallow, fiddle with the ends of my robe's belt.

But I thought...

Another flash of lightning. My breath catches in my throat.

I flip up the lock of the door, and suddenly I've pulled the door open, the sash in my hand. And before I know it, I've moved, unthinking, out onto the back porch, and down the three steps and I'm standing on my soaking lawn as the rain roars down around me, beating against me like the crashing wave of a tsunami.

The sound of metal against metal clashes out. I see a spark in the darkness as I run across the grass, angling toward the back of my yard.

"Stand and fight me, bastard of darkness!"

This makes me stop, makes me skid to a halt. It was a woman's strong voice, ringing in a bellow, rising loudly around me.

Another bolt of lightning hits a nearby tree, or it must have hit something nearby, even though I didn't see the bolt connect. Because the crash and sparks that follow almost deafen and blind me.

But as I stand there, rubbing at my eyes, the rain pouring around me, I see something move in the backyard again. What I thought I'd only imagined. What can't possibly be there.

What can't possibly *exist*.

It's as tall as my house is my first thought, an abstract thought that slowly prostrates itself in my head and dies as the fear takes over, the fear that rises in me until it seems that all I am is fear. Because whatever that thing is, it's *as tall as my house*, and it's dark, and it's enormous, and I think those are *teeth* in a gigantic *mouth*, and if those *are* teeth, then they're as long as my arm, and the mouth is as big as my *car*, and *what the hell am I staring at* as it rears up like some strangely misshapen dinosaur.

I'm staring at something that I *know* doesn't exist, but at the same time...I'm *staring* at it.

And it's then that I notice the person-sized shape at its feet, and thanks to another dangerously close lightning strike, I see the person-sized shape raise something that if I did not think that I was absolutely dreaming, right in this moment, I would say it was...well.

A sword.

"*Fight* me!" comes the woman's voice again, demanding and absolute as she brandishes the sword overhead, pointing it at the sky. But the lightning flickers and is gone, and there's suddenly too much darkness to see anything. But I can *hear* everything. I can *hear* the sound of metal against metal, the clanging, the hot hiss that sounded a lot like the air being punched out of a tire.

There's the roaring silence of rainfall and

nothing else besides for a long moment, as my skin crawls, and I try desperately to see something—anything—in my dark backyard.

That's when I hear that sound again, the sound that first brought me to the door, the bellow/scream/growl/hiss that really does sound like the cross of a tyrannosaurus rex (if Jurassic Park movies actually got that sound right) and a tiger, and it rises all around me, that terrible, nightmarish scream, and then there's a *crunch*, and a slithery *shushing* that makes my entire body shudder involuntarily...

And then the silence of the pouring rain.

More lightning. The...whatever-it-was is gone. There's nothing in my backyard now but that person-sized shape, and it's no longer standing—it's kneeling, crumpled.

Pure instinct takes over, makes me put one foot in front of the other, and I'm running the rest of the way across the yard.

If this is a dream, it's a very real one as I draw closer, because she looks up, this woman who's crumpled on my lawn, and she says with a strong voice that shakes only a little, and only at the end: "M'lady, don't draw closer...the beast could still be about, and it's very dangerous..." She can hardly get out that last word as she uses her sword—*oh, my God, she has a sword*—to try and lever herself into a standing position, but her hand slips on the hilt, and she crumples further, to her hands and knees. "Please leave, I will give it chase, and I will..." She coughs a little, and then she's fallen over, onto her back, sinking down into the mud and grass.

I run the rest of the way and kneel down beside her, sinking down into the mud, too, as I stare down at this woman, my heart beating so quickly, I think it's going to erupt from me, squeeze out from between my ribs and run around in the grass screaming. Her eyes are closed, her brow is lined, and her lips are crumpled in a cry of quiet pain, but her eyelids flutter for just a heartbeat, and she gazes up at me.

Her eyes are so blue, they're like ice.

No.

Stars.

Yes, they're like stars. Bright, burning, ice-blue stars.

Everything else disappears in that moment, the pouring rain, the squelching mud that clings to my legs, the fear that was everywhere a handful of heartbeats ago as I stare down into her ice-blue, star-blue eyes.

But then it's over, and reality comes crashing back as she closes her eyes and folds forward a little, and that's when I notice that she's wearing...well, I don't really know what she's wearing. It looks like armor, but it isn't, really: it seems to be leather and metal combined together, and it covers her chest and shoulders, and she has a fur capelet and a cloak. Her sword, still gripped in a white-knuckled hand, is currently blade-deep in the mud. As I stare down at this woman, this ridiculously beautiful woman wearing armor and wielding a sword in my backyard, I realize that she must be from the Knights of Valor Festival. Of course she must be. And there's something wrong with her—she looks like she's hurt.

"Are you okay?" I ask, my voice shaking, my teeth chattering together. The rain's too cold—it's early July, but the rain that pelts down around us is as cold as the water I store in a pitcher in my fridge.

She doesn't respond. Her eyes are closed, her

long lashes resting against tanned cheeks, her full lips parted, and her breath coming in low, harsh pants.

I think she's unconscious now.

Well, shit.

I don't know what to do. They say to *never* move someone who may have sustained trauma, but really, what could she have sustained trauma *from*? And isn't this a dream, anyway?

I glance up at the dark sky, squinting my eyes against the rain, but the lightning seems to have stopped for the moment. But even if there was lightning, what would it illuminate? What was that...thing? What did I actually *just see*?

A...monster?

I bite my lip for a moment—I honestly don't really know what to do—and then pure instincts take over again. If this is a dream (and if this *is* a dream, it's the realest dream I've ever had in my life), then it won't matter what happened in it once I wake up. And if it *isn't* a dream, I've got to do something about her injuries. Or at least figure out what her injuries are.

I roll the woman over as gently as I can, then try to leverage her upper body into a seated position so that I can lift her arm and put it around my shoulders, help her stand, or at least get her into a position where I can drag her as gently as I can into the house. But I guess her armor is heavier than I thought, and she's taller than I thought, too, and she seems to be made of *one pure muscle* since she's so ridiculously heavy that I can't even lift her upper body even a little, and the arm I'm trying to get around my shoulder is as hard as a rock. I grapple with her shoulders for another moment, but because I'm trying to be careful, and because her armor is wet and slippery, she slides right out of my hands, and I catch her head before it lolls back against the soaking mud and grass, my fingers tangling in her soaking ponytail.

Her eyelids flutter, and she opens them a crack, breathing out and groaning, her forehead furrowed. "M'lady, *please*," she mutters, her voice low and velvety. She tries to turn over, push herself to her hands and knees again. "You need to get inside, so that I can—" She begins to cough, her voice catching. She spits something out of her mouth, something dark that, even in the night, I realize is probably blood. She shudders and takes another ragged breath, shaking her head.

"You're hurt. I think." I mutter to her, again tugging at her arm so that I can loop it around my neck and shoulders. "I'm trying to get you inside okay? I want to help you."

"M'lady..." She grips my wrists tightly with leather gloved hands, glancing at my face before closing her eyes again, groaning under her breath. She reaches down, grips her side, taking a deep breath. "It's not safe," she whispers then, her low voice catching. "Please, go. I will...I will..."

Her gloved hand comes away from her side, and I grip it tightly. My hand is slippery against her glove, and I glance down at my fingers.

There's so much blood.

"It's okay," I soothe quietly. Maybe she has a concussion. (*Or maybe she's talking about that thing you refuse to acknowledge you saw,* I think to myself.) "We'll get you inside. My house is right here. It's perfectly safe."

Maybe she doesn't have enough energy for more words, because she doesn't say anything else, only breathes heavily as she finally acquiesces, shifting her weight on her knees and leaning heavily on me just then. I fumble with cold hands, but manage to grip her wrist and pull her one arm over my shoulder (God, she really *is* super muscular—her bicep alone is rock-hard and larger than normal. Maybe she lifts weights?), and then manage to place my other arm around her waist. The fabric of her shirt not covered by armor is hot to the touch, and when my grip slips for half a heartbeat, my fingers connect with skin. Smooth, soft skin that's so hot it's burning under my fingertips.

And, as odd as the situation is, as cold as the rain that pours around us...I still find myself blushing when my hand curls over that warm skin.

God, seriously, Holly, I groan to myself. What a moment to realize that I have my arm around a gorgeous woman.

I manage to leverage her up to a somewhat standing position, though I'm not even really sure how I did it. Probably the pure adrenaline that's pounding through me helped me, because this woman is taller than me, more muscled than I am, and wearing really heavy armor. I can't breathe, there's rain in my eyes, my nose, my mouth, and we stagger toward the back door as I splutter, do my absolute best to try and hold her up.

Shelley choose that exact moment to come *tearing* out of the house through the sliding glass door that I, like an idiot, left *completely open.* The lightning must have kept her inside until now—it's really the only thing that frightens my over-exuberant ball of energy.

"Shelley!" I hiss as she comes bounding joyfully up to us. "Baby, get back inside *now,*" I mutter, but when has Shelley ever listened to me for a moment in her life? She continues to spring alongside us, leaping up and trying to sniff the dangling drenched bits of fur from the woman's capelet.

I drag the woman up the three steps to my back porch, and then across the porch and through the sliding glass door, and—blessedly—we're out of the rain. I help her limp to the couch, and then I let her slump down as gently as I can onto its cushions. I rush back to the sliding glass door and whistle for Shelley, who comes darting inside and shaking, rain water and wet dog smell everywhere as I pull the sliding glass door finally closed.

When the door is shut, when the insistent pulsing of the rain and thunder and lightning and the overwhelming nature show is safely behind glass once more, I turn around slowly, and I try to flick on the lights.

The power must have come back on. Because somehow, magically, the lights flare to life.

The woman pants on my couch, her chest heaving as she tries to breathe, as she presses one gloved hand against her side.

God, there's so much blood.

Shelley's sitting in front of her and wagging her tale like the crazed dog she is as she insistently licks the stranger's outstretched fingers of her other hand. The woman is watching me, her face creased with pain, but as I cross over to her, sink down in front of her and stare up at her strange outfit, the bits of armor and fur capelet and soaking cloak and leather boots, I realize abstractly that she looks like she stepped out of a medieval painting, *sort* of. The armor is too modified to be truly medieval, but I have to admit—it's the best modification job I've ever seen. There's metal bits, intricately spiraled and molded, to go along with the leather that's been burned with careful patterns. She has a breastplate of that mash-up of leather and metal, and she has *leather pants*, oh, my God, and metal plates that form a sort-of short skirt over the pants, and leather wrist-cuffs that extend up to her elbows and well down and over her wrists to shield the back of her strong, broad hands that she reveals as she slowly takes off her blood-soaked leather gloves.

I can't bear to look up at her eyes, her face, because when I do, my heart does this dangerous little dance again, and I really need to get it together, because she's staring down at me, eyes wide and intense, and I swallow, breathe out, and it turns into a little cough.

She's gorgeous in a way that's difficult for me to understand, a wild kind of gorgeous that I don't think I've really seen in any human being. She's got the intense stare of a creature who hunts for her food, who should never be messed with, but there's also a gentleness to her gaze when she looks at me.

And *oh my goodness* is she intense as she stares down at me, still panting. Her face is creased in obvious pain, yes, but it's still easy to see how full her lips are, how inviting the curve of her jaw is. The brightness of her blue eyes is almost bewitching. Her long black hair is drawn up into a very severe and high ponytail, and she has a bit of fur wrapped around the thong that keeps her hair up, that drapes down next to her hair and over her shoulder. It's gray fur, like a wolf's. I'm trying not to notice the strong, tanned curve of her neck, the way it slopes down to the breastplate, and it's then that I sort of wake up, because I glance down at the rest of her body again and I see her leg, the hole in the leather of her torso, and the leather on both her thigh and her stomach have tears in it, but the most obvious thing to see is that *she has a gigantic wound* on her leg.

There's blood everywhere.

I breathe out again through my mouth, try to think about things other than blood as I get a little light headed, and I stumble to my feet, rush to the kitchen, and I'm back again with an armful of paper towels as I kneel beside her, offer them to her, then crouch down in front of her again, holding out the armful of paper towels.

I have no idea how much pain she's in. But judging from her grimace, from how white her skin is under that tan...probably a lot.

"Oh, my God," I mutter, holding out the paper towels to her with a shaking hand. "Are you...are you okay?"

It's then that she cracks a little smile, her lips turning up at the corners for a heartbeat as she chuckles with her low, velvet voice. She shakes her head as she grimaces, paling further as she leans forward a little at the waist.

"No," she answers, and it's smooth and easy that word, a little rich, low laugh following it. She flicks her gaze up to meet my eyes, her own blue eyes flashing brightly. "Thank you for your concern, m'lady, but in truth, it's just a little thing."

We both stare down, just then, at the wound in her leg as the blood oozes over her skin and pants and *plinks* onto my couch, kind of soaking the dull, gray cushions with bright crimson.

"Not exactly *little*," I mutter, and lean forward, poised with the paper towels. She reaches out, wraps her fingers around my wrist, and I shudder at her touch—her hand is *so hot*—but I also shudder, because it's so gentle, those strong fingers that touch me so softly that it's almost like she isn't touching me at all.

But I notice, very, very much, that she is.

She grips my wrist gently, shaking her head. "Don't concern yourself with me. I shall be well in the morning," she mutters, breathing out, locking eyes with me. We stare at one another for a long moment, and she sort of leans back against the couch, letting go of my wrist gradually as if she's lost the strength to curl her fingers. "Where am I?" she asks then, sighing out and glancing past me to my living room, to Shelley who's wagging her tail so hard, it's in danger of falling off.

"Um. On East Linden Street," I say, which is the first thing that comes to mind, but sounds really stupid after I utter it. "Um. Where do you think you are? Are you concussed, maybe?"

She breathes out, grimaces again, and then I remember the paper towels and very slowly, very carefully, press them to her leg. She makes a low groan but doesn't move a muscle, and I feel like I'm going to be sick for a moment, because the towels soak up *so* much blood. I glance up at her—she's gone pure white for a moment.

Her gaze flicks to mine, and though she's obviously in a great deal of pain, her full lips curl up at the corners again into a small, soft smile.

"Thank you," she whispers to me, her voice so low that before I can catch myself, I shiver a little at the sound of it.

"I...I haven't done anything," I manage, patting the paper towels onto her leg. If I stare down at the paper towels, maybe the warmth in my cheeks will lessen.

"Yes," she whispers, and suddenly her hot

fingers are beneath my chin, and she gently leverages my gaze upward. She searches my gaze, her own eyes so intense and burning that I feel transfixed beneath them. "You saved my life," she whispers.

The spell is broken, because she leans back suddenly against the couch with another low groan, holding tightly to her side. Bright red blood, *fresh* blood, begins to leak out between her fingers and over her hand.

"Oh, my God, I've got to get you help…" I gasp, staggering upright and running toward my purse, my cell phone, that I left on the little table in the entryway. "I'm going to call for an ambulance, and we can get you to the hospital, and you're going to be okay, okay? I promise—" I begin, but I'm cut off.

"Hospital? What is a hospital?" She shakes her head, leans forward again as I fish my phone out of my purse and come back to her, crouching down in front of her again. Now I can see that there's a wolf tail woven in with her ponytail, the silver pelt bright against the darkness of her hair. I stare at that wolf's tail for a long moment before I punch "911" into my phone.

She reaches across the space between us and takes my hand, curling her fingers over my phone, tightly this time. "Please," she says then, her voice so tired and quiet, "what is a hospital?"

"You must be so badly concussed…" My hands are shaking, and I keep swallowing—my mouth has suddenly gone completely desert-dry. "You know…a *hospital*." I turn my other hand in the air as I grapple with the words. How do you describe what a *hospital* is to someone? I just want to jog her memory. Maybe if I can jog her memory…maybe she has amnesia? "A hospital," I tell her, licking my lips. "It's where they can fix you, make you better, stitch up your leg—"

"No," she growls adamantly. This causes her to cough, which she does twice, then doubles over for a moment, holding tightly to her side. She flexes her jaw, gritting her teeth together as she sits up again, pinning me to the spot with her gaze. "I cannot go there—I have not *time*..." she shakes her head, locks eyes with me again as she trails off. What she asks next comes completely out of left field: "What is your name?"

My heart skips a beat, and then it decides to catch up with the beat it missed by pounding blood through me at a heart rate that should probably kill me. I'm flushed so red by that simple question. God, I'm hopeless.

I'm so attracted to her that I can't even bear it.

"Holly," I whisper. I clear my throat, try again: "My name is Holly."

"Holly," she whispers back to me, voice low and velvety like a growl. Hearing her say my name, tasting the sound of my name, does something inside of me, and a small shiver moves through me as she squeezes my hand gently. "Please don't call for the hospital," she says then, her voice still low as she continues to search my eyes, holding my gaze with her own piercing one. "Please. I do not know where I am, but I am certain that I should not be here, and going to the...the *hospital* would further complicate matters that are already *very* complicated."

She flexes her jaw and grimaces as she presses her hand over the hole in the shirt beneath her armor, the hole that blood keeps pumping through. "I must make chase after the beast. I have no idea where he is, what damage he may be causing, and it's my responsibility..." She actually tries to stand just then, rocking back and then forward. I'm too shocked that she's even trying to jump to my feet and try to help her, but she doesn't get very far. She grimaces and slumps back against the couch cushions, making a soft, sort of strangled cry, going even whiter, if that was possible as she sinks back.

She actually looks like she's going to black out as she leans forward a little, her strong jaw clenching to keep in another cry, and I don't know what to do, so I run my fingers through my hair, shake because I'm absolutely freezing in my soaked bathrobe, and—I realize just then—absolutely nothing else. I'm only wearing a soaked bathrobe in front of this stranger, not that it really matters. But still, I gather the robe closer about myself with shaking fingers as I try to figure out what I should do.

"What's your name?" I murmur, the only normal words I can think of in a completely abnormal time and place and situation as she stares at me with her ice-blue eyes that I keep falling into.

"Virago," she murmurs, closing those eyes as she whispers her name between us.

"Um..." I falter, blinking. I keep being mesmerized by her lips, by her voice, and it's then that I remember that she just said "beast." "Is that your stage name? Um..."

She sinks back into the couch, closes her eyes, breathes out for a long moment. "I have to find the monster...it's my responsibility..." she repeats. She's shaking, and her tan looks so sallow now, in the light. She's too pale—she's pale because she's losing so much blood. But she's so adamant about not going to the hospital. "I must find it..." she whispers again.

It. The beast?

Beast?

I don't know what to do. I get up, pace across the living room as I hold my robe tightly around me, pace back across the small space as Shelley whines, glances out the back door.

Beast? Is that what I saw out in the backyard? The enormous thing with enormous teeth?

Could this be a dream?

I cross the room to the sliding glass door and draw the blinds down on it, pulling the curtain closed after the blinds. Still shaking, I run up the stairs to the bedroom, pull out my too-large fleece jacket I got from the local Shakespeare club, my fleece pajama bottoms with the cowboy hat print, black fleece socks with pink polka dots, dive into everything, then dig through my closet until I find the knock-off Snuggie that Carly had thought totally appropriate as a gag Christmas gift a few years ago. It's covered in cartoon cats. I silently thank her, and take it downstairs.

The woman—Virago, I suppose, for now—is fast asleep. Hopefully not unconscious. Hopefully she didn't just faint on my couch from loss of blood.

I mean, I don't know—maybe she took some drugs, and doesn't want me to take her to the hospital, because they'd find them in her system? It's a plausible answer, and it dances around the idea of "beasts" quite nicely. Maybe she doesn't have insurance, and she can't afford paying for a trip to the hospital. Maybe she's…foreign? Doesn't really understand the concept of what a "hospital" is, because she's not familiar with the word? She does have a soft sort of accent that I can't exactly place.

I drape the blanket with arms over the woman,

and then I turn up the heat, sit down in the chair across from her. I try to figure out what to do. I want to take her to the hospital. She's breathing evenly now, looks peaceful, but that doesn't mean anything. She could be losing a ton of blood, still, even though the wound is sealed.

I fret about this for a long time. And then I don't know exactly how it happens—maybe because of the adrenaline or the fear or the completely rotten day. Or the chamomile tea.

But despite everything...I fall fast asleep.

Chapter 4: Another World

I wake with a start and a rush of breath. My neck hurts so much as I open my eyes, sit up...but it probably hurts terribly because I fell asleep sitting up in my comfy chair, my head falling back against the chair top like I'm a ninety-year-old woman.

I rub at my eyes with the heels of my hands, yawn and stretch overhead a little, my head to the side as I massage my right shoulder. Huh. What a weird night. I had the strangest dream, and...

I blink and stare at the couch across from me for a long moment, breath coming in short gasps as my heart rate increases.

There's a puddle of dried blood on the cushions.

Okay.

So it probably *wasn't* a dream then.

I stagger upright, which doesn't last long, because on my first step, I'm tripping over Shelley who was fast asleep on my feet, and I sprawl on my living room carpet. Shelley yelps as I wake her up ungracefully from what was probably a lovely dream about excess kibble. She scrabbles beneath me, and I crawl off her quickly, but she doesn't seem to mind much, as she instantly bounds up, shaking her puffy coat, and then she's wagging her tail hard again and pointing her long nose up with one of her cute doggie grins as she stares up at...

"Are you all right?" There's a strong, warm hand at my elbow and my waist, and then gently, I'm turned over and raised in muscular arms, and I'm held in this incredibly gentle embrace...

And *oh, my God*, it's the woman from last night.

She's standing in my living room.

Holding me.

My eyes are drawn to those beautiful, full lips that are curled upwards in a graceful smile. Her eyes, crinkled at the edges as she grins down at me, are the most intense blue I've ever been witness to, made even more intense by the daylight, as if that were possible. They seem to glow from within, an ice blue that's clear and vibrant beyond description. As I stare up at her, at her gorgeous face with her lovely, strong high cheekbones, her graceful jaw and full lips I'm trying to memorize, she gently lets me go, steps away from me, gazing at me and clearing her throat softly, brows up and still smiling as she inclines her head toward me.

"Um," I breathe out, as I stand there with my mouth open. Very articulate. "Um..." My voice trails off as my gaze drifts down, and I stare at her leg, at the gigantic hole in her leather pants.

At the complete lack of blood.

And, you know, at the *lack of wound*.

The wound is gone.

"Are you all right, m'lady?" she asks then, cocking her head. She's taken off her fur capelet and cloak, and stands in her armor over her shirt and pants and leather boots, one hand on her hip, and one hip cocked up. She's standing there in front of me with such an aimless surety, actually, and this raw sort of sensuality that my breath catches in my throat, and then I'm swallowing again, my mouth suddenly and instantly as dry as any desert I can think of.

Virago, I remember, grappling with my brain. She said last night that her name was Virago.

"Virago…" I mutter, clearing my throat. I can't stop staring at her muscular, tanned leg through the hole in the *leather pants*. (I'm kind of fixating on the leather pants thing, I realize.) "What…happened? Where's…I mean, didn't you have a really bad wound there last night?" My eyes drift back up to her face, my cheeks reddening because my gaze pauses for a long moment on her armor-clad chest. The wound on her stomach is also completely healed—I can see the bare, tanned skin through the hole in the shirt beneath her armor. It's as if she was never wounded in the first place.

"I healed," she says simply, gazing at me with brows raised, as if that statement was the most natural thing in the world. She strides past me with the same practiced ease as a wolf, running her long fingers over her head and through her ponytail and over the wolf's tail dangling over her shoulder. "M'lady Holly…I need to speak with you."

"You healed," I repeat flatly, and then I'm sitting back down in my chair again quickly because my legs apparently no longer want the job of holding me up. Shelley noses at my hand with her long muzzle anxiously to be let outside, and that's what brings me back to reality. My dog needs to pee. You can't get more reality-based than that.

"Um. Just…wait a second, okay?" I tell the woman in armor standing in my *living room*. I get up ungracefully from my chair and make my way to the back sliding glass door, tugging back the curtains and then cautiously pulling up the blinds.

I'm cautious and uncertain about these things, because part of me doesn't even really want to glance at my backyard. Because I'm not really sure what's going to be waiting for me outside.

But it's just my normal backyard out there, with its closely cropped grass, still glistening with the previous night's rain. It's stopped raining, thankfully, and the sunshine filters down into the backyard like a spotlight, highlighting the tall maple trees behind the fence in my neighbor's yard. There's some divots in the backyard, in the grass. I open the door, and Shelley bounds out happily, sniffing around in the damp grass, her white-gold tail wagging. I watch her prance across the lawn for a long moment.

"Holly, it is quite urgent that I speak with you," says Virago, suddenly very close to me, staring down at me with wide, ice-blue eyes, her fingers gently at my elbow again as her hand curls around my arm. I stare up at her.

"I'm listening," I murmur.

She nods, searches my eyes. "I need to leave immediately, need to find the creature, as it is my responsibility that it's here, and if anyone is injured by it…" She swallows, and her eyes flash as she breathes out slowly, her jaw working. "I need to do right by this," she finishes, voice strong and low. My heart begins to beat faster as she inclines her gorgeous head toward me. "I must thank you for last night," she whispers, searching my eyes with her own. "It was you who startled the beast. Without your help—"

I swallow, suddenly going cold. There's that word again. "Beast."

"This is all just…very, very strange," is what I

manage to say then, hardly capable of getting the words out. "Um…your leg just *healed*? Wounds don't…they don't heal overnight. What's going on? Who *are* you? I don't understand…" I trail off, searching her face, ready and waiting for her to tell me that this has all been an elaborate stunt for the Knights of Valor Festival that somehow went very wrong. That maybe they have a motorized "beast" that they're going to start including in shows, and that it had, somehow, wound up in my backyard…

But I have a very strange feeling that this isn't what she's about to tell me.

Virago sighs, gestures back to my coffee table. "I have been looking through your books, and I think that it is safe to say that I am no longer in my world, and that what we attempted to do to detain the creature did not, in fact, work." Her glittering gaze flicks back to my eyes and pins me to the spot as she straightens, drawing herself up to her full height and crossing her muscled arms in front of herself. "So to begin with, we must start at the beginning. I must know—what world am I in?"

"Earth," I blurt out, before I realize in the next instant how *absolutely crazy* this is. What *world* she's in? "Virago…" I splutter, "you can't possibly…" I settle on the only rational thing that comes to mind: "I thought you were from the Knights of Valor Festival?"

She stares at me blankly, head to the side.

"I mean…just look at you…" I say, throwing my hands to the sides and indicating her armor, her capelet, her cloak. Her friggin' *wolf's tail* that's dangling over her shoulder from her ponytail. "You can't…you can't *possibly* expect me to believe that you're from another world." I pale, and clear my throat, stiffen when she continues to watch me with guarded eyes, her arms crossed. "Wait, did someone set you up to this?" I ask her, anger making my voice shake. "Because if they did..." She remains silent, watching me, and I go quiet, watching her, too.

"M'lady, would that I had a simpler explanation for you," she remarks wryly, again with a small, sideways grin as she shakes her head. "But it seems that I am out of my element, at the present, and can not present you with anything but the truth. I am no longer on my world. As is my beast, who—right now—may be wreaking havoc and hurting innocents." Her face goes grave again, her ice-blue eyes flashing, and she sighs, pushes her broad shoulders back, the pads of her armor moving with her. "I need to track him down and destroy him—exactly what I was trying to do last night before my unfortunate wounding. Neither I nor the beast expected to end up here, and I think he simply recovered quicker than I might have, and—"

I can't believe I'm actually saying it, but I blurt out: "Whoa. Wait. Start at the beginning."

Virago draws herself up to her full height (which is a full head taller than me), and nods genteelly, that graceful arch of neck and jaw a gravity that my eyes are compelled to follow. She indicates the chair I slept in all night with a gentle wave of her hand. "If m'lady would take a seat, I shall recount my journey here as best as I'm able."

I sit down quickly.

In one smooth, fluid motion, Virago is crouching down in front of me on one graceful knee. She is *kneeling* in front of me.

"I am Virago of the Royal Knights of Arktos City, capital of Arktos," says Virago, her voice strong and clear. She touches the place over her heart with long fingers and inclines her head to me in this sweeping bow, causing my own heart to beat even faster as I try to understand what she just told me.

And then with a dancer's grace, and still down on one knee, she takes the hand that had touched her heart and proffers it out to me. In a stunned sort of silence, I give her my hand, because I assume that's what she wanted: me to give her my hand. And, God yes that's exactly what she wanted, because *she's kissing the back of my hand*, her lips just as soft, just as warm as I'd imagined. Her hot, satin mouth lingers against my skin for a single beat too long, my heart thundering against my chest like it's going to stop working completely.

She's smiling softly as she lets her warm fingers trail over my palm, her bright blue eyes gazing at me unwaveringly and then she lets go of my hand, and it falls back into my lap, and it's all warm and tingly from where her lips brushed against it.

Virago stares at me intently, this gorgeous woman on one knee in front of me, perfectly balanced and steady, with her elbow on her knee, her *armored* elbow. She breathes out softly, slowly, and straightens, then, as she sits back on her heels in a single fluid motion, I find I can breathe again. Just barely.

"I have been a knight since I took my oath to Queen Calla in my seventeenth year," she tells me, her face serious and impassive as she says the words with a quiet strength. "It is my solemn and sworn duty to protect the people of Arktos City, and the kingdom of Arktos, and that is what I have done to the best of my ability. Until last night." She grimaces, sighs, places her hands on her legs—one on the bare skin of her thigh, actually, since there's still a gaping hole in her pants. Not that I'm still paying attention to that, obviously.

She searches my gaze, her beautiful, full lips beginning to turn downward into a frown. "We received word in Arktos City that a great beast was terrorizing the peoples of the northern mountain range," says Virago, raising one brow as she growls out the words. "So a group of my best fellow knights and myself were asked by the queen to journey and stop the beast in its tracks, before it had cause to reach more populated areas. You see, we'd received more than one story like this, stories that had come in from many different places, different villages and towns—there was even word that an entire village may have been wiped out by the creature. So we went quickly, and we engaged it in battle. But this..." She pauses for a long moment, searching for the words, her bright white teeth worrying at the edge of her full lip. "This was a very different creature than any we'd ever encountered before, and it didn't respond to swords or spears or arrows, not to axes, and not even to magic when we used it."

I stare at her, my mouth open, as she pauses, clears her throat. She said the "m" word. Magic.

"So we concocted a plan..." she continues, raising her chin. "If we could open one of the portals from our world to an in-between place between worlds and lure the beast through the portal, it would be trapped where it could not destroy or harm anything or anyone, ever again. We believed, you see, that this was no ordinary beast, but a construct, built of magic. Dark, evil magic."

"Magic," I repeat softly. "And...and portals." Virago is watching me, head to the side, and she nods slowly, thoughtfully.

"So we sought the only local witch that we could find…"

"Witch?" I manage weakly. She ponders this for a moment.

"They do magic…" she turns her long, graceful fingers in a circle. "Sometimes, they're called sorceresses."

"Oh," I reply, swallowing. Sure. Actual witches. *Sorceresses.*

"…and there aren't that many villages in the northern mountain range, so it was hard to *find* a witch. Thankfully, she was near where the portal was located. You see, only a witch can open a portal, and—"

"I'm sorry…" I mutter, standing, spluttering. Virago's brows both go up, but she watches me quietly from her position, crouching on my living room floor, her elbow on her knee like she's just been knighted. "But…" I splutter again and fall silent, staring down at her ice blue eyes, her set, strong jaw. I swallow, continue quietly: "You can't *possibly* be asking me to believe that you're from another world," I tick off my fingers, "that you're a *knight* from a *kingdom*, that you came here with a *beast* that happens to be a *construct of sorcery*, and—"

Virago stands too, then, her eyes flashing as she spreads her long-fingered hands. "I am sorry, m'lady, but it is the only explanation that I can muster. I do not know why it went wrong. Why I came here. I only know now that I am here, and that there is a beast that I brought with me that may hurt or kill others. I will be responsible for this, and I must not let that happen. I will not let innocents suffer because of me," she says, her voice low, passion making her words break at the end. She searches my eyes. "M'lady Holly…I do not know *why* I came here, but I arrived here…you were there when I came through…" She trails off, and I'm not certain what she's going to say next, but my heart's beating so quickly, I can hardly breathe. We're so close to each other. So close. I can smell the scent of her, leather and metal and something a little like sandalwood, and the warm, sweet scent of her skin. She works her jaw, and she stares deeply into my eyes.

She's waiting for me to say something, I realize.

And I hate myself for what I say next, but it's the truth. "How can I believe that?" I whisper, balling my hands into fists. All of the fight is knocked out of me, but I have to speak the truth. "How can I believe that you're from another *world*? That's…that's not possible."

We stare at one another for a long moment. Her eyes are wide, pained, and then something comes across her face, and her jaw hardens, her expression hardens, and she grimaces, shaking her head, shifting her weight back onto her heels.

"M'lady Holly," she says stiffly, standing at attention and staring straight forward, over the top of my head. "I realize that I have troubled you too greatly. You have been quite kind in all of this, and I do not wish to further trouble you. I will be on my way, then."

I swallow as she turns, taking up her still wet fur capelet—it lays across her arm like a sad, unconscious animal—and her still wet cloak. "No. Please. Wait…" I mutter, stepping forward, putting my hand on her warm arm, my fingers against muscled skin that's surprisingly soft to the touch. "Please…" She turns to look back at me, her blue eyes a gravity that pulls me down and into them, and that gaze again…the jolt of it goes all the way down my toes and back again. When she looks at me, it's as if she can see into the very heart of me.

Her gaze packs a punch.

"Okay," I say slowly, breathing out. "If all that you say is true…" (*Oh, my God, Holly, oh, my God*, I think to myself, but I push through all of the doubt and keep talking.) "If all you say is true," I repeat, and gulp, "then how did you end up with that thing…that 'beast,' here?"

"Well," says Virago heavily, licking her lips as she shakes her head, rolls her shoulders down, "the witch was supposed to open a portal to the in-between place between worlds, but she opened it to here…I suppose. 'Earth.' And she was trying to change the direction of the portal when the beast—which, unfortunately, our knights could not control nearly as well as we'd hoped—broke through our ranks, and pushed through the portal. Dragging me with it. In its mouth," Virago adds helpfully, patting her leg, and the wound that had sealed in her skin. A wound from a gigantic mouth and teeth, I now realize. "And then the portal was closed. And it still is," she folds her arms, her leather gauntlets creaking against the fluid motion as she sighs again. "But it doesn't *matter* if the portal is closed or not, because I have to find *another* portal, and *another* witch, so that I can do what we set out to in the first place: trap the creature in the in-between space. Or it will wreak havoc on your world. And destroy it," she says, words weighty and final.

I breathe out, run my hands through my hair, sink back down in the chair again. "Destroy it," I repeat, gazing up at her, and she nods, hands on her metal and leather-clad hips.

"So you see, it is quite imperative that I find the creature. And a portal. And a witch," she says, kneeling smoothly down before me again on one knee. She leans toward me, her bright blue eyes trained on my face, her full lips downturned as she murmurs, beseeching, her low words strong and intense: "M'lady Holly, I beg of you...I am a stranger here. I do not know the ways of your kingdom, and we are running out of time. Please help me find these things?"

I splutter, swallow, try to form coherent words. "But...there just aren't any witches on my world. I mean..." I trail off as she shakes her head, her ponytail moving softly over her metal shoulder, the dark hair drifting over the metal like dripping ink. I follow the motion with my eyes, mesmerized, but then my gaze is irrevocably drawn back to her own, to her bright blue eyes that seem to burn themselves into me.

I swallow as I watch her lean forward a little.

God...am I actually beginning to believe her?

"*Every* world has witches, I promise you that," she says with conviction, nodding her head slowly, jaw set. "Just because this is not Agrotera does not mean that witches don't exist here. *Every* kingdom possesses them."

"...Agrotera," I repeat, tasting the word.

"My world," says Virago, smiling proudly. "My beloved world," she says it softer, her deep, rich voice making me shiver with delight. "Please, m'lady Holly..."

"It's just...just Holly. Please," I say, and in spite of myself, I'm returning her smile weakly. I sigh, take a gulp of fresh oxygen, grapple with what I should do, my thoughts racing.

"Holly," she whispers then, taking my hand in

her own strong one, her tan fingers cupping my hand, her thumb tracing a pattern over my palm. My name on her tongue is electrifying. She says the word so soft and low that it seems to reverberate deep inside of me. I shiver, again, in spite of myself and clear my throat.

I sigh.

"Okay. Here's what we're going to do," I mutter, standing, smoothing out the folds in my pajama pants, suddenly acutely aware that I'm wearing an entire fleece collection of mismatched, crazy prints in front of this incredibly gorgeous creature dressed in *leather and armor.* "I'm...I'm going to bring my dog back inside," I start, because it's really the only thing I can think of in the face of all of this new—and completely out of this world—information.

I cross the room to the sliding glass door as Virago folds her strong arms, nodding to me. I pull the door open, clear my throat, and say loudly out into the backyard: "*Shelley!*" But, of course, my dog is paying me absolutely no mind as she stands out in the back industriously licking something.

"Just a minute!" I tell my guest with what I hope is a cheerful tone. I shove my garden clogs onto my fleece-covered feet and stalk out into the wet backyard and the bright morning sunshine.

Just like any other day.

But...not really.

Okay, I think, as I pace across the backyard, my socks becoming instantly soaked in my clogs from the wet ground as I make a beeline toward my stubborn dog. *So Virago thinks she's a knight from another world. That's...that's mentally unstable, just a bit. But, I mean...at least she doesn't think she's the messiah or something, right? From another world we can handle, can't we? I'm sure she's* actually *from the Knights of Valor Festival, and if we go visit them, we can get this all sorted…I mean, she* has *to be from the festival. Her clothes, the fact that she had a sword…*

A sword.

I stare.

What my ridiculous dog is busy coating with slobber is, in fact, a sword, stuck in the ground like a cheap knock-off prop of the Arthurian sword in the stone legend. But I can tell immediately that the sword itself isn't cheap. I've seen replicas of medieval-era swords before, and this…isn't like them. That's the thing. It doesn't *look* like a replica at all, because most replicas are built of cheap metal with a possibly molded rubber handle or the words "made in China" printed along the blade.

This sword looks like the *real thing*. Like the swords I've seen in museums. For one thing, real swords have little nicks out of the blade (from actually being used in combat) and have an incredibly sharp edge, or a sharp edge that's been dulled with time and sharpened over and over. Exactly like this one. I take Shelley by the collar and pull her back from the sword (at least she was only busy licking the hilt. She is *so weird.*). When I make certain my dog isn't bleeding anywhere, I turn back to the sword, staring at it for a long moment. And then I reach forward, curl my fingers over the hilt and yank the blade up and out of the ground.

The blade is so bright that when I turn it, it reflects the sunshine into my eyes, temporarily blinding me. It's so *heavy*, that it's actually hard to lift, and when I can see again, blinking away the spots in my vision, I notice the gem in the pommel, what I thought was a rhinestone when I first picked it up. But no. This doesn't really look like a rhinestone. It looks, instead, more like a gem, like, an *actual precious stone*. It's clear, like a diamond, but it also has this weird blue-green flash of color deep within...

The flash of the gem almost blinds me again, but I turn my eyes at the last second, rest my gaze on the ground.

I blink for a long moment, still staring at the ground. Because there's something on the ground that's even more fantastical than this massive, heavy, too-real sword in my hands. Something utterly...impossible.

I move the sword so that the point rests against the earth, and the pommel is leaning against my side for a moment, because I've suddenly lost a great deal of my strength, and I can't hold the sword up anymore. My legs are buckling under me, but I tighten my knees, stare down at the ground. Beyond the sword, in the grass of my backyard, are the divots I saw from the back door. But, this up close, I can actually see them much more clearly, can see the details.

They're not divots.

They're...tracks. Animal tracks, I realize, as my brain tries to make sense of what, exactly, I'm seeing.

They look a little like a Tyrannosaurus Rex's footprints, is the first thing I realize.

And then I realize that I'm comparing *fresh* footprints in my *backyard* to those of a *dinosaur*. But really, what else in the whole world could I compare them to? Each individual print (and there are three perfectly clear ones and a few smudges into the earth, I realize, as I count them up) is about four feet long. Four *feet*. That's about how long my *dog* is.

I glance up after a long moment and stare thoughtfully

at my shed. Or, rather, what used to be my shed. Because the useless little building that I always thought only existed to house snakes and spiders (and would never, ever house my little lawnmower for those exact reasons) is now flattened, boards everywhere in tangled stacks, and the roof smooshed into the ground.

Really, the best word to describe it is *obliterated*.

For a single heartbeat, I wonder if it was destroyed because of a lightning strike. I wonder if lightning hit the roof of the shed and it just sort of…exploded. And then I think better of it, because, seriously—I know better. It wasn't because of a lightning strike that my shed is now a pile of kindling in my backyard.

I stare at what was once my shed and swallow, my heart starting to pound inside of me.

Is it actually possible that Virago could be telling the truth?

I mean…I know that I saw something last night, something that can't really be explained. It was enormous. And it was out in my backyard. So, no, I don't know exactly what I saw, but it couldn't possibly have been a hallucination—could it have? It seemed so real.

I stare down at the footprint.

That certainly seems real enough.

I turn around and stare at the woman who stands in the doorway easily, leaning against the frame with raw grace, one hand on her leather-clad hip, her head to the side, her silken black ponytail pooling over her shoulder as she watches me intently. A little shiver runs through me, and I close my hand around the pommel of the sword that leans against my side.

I saw Virago's wound last night. I saw the

blood, the blood that leaked onto my couch, the evidence of which is *still there*. That wasn't faked—it was *real*. And now, somehow, the wound is healed, the wounds in both her side and her thigh completely gone, as if they'd never been there.

And then, of course, there's this sword. I look down at it, try to lift it again, but I can't, really, because it's solid metal. This isn't a fake.

It seems real enough, too.

Okay, Holly, what are you going to do? I think to myself. I worry at the edge of my lip with my teeth, and then I take a deep breath and start back across the lawn, half-dragging, half-trying to carry the sword after me. Shelley follows along, leaping alongside me, the happiest I think I've ever seen her, her luxurious furry tail wagging and waving behind her like a fan.

"She really likes you," I grunt, heaving the sword after me as Shelley and I traverse the three steps up onto the porch. Shelley prances right up to Virago and sits down in front of her, her tail wagging so hard and so quickly that it makes a little, faint *thump* against the floor.

Virago smiles affectionately and crouches down, tousling Shelley's head with long fingers and ruffling the tufts of hair behind her ears.

"She's a good beast," she says easily, even as Shelley's face darts forward, and she begins to bathe Virago's cheek and chin with her bright pink tongue. Virago laughs with delight, and I'm frozen to the spot as I watch this exchange. Yes, Shelley loves a lot of people, but she's also a pretty good judge of character. Nicole hates Shelley, and Shelley isn't too keen on Nicole.

Now, Virago chuckles, sits back on her heels,

and she glances up at me with her ice-blue gaze as she ruffles Shelley's ears again. "What is the beast's name?"

"Shelley," I say hesitantly, still watching their interaction for a moment. Then I shake myself out of it, offer the hilt of the sword to Virago. She rises in a single fluid motion, and takes the hilt from me, those long fingers now wrapping around mine as she lifts the blade out of my hands, her warmth lingering against my skin for a moment as I watch her heft the sword into the air. She lifts it up like it's about the same size and weight as a piece of *celery*. "Like in…Mary Shelley. I named her after Mary Wollstonecraft Shelley," I say, trying to stick to things I actually feel like I understand at this moment. "She wrote *Frankenstein*," I continue, as Virago raises her brows questioningly. "It's…a very good book. One of my favorites."

"Ah," says Virago, and ruffles Shelley's head again with a small smile. "Named after the maker of a good book. A good name for a good beast," she finishes, smiling at me then, her full lips in a gracious curve. "Thank you for retrieving my sword," she says, stepping back genteelly to let me in through the door, holding the sword so that the blade is pointing down and to the side, at ease. "If I may, perhaps, have a cloth to clean it?"

"Sure," I say, because why not? I wander in past her.

I am so in over my head.

I find the roll of paper towels on its side on my counter from where I ripped some off last night to staunch the flow of Virago's blood, and I bring in a handful of them to her. Virago's seated on the couch, sword resting lightly on her knees, and she takes the towels from me, nodding and smiling her thanks. *Holly, seriously, oh, my God, get it together!* It's just so *hard* to get it together, because every single time Virago looks at me, or her gaze lingers on me, I find that it's difficult for me to form a complete thought, let alone complete sentences, but there are so many problems with that fact, because—first and foremost—*she thinks she's from another world*, and though I'm going to be breaking up with Nicole, right now I'm still in a relationship with her, and...

Okay. Let me just be completely honest: the worst problem, the insurmountable problem? There's really *no* possibility that Virago is gay. I watch as she begins to stroke the wad of towels deftly along the length of the blade, rubbing off the mud and bits of grass, making certain they don't fall on my carpet. I mean. *Maybe* there's no possibility that she's gay. She certainly gives off the gay vibe, and I've always congratulated myself on my impeccable gaydar. But how can I be having these thoughts about someone who *genuinely believes* she's from another world?

Because she's gorgeous and kind and chivalrous, I think in the back of my head.

And, anyway, I realize, reeling myself in and depositing myself back on the sad, desolate earth. I have Nicole.

...Nicole. *Shit*. Shit. I was supposed to call her, and then never did, and last night was *terrible*, I remember clearly. Everything about yesterday was pretty darn disastrous. I straighten, clear my throat, take a step back. "Um, I've...I've got to call my..." Virago looks up questioningly, and I falter. "Um. I have to call someone," I tell her, and she nods, and I slime away, feeling like the worst traitor on the face of the planet. Nicole is my *girlfriend*, I should have told

Virago that I had to call my *girlfriend*, but...

But what? I don't want Virago to know that I have a girlfriend? I mean, for how much longer am I going to *have* a girlfriend?

And Virago's *not gay, Holly, would you stop drooling all over her?*

I sigh, hit Nicole's speed dial, and wander up the stairs and into my bedroom, shutting the door behind me.

Of course she doesn't pick up. Of course I get her voicemail. It's Saturday morning, and she's probably still in meetings, but everything around me just became so strange, that I realize, my heart aching inside of me, that I really needed to hear her voice just then.

But she probably doesn't even want to speak to me right now, what with Carly volunteering her to make a fool of herself on stage.

Maybe she realized last night, too, that we have to end this.

"Hello, you've reached Nicole Harken," her voice mail message says breezily. "Please leave a message and I'll return your call as soon as possible."

I breathe out.

"Hey, it's me..." I mutter into the phone. "Um. About last night..." I trail off. I remember the way she looked at me yesterday. She'd looked so angry. So put out. This isn't really something that we can talk about over voicemail. I swallow, try to think of something to say. "Just call me back, okay?" I manage, and then I hang up.

I rub my hand over my face in frustration, go into the bathroom, stare at my reflection in the mirror.

God, I look *terrible*. I didn't take my makeup off

from last night, and because of the rainstorm and the bath and everything else, I sort of look like a very deranged clown, the blue eye shadow creased with the glitter I'd applied for the Renaissance Festival now congealed next to my eyebrows and my eyeliner running down the sides of my nose. My wavy red hair is all tangled, and sort of standing up around my head like a puffy, messy halo. I turn on the hot water, get my hands soapy, wash my face slowly and methodically, relishing the warmth against my skin. It draws me back into the moment, helps me think.

So yeah, I looked terrible, but it doesn't matter if I look attractive or not, because Virago isn't gay, and she thinks she's from another world. Okay, good. I scrub at the eyeliner that leaked down the side of my nose. And, anyway, I'm with Nicole. I pause, wiping some soap off the tip of my nose. But I'm not *really* with Nicole, because I have to break up with her, and if last night was any indication, I have to break up with her pretty darn soon.

I turn off the water, reach for the hand towel and rub my face vigorously with it. I hang it back on the rail and grimace at my freshly scrubbed reflection in the mirror.

I need to be completely honest with myself: I'm really attracted to Virago.

But she thinks she's a *knight*, for heaven's sake.

I take another deep breath and stare at myself in the mirror as my eyes widen.

Okay. Yes. I have a total thing for knights, obviously. But that doesn't change all of the facts.

I peel off my fleece shirt and my fleece pants, and pull on jeans and a bright blue tank top that reminds me a little of Virago's eyes, which I fully admit to myself. Then, with a long sigh, I take the tank top off and put on a bra, then put on the tank top again, and pull my hair in a pony tail. Then I take my hair out of the pony tail, then put it back into the pony tail, with another long sigh. I think about taking off this plain white bra and putting on one of my black ones, but I realize I'm being ridiculous and don't, in fact, change my bra. I trot downstairs, trying not to care how I look, and at the foot of the stairs, I stop.

The sword is now in the scabbard on Virago's back—the scabbard that I didn't notice until now—and Virago is talking very quietly with Shelley.

My dog, my dog who's never paid rapt attention to anything other than food in her entire life, is sitting at attention at Virago's feet, her front paws even together, her long snout angled up toward Virago and her bright brown eyes wide as she stares up at the woman, eating up every single word that Virago tells her.

"...and you are a very good beast to the mistress Holly," says Virago softly, her low voice like a big cat's purr. She nods, the wolf tail moving over her shoulder with her long black hair fluidly. "What a very, very good beast."

Shelley's white-gold tail has not stopped wagging.

"Wow...she never even looks at *me* like that," I manage, putting my hands in my jeans pockets as I step down to the staircase landing. Virago rises and turns, her head inclined toward me with a nod.

"I have always loved hounds," she tells me with a soft, indulgent smile as she shrugs toward Shelley. "And they tolerate me, for the most part." She rolls her shoulders back, stands at attention, but not before I notice something that makes me practically speechless. As she stands at attention, her bright blue gaze roves over me. Literally. Her eyes actually travel—slowly—down my face, over my chest and stomach and hips and legs, and then slowly back up.

Did she…just check me out?

My knees feel weak as her gaze flicks back up to my eyes. Her mouth is turning up slightly at the corners now, but that doesn't mean anything, does it?

Did she *just check me out*?

Virago clears her throat, nods toward me. "Now, m'lady Holly—"

"Remember…it's just Holly…" I manage to tell her, and then I realize that my cheeks are probably bright red, and I don't want her to see that my cheeks are bright red. So I wander past her into the kitchen.

Okay, I'm too old for this schoolgirl crush thing that seems to be happening, right? I mean, I'm thirty-two, and I'm acting like I'm seventeen and some gorgeous girl just looked me over when, in fact, I'm thirty-two, in a relationship, and a woman who claims she's a knight from another world just looked me over.

I bite at my lip as pure delight rushes through me. Okay, yes. All of those things are true.

But I really and totally think she did, in fact, check me out.

"So," I say loudly, clearing my throat and trying to act (and failing to act) casual. "I think we need some breakfast before we can begin…whatever it is that we're beginning."

"Finding the beast, and the portal, and a witch," she says effortlessly, striding with ease over to my kitchen counter and leaning down on it, her broad shoulders curving toward me beneath the metal slopes of her armor. I wonder if she knows how easy and effortless she makes everything look, even turning *leaning on a counter* into something dripping with raw sensuality and gorgeousness. I avert my eyes and open my fridge door, grateful for the fact that it blocks my still red face from her.

"Great," I mutter, peering inside at the almost completely empty shelves. I'd forgotten that I was supposed to go grocery shopping this weekend. "Okay. So I have soy milk. And…and ketchup. I'm kind of low on everything because I wasn't supposed to even be here this weekend…" I trail off, shut the fridge door as I bite my lip.

I wasn't supposed to be *here*, because I was supposed to be spending the weekend at Nicole's.

You know. Before the complete disaster that was last night.

"Anyway, I'm sorry I don't have much. I wasn't prepared to have a…guest," I tell her, rubbing at my bare arms absent-mindedly. "So we need to go get some food. Some breakfast." I take up my mug from the night before, with its half-finished tea, and bring it to the sink. "Does that sound all right to you?"

"Yes, if we can then start the quest immediately after," says Virago quietly, inclining her head. "It is very…kind of you to be assisting me in this, my greatest trial. I hope you know that I am indebted to you because of this…" she trails off, pushes off from the counter, comes forward around it, moving slowly, like a big cat would move, I think, slowly, in a sensual prowl. As she steps toward me, everything seems to slow, and time lengthens. My heart is pounding loudly against my chest, again, like it's knocking on a door. "Holly…" she whispers, stepping closer slowly until she's only an inch or so away from me. She inclines her head toward me, a graceful curve of neck and shoulder.

This close, the scent of her fills me, that rich, dark scent of leather merging with sandalwood, the bright tint of metal from her armor mixing with the scent of her skin.

My chest is rising and falling quickly with my breath. I try to get a hold of myself, but I fail to, swallowing.

She's close enough to kiss as her ice-blue eyes search mine. The warmth of her body, even though she's still a few inches away, is still electric against me, and every hair on the back of my arms is standing to attention.

Everything about her draws me to her. The curve of her mouth, the intensity of her gaze, the scent and sound and sensation of her closeness. She speaks so formally, but passionately, and she's wearing armor and a sword.

She is, literally, my perfect woman.

A knight in shining armor.

"Um," I whisper, blinking as I try to clear my head from all of the thoughts that I'm powerless against—the chief one is the one I'm absolutely not supposed to be thinking about and involves me leaning forward and capturing Virago's mouth with a kiss. I lean back, away from her, dodging the bullet. "I'm, um, really hungry. Are you?" I manage.

Her left brow raises, but then she smiles at that, her mouth quirking sideways, and she nods, chuckles, steps back. She was close enough that if I'd stepped forward, we would have merged together, my arms wrapping around her waist, and then...

"Yes," she murmurs, her intense gaze still

pinning me in place. She searches my eyes, and then turns away, her chin down as she takes a deep breath, rolls her shoulders back again. "My apologies. I am quite hungry."

"Okay. Great. Let's go get some food!" My voice is shaking, and my hands are too when I take my favorite black cardigan from the coat hook by the door. "Um..." I glance her and her armor up and down, grabbing my purse and the keys from the dish. I smile brightly and clear my throat. "We'll go through the drive through."

Chapter 5: Modern Miracles

"…And a large soy caramel frappe with an extra shot," I tell the bright yellow microphone box loudly, turning to my companion. Virago is seated beside me, armor uncomfortably strapped to the back of the seat because the seatbelt is too big to go across her breast plate. Virago raises her eyebrows at me as I smile at her. "Virago," I ask, trying to figure out what, exactly, on the menu of Starbucks she might actually enjoy. "Do you like…bread?"

"Surely," she replies, leaning forward to fiddle with the knob on the radio again. She's been playing with it this entire drive because it fascinates her so much. I guess, if I were from another world, music coming out of a dashboard would be pretty impressive, too. Now she presses the forward button again, and classic rock music blares out of the speakers because she turned the volume up so loudly. I quickly turn the dial down as the barista chuckles through the speakers.

"…And you want a side order of Bon Jovi with that?" crackles out.

"Sorry about that!" I tell him, but I'm laughing, too. Virago shrugs and smiles handsomely. "And two croissants?" I tell the barista.

"You got it! That'll be thirteen eleven, you can pull up!"

I roll up the window and inch forward in the

line of caffeine-deprived drivers. It's a Saturday morning, and the line in the Starbucks drive through was so long, I almost contemplated pulling into a parking space and just going in myself. But if I couldn't leave Shelley in a parked car on a warm day, I sure as hell wasn't leaving a ridiculously gorgeous knight alone. Even with the window cracked open.

I cast another sideways glance at Virago, and she smiles at me again, leaning back in the seat and tugging at the taut seatbelt.

"So, what sort of witchcraft is that?" asks Virago, mystified, as we ease up to the bumper of the car ahead of us, and I fish through my purse for my wallet.

"Um. It's called a 'drive through.' You order at that microphone back there, and then you pull up, and they give you the food and drinks you ordered, and you pay for it at a window," I tell her distractedly.

"I am thinking," says Virago, head to the side, "that it would be a great addition to the tea houses in Arktos City. I cannot tell you how many times I've tied my horse to the hitching post out front, and—you must realize she is a lead mare caught and tamed from the northern herds, and she is quite ill tempered and not fond of waiting—and I come out, and she is gone. And *then* I must find her in the whole of the city, and I am quite held back, being full of tea," says Virago with a small chuckle, her hands spread, the metal spirals on the edges of her wrist gauntlets sparkling in the morning sunshine. "You can imagine that this is not my favorite occupation—trying to find my mare in the city. So this is quite innovative," she finishes as the car ahead of us pulls out, and we pull forward. I'm grinning, because I'm imagining Virago prowling through the streets of some fantastical city, whistling for her mare.

We're finally next.

"Hey, Henry!" I greet my favorite barista and hand over my debit card.

"You're not usually with such a foxy lady!" he says, leaning down in the window, feathered blonde hair falling into his eyes as he peers at my passenger. He's wearing a cheesy grin and eyeliner. "You must introduce me! Why didn't you come in? Why is she dressed like a knight?"

"Oh, well, you know the Knights of Valor Festival is in town!" I admonish him, but I sound a little fake and desperate, even to my own ears. He raises an eyebrow, runs my card through, and starts to hand out little bags and drinks. He winks at me when I start to pull away. The kind of wink that indicates "good job, nice catch." I grimace a little at him, but then I'm pulling away.

"Okay," I tell Virago as we edge out onto the street into the line of traffic, and I start guzzling my frappe like there's no tomorrow. "We're going to get you some clothes. Help you blend in a little more." I glance sidelong at her. Clothes might not really help the "blending in more" thing. She radiates a sort of power and intensity that most people just don't carry around with them.

"Holly," says Virago, patiently holding all of the little bags of breakfast in her lap. "Clothes are not nearly so important as finding the beast, the portal and a witch. There are people in peril out there, and—"

"Don't worry—I looked it up on my phone," I begin, and when she stares at me blankly, I bite my lip, reconsider what I'm saying. "I...I looked to see if your beast has been causing trouble on something that would be…able to tell me if he was causing trouble or not." I think of my news app and realize there's no better way to explain it to her. "Anyway, there was nothing about it anywhere, not on the news, not *anywhere*. And I would assume a nice big beast causing havoc would be kind of newsworthy. So I don't know. Maybe it found the portal on his own, went back to your world? Or something?"

I try not to think it, but there it is: *Maybe it didn't exist in the first place?*

"No…" Virago muses, chin in hand as she thinks, gazing out the window. "But it may have gone into hiding to try and heal. I *did* manage to stab it through a crack in its chest scales, and the wound was quite close to its heart, but I didn't think I'd gotten it so badly…" She thinks for a longer moment as I take another sip of my frappe, letting the sweetness roll into my mouth. "I did cut off a bit of its tongue," she says then musingly. "Maybe it didn't quite like that. Good to know that it might have something of a weakness," she adds, gazing sidelong at me.

"Maybe," I tell her, but I'm so unsure. There are those tracks in my backyard. They're *definitely* there, but are they *definitely* real? But how could I have imagined what I saw last night? I know that I have a great imagination, but really—the image of the massive beast, hidden mostly by the rain and the night, but bits of its scales glinting, teeth flashing in the darkness…that would probably haunt my nightmares for my entire life.

Virago visibly relaxes next to me, leaning her head back on the headrest. "This gives me great comfort," she says then quietly with a low sigh. "I had been considering what it might be doing to innocents…" She shudders in her seat, shakes her head. "I am glad that, like me, it is rallying. We can meet each other in dignified combat, then, face one another as equals upon the battlefield…" She trails off, lifts her chin, her blue eyes taking on an edge of steel to them. "This time, things will go differently."

I work diligently on keeping my eyes on the road, because when she talks like that, a little thrill runs through me, and I try to repress a shiver. Instead, I lift up my frappe cup again and take a quick, chilly swallow of the sugary beverage.

Virago's brows raise and her full lips curl into a grin. "You…quite like that."

"Mm?" I swallow another mouthful. "Oh, this." I smile a little, glad of the distraction. I tip the cup toward my face, inhale the fragrant aroma and…end up with a bit of whipped cream on the end of my nose. I wipe it off with the back of hand self consciously. "It's only my favorite thing in the entire universe. I mean, not really. I rather like Shelley and my books, too. But when things are overwhelming and I have a soy caramel frappe, the world suddenly starts to make a whole lot more sense. Do you want a sip?" I offer her the plastic to-go cup.

Virago stares down at it, her brow furrowing. "I do not know what manner of drink this is…" Virago tells me, picking up the cup and sniffing at the domed lid. "What's this white stuff on top of it?"

"Oh, whipped cream. That's the best part." I glance sidelong at her, too, and then I'm snorting down an unexpected chuckle. She's trying to upend the cup to drink out of the top hole of the domed lid, ignoring the straw. "No, you drink through this…" I tell her, pointing to the straw. "Try sucking up on it. Put your lips around it…" I trail off, clear my throat.

Describing how to use a straw? It sounds kind of like a come on when you think about it. I realize that I'm turning a very warm shade of red as Virago lowers her head to the straw, putting her full lips around the plastic and, as I instructed, sucking up on it. God, I *really* need to pay attention to the road, because for a heartbeat, all I can stare at—my heart thundering inside of me—is this gorgeous woman, drinking out of a straw seemingly for the first time.

Virago has a very strange look on her face as she sets the cup back down into its holder. "That was very cold," she says, licking her lips and smiling. "But also quite delicious. I can understand why you like it so much. It is very different from tea."

"That's because it has espresso in it, not tea," I tell her with a small smile. I put on my blinker, turn down the next street.

"Espresso?"

"It…um. Espresso…" I trail off, then shrug. "Well, it helps you do things faster."

Virago raises one brow, her head to the side as she considers the cup. Then she picks it up, takes another sip from the straw, holding the cup aloft like she's toasting me. "All right, then, Holly, I shall put this to the test!" She sets the cup back down and rolls her shoulders back against the seat of my car, leaning back to regard me with a brow raised, a smile tugging at the corner of her lips. I try not to stare at her too much. She practically purrs: "I am always looking for ways to be faster and better."

"This might help you with that," I'm chuckling as I put my eyes back on the road, try to sound normal and not squeaky. I have to ignore the fact that this incredibly gorgeous woman is practically lounging in my car if I don't want to get into an accident, which is becoming increasingly more possible the more I stare at my passenger. I clear my throat. "I still remember when my brother gave me my first cup of coffee..." I trail off after a moment, as I consider an odd thought. "Hey. Actually. My brother, Aidan..." I frown. "I mean, this is kind of a weird idea. He's going to think I'm nuts," I mutter as an afterthought. But, actually, maybe not. It *is* my brother I'm talking about, after all—he's kind of the king of weird ideas.

"What is it, Holly?" asks Virago, then, her voice deep and soft and encouraging.

"Well," I answer, taking one of the bags from her lap and opening it up. Because I'm still staring at the road, I manage to brush my fingers against the warm skin of her leg through the hole in her leather pants. That skin is so soft, it's surreal, but beneath it is a ripple of hard muscle. "Sorry," I whisper, retracting my hand, but she doesn't seem to notice, or, at least, I think she hasn't noticed until I chance a sideways glance, and see that she's trying to suppress a smile as she stares out the window. I feel my cheeks redden, and the scent of warm croissant fills the car as I open the bag.

"Okay," I tell her, handing her one of the warm pastries. She takes it, her fingers brushing against my palm as she lifts the croissant up to her nose and inhales the mouth-watering aroma, mystified. "First," I brandish the second croissant, "we eat. Then, we'll get you some clothes. You really need to not be a walking advertisement for the Knights of Valor Festival. At least it's in town, so people won't think you're from a television show or…or something…" Yes, what *would* people think she was? I trail off, take another sip of the frappe. "And then, I think I'm going to take you to see my brother."

"Oh?" asks Virago, and then she takes a bite of croissant, chewing thoughtfully.

"If anything," I say with a brow raised, "he can help you clear your chakras. And who doesn't like cleared charkas? You like?" I ask her, indicating the already three-quarters consumed croissant in her hand.

"It is perfect," she tells me, taking another bite. But she's not looking at the croissant when she says it. Instead, she's staring intently at me, her bright blue eyes tracing over my face.

My hands grip the wheel a little tighter, and I train my eyes back on the road, flush rising in my cheeks.

She totally didn't just come on to me, right? Right?

…Right?

The croissant is gone, and Virago licks her fingers slowly and sensually, brushing the remaining crumbs off her leather-clad lap. "Good plan," she tells me then, leaning back in the car.

"We're almost to the mall," I tell her, wracking my brains as I try to figure out if she did, in fact, come on to me, then decide I'd really better stop thinking about this. It can only lead to heartache.

I pull into the parking lot, start the search for a parking spot, which makes me focus on something that doesn't involve the smoldering individual seated to my right.

Getting angry at not being able to find a parking spot is far preferable to the erratic heartbeat and sweaty palms that should, by all rights, only ever be sported by a teenager.

Okay, so I'm not a mall person. There. I said it. But I can't really think of a better place to take Virago clothes shopping. Every year, there's usually people from the Knights of Valor Festival stationed at the mall as a publicity move, handing out brochures to the bored mall walkers, so it'll be easier for her— somewhat—to blend in. People can think Virago's a promotion for the festival.

Either way, it makes more sense to me than dragging her into Wal-Mart, which would have a host of problems on its own, the least of which would be getting Virago in her full armor past the greeter. (Somehow, I think that the usual little old lady—who happens to be as sharp as a fox—wouldn't let Virago in based on how dangerous her boots look alone.)

So we're going to the mall.

I sigh as I park at one of the farthest spots away from the actual mall entrance, what happens to be the only available parking space, which we found *only* after circling the mall twice. I forgot it was Saturday morning—what a lovely time to go to a mall! If by "lovely," I meant "packed and unnavigatable," then yes. We get out of the car, me clutching my almost-empty frappe cup, Virago holding her bottle of water casually as she glances up at the concrete building with her head to the side, as if she's sizing up a soon-to-be-conquered beast. Her ice-blue eyes glitter in the sunshine, and I can't help but stare at her for half a heartbeat as she leans against my car door languidly, her scabbard *thunking* gently against the door.

"Um...if you could leave the sword in the car..." I gesture to the empty back seat with my frappe cup. "Mall security might not take too kindly to it."

"Holly, I can't leave my *sword*," she says with a wry smile, shaking her head, as if I've said the most amusing joke as she reaches over her shoulder and pats the hilt. "A knight *never* leaves her sword behind when beginning a quest," she tells me like she's quoted that particular rule perhaps a million times.

"Well," I say, my tone wheedling, "this isn't necessarily a *quest* so much as a journey to buy you pants," I point out. "And you really won't need a sword in there. I promise."

Virago folds her arms, her leather gauntlets creaking as she narrows her eyes. "I am a knight with a maiden, and—as such—it is my sworn duty to protect you."

My heart is beating so quickly it's in danger of attacking me. I breathe out for a long moment, try to keep my jaw from dropping onto the ground. *Maiden. Protect* me? The idea of her protecting me shouldn't ignite a very serious fire that races through my heart (and between my legs), not because I need protecting...but that she would have thought of such a thing in regards to me. Like she's actually thinking about me. And my safety.

That's so...thoughtful.

"That's very sweet of you," I manage, then, not exactly certain what to say. "But...I don't need protecting. And it's a mall. The only slightly aggressive thing in there is the lotion salespeople."

Virago gazes at me with her piercing blue eyes, and then nods her head, inclining it toward me with a graceful bend, her wolf tail and long, silken black hair pooling over her shoulder and over her right breast. "I will do as my lady asks of me," she says softly, and then she's unbuckling the scabbard from across her breasts, and pulling it over her head in one smooth motion that, for the rest of my life, I'll see in my happiest dreams. She's grace personified. I wish I didn't notice that so much.

"Thank you," I manage, unlocking my back door and opening it for her. Virago sets the sword down gently on the back seat, as if she's setting a relic on an altar and not a gigantic sword on a polyester car seat that's covered with clumps of shed dog hair.

And then we're headed, together, for the mall.

"So we'll get you a jacket, and a shirt, and pants, and some shoes and some underwear…" I tick the items off my fingers and hold the door open for her. Virago stops at that, brow raised, and does a little bow, then, hand at the top of the door, the curve of her body complementing mine as she leans over me, the heat of her skin so close I can feel it.

"After *you*, m'lady," she says, inclining her beautiful head and leaning down a little as she whispers those soft, low words into my ear.

Okay. Would *that* be considered a come on? Could it be anything *but?* I shiver a little as her warm breath drifts over the skin of my neck, and I breathe out, walking through the door, trying not to redden. But after I walk through, Virago continues to hold the door open for a woman and a stroller, and a gaggle of teenagers, and then a little old man who pushes his walker ahead of him. So I really shouldn't feel special. But she certainly didn't whisper in anyone else's ear! Right?

Holly. Seriously. You're grasping at straws here. I hold onto my frappe's straw, actually, taking another sip. I realize at that moment that I am *literally* grasping at straws.

"Are you from the Knights of Valor Festival?" asks one of the teenagers, a slight brunette with a boy-band-of-the-hour t-shirt and braces, beaming up at Virago as she pauses in the mall's entryway. Virago follows her through the door, head cocked, looking to me with brows up, eyes appraising.

"Yes! She is!" I tell the teen, and I take Virago's arm, my fingers curling around the smooth, warm leather of her gauntlets as I lead her through the second door, into the mall proper, leaving the teenagers behind.

I'm about to start power walking down the mall corridor toward J. C. Penney's, but I pause, because Virago is pausing. She's gazing out at the mall that opens up in front of us with wide eyes, with perfect full lips slightly parted in wonder.

Huh. It probably would look kind of weird to someone not from this world.

It's pretty much like any mall I've ever been to. There are free-standing particle-board kiosks with people hawking cell phone cases, overpriced lotion and free piercings to go with your new silver earrings. There's the fountain in the middle of the mall corridor, right beneath the big skylight dome that looks as if it was (and it really *was*) built in the eighties, with the cartoon characters sculptures that I remember from my childhood—which now, in adulthood, look a little creepy since they're so old and flaking paint. The statues stand about a foot shorter than me, in various uncomfortable looking poses, the most deranged one— a Ronald Duckington from a Disney copy-cat cartoon—looks like he has sharp teeth on his beak now, because of how the paint flaked off his face.

The openness of the middle of the mall shows off the golden bird shapes hanging from the skylights overhead, the skylights covered in bird poop that still lets in a great amount of light to show off the columns and cheap plastic cell phone cases directly beneath them.

I mean, it's not the Grand Canyon, but if you were from another world, it'd probably look magical to you, too. The shininess of the plastic alone would probably do it for me.

"Come on," I tell Virago with a smile, tugging gently on her arm, and we begin walking down the length of the mall, toward Penney's.

For a Saturday, the mall is packed even more than usual, and entire groups of people look at Virago, openly staring (some of the teens even taking surreptitious pictures of her on their cells), but she's not paying them any sort of attention, instead staring at the mosaic floor, and up at the hanging seagulls. We pause as we pass the fountain because she's practically obsessed with Larry the talking cartoon cat.

"It speaks," she breathes, staring up at it as if it were a statue of a deity.

"Always wear helmets, even for short bike rides, kids!" says Larry the talking cartoon cat in the same deranged, slightly out-of-tune recording he's been repeating for over thirty years.

"Yeah, it does," I tell her sheepishly, and then, glancing at the fountain in front of us, I dig around in my purse for a penny before I realize what I'm doing. I'm too much a sucker for tradition. My fingers brush against a penny at the bottom of my purse, next to my usual nest of pens and straw wrappers, and I dredge the thin copper coin out, pressing it into her warm palm, as

I glance up shyly at her questioning gaze. "I know it's silly, but ever since I was a kid I do this. It's this silly thing," I tell her, licking my lips, "but if you toss it into the fountain," I explain to her, "and make a wish, maybe it'll come true."

"You have water spirits here, too?" she asks me, one brow raised, and I cock my head for a long moment, not understanding.

"No—"

"Then how does the wish come true? That's how our wishing waterways work. A water spirit accepts the offering of coin and lends us a small amount of her magic to create or accomplish the wish."

I stare up at her unblinking for a long moment, then clear my throat. "I never...thought about it. It's just a superstition, really. It's not supposed to actually *work*. I mean none of the wishes I made here, throwing a penny into a mall fountain, ever actually come true..." I say quietly, trailing off.

Virago stares down at the penny in her hand and seems to reach a decision of her own, for she nods, curling her long fingers over the coin. She closes her eyes, places her fist over her heart, and then the penny is arcing through the air, glittering in the morning sunshine that drifts down through the skylights. The penny settles with a *plop* in the water, shimmering as it nestles instantly among the other coins there.

"It is done," says Virago, smiling at me. And then she takes up my hand and threads it through her arm again, the curve of her breast pressing against the back of my arm, and we continue walking through the mall like walking arm in arm with a lady knight past the sporting goods store is perfectly normal.

I take a deep, wavering breath, and another sip

of frappe to calm my nerves. Because, of course, my overactive imagination is jumping to all sorts of conclusions. But I have to remind myself that just because Virago took my arm back doesn't mean anything. It's a very chivalrous thing to do, and she's kind of implied that she thinks she has to protect me. Which…while being chivalrous and sweet, still isn't remotely true. Maybe the reason she took my arm is that she thinks I'll trip on a candy bar wrapper, and she's just heading off having to dive to catch me. Yes. That's totally it. I mean I *was* totally graceful this morning when she picked me up from sprawling on top of Shelley.

I grow even redder remembering that.

By the time that we reach the escalator by Penney's, my heart is beating too fast, and I wonder if drinking so much espresso so quickly was the best idea. I toss my empty cup into a garbage can and wipe my damp palms on my jeans. Virago has (sadly) let go of me to stare at the escalator with her arms crossed over the breastplate of her armor, and a single, imperious brow raised.

She looks so out of place here, the wolf's tail (or, at least, I assume it's a wolf's tail—I should ask her about that sometime) over her shoulder, the silver of the fur mixing with the ink-black of her hair, her leather boots straight out of a fantasy novel, her armor scratched and banged up, attention to detail stuff you don't usually see on replicas. The thing is, I'm starting to realize *this is really not a replica.*

People keep staring at her, but not really like she's an oddity. More like she commands their gaze to gravitate toward her with her regal presence alone. She's languid and sensual as she strides forward, graceful as a dancer, strength and power radiating off of her like a shimmer. She's standing with her feet hip-width apart now, as she stares at the escalator, that power drawing me in, and I'm kind of weak in the knees as I edge over to her from the garbage can, clearing my throat.

"What is this contraption?" asks Virago then, indicating the escalator with a wave of her hand.

"That's…a sort of movable staircase," I tell her, my eyes flicking to the second level of the mall. "It'll take us up to the second story where the store is."

"Oh no. No," she tells me firmly. I stare at her perplexed as she frowns. "They used witchcraft to try and make movable staircases in the palace in Arktos City," says Virago, shaking her head ruefully. "It didn't work. They are not to be trusted, Holly," she tells me completely seriously, her bright blue gaze searching mine.

I should laugh at that statement, but she says it with such strong conviction that I sort of stare at the escalator for a moment, uncertain of what to do.

"We…um. We could walk all the way to the other end of the mall. It's where the stairs are," I tell her, chewing at my lower lip. "Or you could give it a shot. I promise, it'll last for only a minute, and it's so quick and easy!" I tell her brightly. "See? Watch me." I step forward and on to the first step, then take a step down, and a step down again as the escalator keeps its slow, careful ascent going. "See? Piece of cake," I tell her with a broad smile, crooking my finger toward her. "Want to give it a shot?"

Virago reaches out her hand, and across the space between us, she takes mine.

Her face is set in steely determination as our

arms draw apart, for the escalator continues in its relentless climb, taking me away from Virago. She breathes out, narrows her eyes and takes one big step forward.

"Great! Now the other one..." I tell her as her other foot remains firmly on the ground below. Her legs stretch out for a moment, and then she takes that last step forward, finally standing with both feet on the escalator.

"This is most undignified," she says, a brow up as she rides the escalator upward with me. I smile at her, shaking my head.

As if *she* could ever look undignified.

And then the escalator ride is over, me stepping off onto the second level, and Virago sort of half stepping/half leaping onto the second floor in one smooth, practiced motion.

"This is a very magical place, and I quite enjoy it. Except for that," she says, hooking her thumb over her shoulder and back at the escalator as she tries to keep from smiling, her lips twitching as I lead her toward Penney's, hiding my own smile behind my hand.

"We'll just...walk around the mall on the way back and take the stairs on the far end. You won't have to take the escalator again," I promise her, and—completely unbidden by me—she reaches across the space between us and doesn't take my hand to thread it through her arm. She simply takes my hand to hold it, her warm palm against my own, our fingers laced together as if they were meant to be.

My heart's still not stopped beating too much, too fast, too loudly. But, somehow, now it beats even faster.

"Okay," I breathe out, dragging out the word as

we walk into the inviting bright light of the department store. The only reason I chose this one over the other stores of the mall is that my mother used to bring me and Aidan here when we were little.

I pause for a moment, my heart still thundering, but for different reasons now. I blink, clear my throat as the memories come rushing back. I have so many of them, all happy memories of Saturday afternoons spent trying on different outfits, my mother and Aidan and I all laughing, getting ice cream after hours of trying on clothes. Just thinking about it, it sounds so idyllic. That was how things *used* to be. Before the cancer took my mother. I shake myself a little, breathe out, look back at Virago who's gazing at me in concern, brow creased, squeezing my hand.

Penney's, as odd as it sounds, had been one of her favorite places in the whole world.

"I have happy memories here, believe it or not," I tell her by way of explanation, laughing a little as I say it—but the laugh sounds wooden as I clear my throat. I tug on Virago's hand and lead her toward the women's section. "Here we are!"

"Oh," says Virago after a long moment as I sweep my arm over the rows of skirts and blouses and pants and dresses. She glances up at the mannequins at the edge of the display, all wearing the summer's latest short skirts and fashionable dresses, her brow furrowed, her head slowly shaking. "I don't…think that any of this is really very *me*," she says quietly, again putting her other hand on her side, her hip leaned forward, curving toward me.

"Oh?" I blink. "I mean, they're not armor," I tell her quickly, but she's still shaking her head.

"They're lovely," she tells me, her voice low as

she grimaces a little, her head to the side. "But do they have anything more...ah..." She trails off, sweeps her hand down to indicate her clothes. "*Less* lovely?"

I blink again. "*Oh.*" I realize what she's saying and glance over the racks. There's really nothing more boyish in the women's section this season. I turn and look toward the men's section, loop my arm through hers. One of my old girlfriends always bought her clothes in the men's section. I nod at her encouragingly. "Let's try here..."

Virago's smile lights up the room as I lead her toward the (albeit man-shaped) mannequins that casually display shirts and pants and jackets and ties. "Yes," says Virago with smooth surety. "This is it."

The salesman in the men's department takes one look at Virago, at her armor and wolf's tail and massive leather boots, his eyes going wide, and then he simply smiles with a small shrug. Maybe he gets all types here. "How can I help you?" he asks us, and I let go of Virago's hand as she prowls forward through the rows and racks of suits and jackets and ties and slacks like she's a woman on a mission.

"She's looking for an outfit or two," I tell him. "There was an...accident, and she lost her luggage. And...she's here for the Knights of Valor Festival..." All of it sounds like a lie, but the man is nodding, his head to the side as he considers Virago, not even really listening to me.

"What are your measurements, ma'am?" he asks, wandering after her with his tape measure.

Virago is feeling the weight and heft of a jacket's sleeve. "I rather like this one," she says, mostly to herself, but she's gazing up at me as she says it, her bright blue eyes flicking to me as if she's considering me, too. She glances sidelong at the man who takes the tape measure from around his neck. "I'd like this one," she tells him, then, but he gestures toward the fitting room, and then back at me, brows raised.

"Would the lady like to…try it on?" he's asking, tilting his head toward the nearest fitting room. "This one is unisex," he says, pointing to it.

"Yeah, try it on," I tell her with a smile, gesturing toward the fitting rooms. I grab a dress shirt, a tie and some pants, guessing on the sizes as I usher her toward the rooms. "You go in here, take off your clothes and try these on. To see if they fit," I explain, when she looks perplexed, glancing over her shoulder at the attendant guy who's still watching us, now both brows up. I guess most people don't need to have fitting rooms explained, but sometimes they do, okay?

"Give us just a second…" I mutter to the guy, and hold open one of the fitting room doors for her, handing over the rest of the clothes.

Virago gazes down at me, head a bit to the side, working her jaw for a heartbeat, before I clear my throat. "Do you need help?" I ask.

"No," she murmurs, her voice husky. She breathes out, smiles softly. "I don't. But thank you, Holly." She pulls the door shut after her, and I lean against it for half a heartbeat, feeling the blood quicken inside of me.

I sit down on the little chair outside of the fitting room, swallow, try not to think about the metallic clangs and noises that sound exactly like buckles being unbuckled from in the fitting room. I try very, very hard not to think about Virago becoming naked in there, but then while I try *not* to think about it, my overactive imagination supplies me with many possibilities, and then I'm bright red.

"Holly?" asks Virago after a long moment.

"Yes?" I squeak, then clear my throat, picking up my purse as I stand too quickly. "I'm right here," I tell her, taking a deep breath.

The door to the fitting room creaks open.

"What do you think?" she asks me.

And there, leaning against the dressing room door is Virago. Sans armor and torn pants and leather boots. Those things are on in a small, neat heap on the floor in the corner of the fitting room.

Instead, she's now wearing a buttoned down cream-colored shirt under a ridiculously pretty, shiny and bold red satin vest. Her muscular legs are clad in a pair of smoothly-creased black slacks.

And over her chest, tied neatly (like she's been doing it all her life), she's wearing *a red tie*. It's expertly knotted and pulled snug against the graceful curve of her neck. She's standing there, her hips to the side, curved toward me again, and her thumbs are hooked into the black slacks' belt loops. She's wearing a confidant, sexy smile as she takes in my appreciative expression.

Honestly?

I've never seen anything more gorgeous in all of my days.

"It's a little more constricting than what I'm used to," she says easily, turning to the side and leaning toward the mirror as she adjusts the buttoned sleeves at her wrists with long fingers. "But, for now, it'll do, I think." She glances up at me, eyes hooded and bright and unwavering as she gazes deep down into the very heart of me. "What do you think, Holly?" Her voice is so soft and low that I almost don't hear her words, but my body still reacts to them, shivering at the sound of her voice.

"Beautiful," is the only word I can think of, the only word I can manage.

At that, she gazes at me, breathing slowly, evenly, her head tilting as a slow smile turns the corners of her mouth up wickedly.

My heart can't possibly beat faster. I feel like it's about to burst out of my chest. I clear my throat, turn a little. "This is great," I tell the sales associate with a shaky smile. "We'll take it. Um, Virago, I'll go pay for it," I tell her, beginning to angle toward the register, but I'm paused, because there's a hand at my wrist, long, gentle fingers curving over my skin with a warmth that makes me shudder.

I turn back, look at this woman with the intense eyes, the woman in the men's clothes, who exudes a sensuality I can do nothing else but respond to.

Her strong jaw works for a moment, and she opens her full lips to say something…but whatever she was going to say evaporates, and she simply shakes her head, just a little, says nothing as the ink-black silk of her hair falls over her shoulder again. She lets go of my wrist and I turn away, feeling the flush move over my skin.

The sales associate's grinning at me, shaking his head, as I hand him my credit card.

"Your girlfriend looks great in those," he says, chuckling a little as I try to gather my wits about me, willing my knees to stop being jello. I take a deep breath, let my shoulders roll back, try to calm my roaring heartbeat.

"She's not my girlfriend," I tell him weakly. He raises a single brow.

"Right," he tells me, snorting.
I stare at him, my eyes wide.
Right.

Chapter 6: Do You Believe in Magic?

"Hey, Carly," I answer my cell phone's insistent ring and murmur into it as I open the doors of my car. Virago straightens her sleeves again proudly, placing her neatly bundled armor and pants and boots in the backseat, then sitting and staring straight ahead thoughtfully in the passenger seat, considering the buttons on the sleeves. I bite my lip, watch her long fingers adjust a single button before I shake my head, press the phone a little harder to my ear. "Hey, now's not the best time, okay?" I squeak into my cell phone before my best friend makes a shrewd little sound.

"Are you *with* someone?" she asks delightedly.

"Carly, seriously…"

"No, *you* seriously, miss Holly! *Are you with someone?*"

"Yes…" I whisper, turning in my seat and putting my hand over the speaker as she begins shrieking.

"Oh, my *God!* Oh, my *God, I knew it.* Oh, my God, what's she *like?* How did this happen? I totally just left you last night…oh, my God, did you go *out* after I left last night? Did you just totally hook up with someone? I'm dying here, I need *details*, you're *killing* me!"

Virago tilts her head questioningly toward the phone because Carly's shrieking loudly enough that she can obviously hear every word my best friend is practically screaming. I smile in embarrassment, mouth "just a minute." I sigh into the receiver.

"Carly, seriously," I whisper, "I'm sorry, I really don't have time to—"

"Okay, okay," she says, still cackling with glee. "But the *minute* you're alone, you'd better be calling me back and giving me *serious details*, or I am going to be *so pissed*."

"Yes, ma'am," I tell her, chuckling in spite of myself.

But, seriously, it's really not like what she thinks it is.

Really not like that.

I hang up with her and turn back to Virago, who's gazing sidelong at me, then, her eyes dark and bright, shining from within. She reaches across the space between us, takes up my hand with her warm, curving fingers, pressing her palm against mine effortlessly. "M'lady Holly," she whispers, leaning toward me, stopping herself at the last moment. We're so close that our noses almost brush, and I breathe in the scent and warmth of her, the sweetness of leather and mint, her lips close enough that if I tilted up my head, pushed forward just a little... "Holly," she repeats, voice low. "Thank you so much for the clothing," she murmurs to me, head inclined toward me, her tone soft, warm, her low voice making me want to shiver, but I squash the urge to do so again.

"It's no problem," I tell her truthfully. "It was my pleasure."

Slowly, regretfully, she straightens in the seat again, shakes her head, her ponytail of ink-black hair pooling over her shoulder, contrasting darkly with the crisp white of her shirt. "Now…" she tells me with a long sigh. "Your brother? I have a job to do," she adds heavily after. With regret.

The job.

The monster. The portal. The witch.

Right. I breathe out, try to still my thundering heartbeat. Fail at that.

My brother's shop isn't that far away from the mall, but it's more in the artistic district of the sprawling suburbs. A few blocks worth of driving, and then I'm pulling up right in front of it.

"So, about my brother…" I trail off, turn off the car engine, hands tapping a rhythm on the wheel. A woman from another world sitting in your passenger seat, wearing the sexy hell out of a tie and men's clothing and looking like the most gorgeous thing you'll ever see is bound to distract you. "My brother might, might, *might*," I stress, "be able to help you. The worst is that at least he won't think you're crazy. Which is a start."

"Why do you think he can help me?" asks Virago as we get out of the car, stare up at the building before us.

"Because my brother's a witch," I tell her, hands on hips as I stare at the very unfortunate sign of my brother's shop:

"Welcome to *The Cat, The Cow and The Cauldron*," I tell her with a smile.

"The…the cow?" she asks, perplexed, following me up the broken sidewalk and purple steps that lead up to the bright purple door of his shop. It's bright purple and covered with glittery stars that Aidan re-glitters every month or so because glitter paint isn't exactly weather-proof. I push the door open, and the bell rings gaily with its fairy-esque chimes as we step into the shop.

Immediately, we walk into a fog of incense and herbs, the default perfume of, really, any occult shop. But I also smell cotton candy. Which is the particular perfume of *this* shop. My brother has an eternal sweet tooth.

"Holly!" hoots Aidan from behind the cash register, erasing something in a notebook with a chewed on pencil. He glances up at me with the wide, usual grin, his dark red hair looking especially unkempt and crazy today as it's on end and pointed in every direction. He's wearing his ever classy *"real* witches do it on a *broom"* black t-shirt, and he has slow, methodic drum music playing in the background, which means he's burning his "Primal Energy" incense and probably working on the bookkeeping for the shop. He's grinning at me, and then he looks past me, and the grin sort of freezes on his face, his pointed little beard quivering. I think he's trying to suppress a chortle of glee as I actually *see* the equation being worked on in his head and coming to a conclusion. He darts forward, his mouth in an "o" of astonishment.

"Holly, did you actually do the unthinkable? Did you break up with the ice queen?" He spreads his arms, all but waltzes out from behind the counter and squeezes me so tightly I can't breathe. His shoulder reeks of incense. "I'm so proud of you!" he wibbles dramatically in my ear, and I punch his shoulder, push him off me with a chuckle and roll of my eyes.

"Oh, my God, Aidan, It's not what you think," I tell him, shaking my head and cutting my finger across my throat at an angle that I hope Virago can't see so that he could possibly shut up. "Aidan, try to get serious, okay?"

"Hah! Did you *hear* what she *asked* of me?" he says, waggling his eyebrows at Virago, who's folded her arms (an action that looks somehow even *more* graceful and sexy as she's wearing a tie and vest while doing it) and adopts a careful expression of neutrality, rocking back on her heels and planting her feet an impressive hip-width apart as she raises a single brow and regards my brother with an expression of disbelief.

This is how most people who enter *The Cat, The Cow and The Cauldron* begin their shopping experience (Aidan's two-man *real* skull collection is the very first thing you see when you enter, positioned on either side of his jet-black cash register) but Aidan—my cheerful, charming brother who could charm the scales off a snake—usually gets to them by the end. As he tries right now, for example, taking Virago's arm gently and leading her along the shelves of tea. What is, arguably, the most "normal" friendly section of the shop.

"Now," he tells her, "can I interest you in some genmaicha tea, perhaps? It's a lovely green tea with the rich, nutty aroma of roasted brown rice," he says, his tone smooth and warm as he rubs at his little red beard with a hand that flashes with rings of various semi-precious stones and purportedly imbued with different magical energies.

The walls of *The Cat, The Cow and The Cauldron* are painted a very esoteric shade of purple, a shade that's a little darker than his front door, and are covered with paintings of black cats, black and white cows (wearing pointy witch hats and superior expressions), and cartoon cauldrons with faces (which are, admittedly, slightly creepy). The shelves are stocked with the usual wares: sparkling crystals, rows and rows of blessed and consecrated candles, packets of incense, statues of gods and goddesses and stacks of tarot cards and books—stuff you'd find in any occult shop. But Aidan loves his little store to the moon and back, and it shows in the handmade items in his cases, jewelry made by local designers of semi-precious stones that have healing properties, and on the immaculately spotless glass shelves rests everything from wire wrapped crystal pendants to handmade bath salts and little hand-sewn goddess dolls.

This place has always made me feel at home, but today…now…the usual comfort from this space drains from me as I remember exactly why we're here.

"Aidan, *seriously*…" I trail after him, popping a piece of hard candy from the dish on the counter into my mouth. Because he keeps the candy in the open air, they often have a flavor of fruit and sugar mixed with frankincense and myrrh. It's not *terrible*. "I have a problem…" I whisper to him, and he finally drops Virago's arm at that statement, turns toward me, and suddenly his big-brother-ness takes hold of him, and his eyes narrow as he hugs me again, tighter and harder.

"What do you need? Tell me what you need," he says, his voice low as he shakes my shoulders gently, and I sigh with relief as I search his eyes. This is pure Aidan at his finest. He may have a great sense of humor and a propensity to be mischievous and funny, but at his very root, he's the ultimate problem solver, and he *always* wants to help.

Maybe he *can* help us.

Aidan's always had my back. *Always*.

"Things are a little…weird…" I tell him, taking a step back as I try to figure out how, exactly, I'm going to tell him everything.

He glances from me to Virago, and then sighs. "Okay. Go to the back room. Turn on the tea kettle." It's his usual battle cry for when the going gets tough. Aidan crosses to the front door and locks it, turning the old metal lock with a satisfying *click*. He even switches the hand-painted "The witch is *in!*" sign (not surprisingly a purple number, covered in gold, glittery stars) over to "the witch is *out!*"

Virago picks up a large chunk of rose quartz, carved into the shape of a skull from the counter. "This is quite like any witch shop that I've been in, back in Agrotera," Virago tells me as she sets the crystal skull back down onto the counter, and we turn and head toward the back room. "They have tea and herbs and candles and spells in their shops, too, so…is that why you brought me here? Because your brother is a witch?"

"Well. I don't think your version of a witch and our world's version of a witch are the same thing," I warn her with a slight grimace. "And I'm really not sure he can help you much at all. But I'm hoping he might be able to help a *little*, at least," I tell her, and we walk through the dark hallway and the shimmering, purple beaded curtain into what my brother has always cheesily called "the Lair."

It's a terrible descriptor that should never be uttered.

Because "The Lair" is a beautiful place.

"The Lair" is the big back room that in front of the *bigger* back stock room that holds all of the random merchandise and window displays that don't quite fit in *The Cat, The Cow and The Cauldron* currently. The Lair is big enough to hold a coven of about twenty people, which is actually about the size of Aidan's witch coven when they all get together for Sabbats and Esbats and the weekly meditation circle that Aidan always makes a point to invite me to. And, surprising no one more than myself, I actually go, every single week, because he's pretty good at leading the circle, and—at the very least—I get relaxed for a handful of minutes.

The walls in "the Lair" are painted black with purple and gold mystical symbols and Goddess figures. The chairs around the edges of the room are all plush and mismatched colors (though, somehow, they effortlessly compliment each other anyway. It's Aidan's interior design superpower), and some of them have holes with stuffing coming out, which Aidan has artfully draped shawls and pillows over, so when he flicks on the dim light, and the string of Christmas lights that he put up around the ceiling of the room, it's one of the most cozy and magical places you could imagine.

And I don't even believe in magic.

When Virago and I enter the room, Virago comes to a complete standstill, gazing around at the paintings on the walls, her bright blue eyes wide. Then she pauses, breathing out softly, slowly as she stares at the painting on the far wall of a goddess—a depiction of Aidan's matron Goddess, Hestia. Hestia's a Greek Goddess of hearth and home (which really makes sense, because Aidan's all about family and home and making his space beautiful and warm. I envy him that, sometimes. And it's why I got him to help me decorate my house), and the painting here, while not actually very good in an artistic sense, is still obviously heartfelt. The mural depicts a naked, disproportionate, curvy woman with curling black hair and loving brown eyes holding a terracotta bowl of fire as she gazes out at the room with an expression of bemusement and kindness. I've always thought that she looks like she's about to step out from the wall to embrace you tightly.

Aidan comes in behind us and blows a kiss unthinkingly to his matron Goddess, and then stops, watching Virago, too. Because Virago is still staring at the far painting, working her jaw, and it's then that I realize there are tears in her eyes.

A single one sheds, twinkling in the shine of the lights as it traces its way over Virago's high cheekbone, and down the softness of her cheek.

Virago kneels, then, gently, slowly, with deep reverence, one hand in a fist over her heart, her head inclined toward the painting, her eyes closed, her jaw set.

Aidan gazes across the room at me, head cocked, one brow up, arms shrugged. "She's a witch?" he mouths to me. I shrug, too, because Virago isn't a witch, but how does she know that this is a piece of sacred art?

And why is she so touched by it?

But then Virago is standing smoothly, breathing out, not wiping away that tear that still remains clearly etched on her face. It remains there, bright and shining, a visible symbol of her strength and humility that she has no problem bearing.

"This is a beautiful place," says Virago, then, to Aidan, her words low and rough, full of emotion. Aidan opens and shuts his mouth, and then my brother *actually blushes.*

"That means a lot to me," he says simply, smiling up at her. "Thank you."

Of course Aidan adores her pretty much instantly. He's my brother. He loves everyone, and everyone—pretty much just as instantly—loves him. But this is different.

This is Virago.

Aidan, who can pretty much tell everything about someone just by looking at them, adores *her*. I glance from my brother to Virago back to my brother again. That's a very good sign. Not that I needed a good sign. But still.

"Who are you?" asks Aidan then, crossing his arms over his chest, head to the side, eyes narrowed as he gazes at her wonderingly. "Have I met you before, maybe at an open circle? Are you Wiccan, too? I mean you reacted to…" He trails off as he gestures to the painting, back to Virago, shuts his mouth. Waits.

Virago looks to me, and I nod, once. Now's as good a time as ever.

And there's really no use beating around the bush.

Which is exactly what Virago does *not* do.

She stands full to attention, rolling her shoulders back, her chin up, and her face resolved. Then Virago reaches over her shoulder and pulls her sword out of the scabbard (that she ecstatically was able to put back on again once we left the mall), now pulling it over her head and *thunking* it down so that the pointed end lands surely in the carpeting at her feet. She kneels down, head against the pommel, touching her heart with her fingers again. "I am Virago, of the Knights of Arktos City, capital of Arktos of the world of Agrotera. The lady Holly, your sister, said that you might be able to aid me in my quest, sir Aidan. I am hoping that you can."

My brother opens and shuts his mouth again, glances up at me with wide eyes, then back down at

Virago. Then he smiles, chuckling a little, sprawling back in his favorite too-stuffed chair (not surprisingly, a velvet purple number). "God, Holly loves all this chivalry stuff," he says then, practically giggling as he hooks his thumb to point toward me. "She has since she was little. You're very convincing, by the way. And I love your sword! I've been trying to order some good swords in for the shop, but…"

Virago gazes up at him, her eyes dark, and she shakes her head only once, my brother trailing off into uneasy silence. "I am not from the Knights of Valor Festival," she says tiredly, softly, as my brother shuts up, his eyes wide. "I am Virago, and I know that this is strange and difficult to believe," she sighs out again, "but I beg of your indulgence to try. I am from the world of Agrotera, and last night, I was fighting a sinister beast on *my* world, and a portal opened, and we came together, the beast and I, to this place. And now the beast has gone missing, and I *must* find it," she says, standing then, feet planted strongly hip-width apart as she hefts the sword up easily from its resting place, embedded in the floor, "and I am hoping that you may help me," she says, eyes steely, "because you are a witch. Can you do magic?"

"Magic?" Aidan splutters, glancing to me. "I mean, I'm a *Wiccan*. I don't go flying around on brooms or turning people into toads, if that's the kind of magic you're thinking." He licks his lips, shrugs, says in a smaller voice: "What kind *are* you talking about?"

"I need you to be able to open a portal to a place between worlds, so that we may usher the beast through, so that it may be contained, and cause no more death," says Virago easily. "Do you have the ability to open portals?"

Aidan is looking at me again as he splutters, tries to find the right words. And then his eyes narrow, too. "Is this woman for real, Holly?" he asks me, voice tight. "Does she *actually* believe she's from another world?"

I shrug, fold my arms. "Yes. She does," I tell him, simply. "Look...she's not crazy. Things really add up. She really might be..." I trail off. I'd have to show him the massive, monstrous footprints in my backyard, and my smashed shed, and—admittedly—he didn't see Virago heal, but maybe he'd believe that she did if I told him. But I shake my head, sigh. "I know it's very strange," I tell him softly, "but she really does need help, and I thought—I mean, I don't know what I thought. You're a witch. You've never talked to me about *portals*, but I didn't know if...maybe..." I wave my hand. "She just really needs help, and I thought of you immediately," I tell him.

His face softens at that, and he gazes back at Virago, then, eyes immediately drawn to her sword.

"So," says Aidan slowly, carefully, "last night, I was doing a spell for prosperity because of the waxing moon..."

I raise my eyebrows at him. "Muggle-speak, Aidan. We're not all witches here. Please translate for us?" I ask him, my mouth twitching into a smile.

He chuckles a little, but it's forced. "I was doing a spell," he says, enunciating the words, "...and the power went out." He points upward. "Which isn't unusual—I mean, it was a bad storm around here last night. But I felt a great darkness come into the city, and I knew something was wrong. And *then* the bowl with my herbs in it cracked in two. And I knew they'd absorbed something dark that was meant for me."

"Aidan…" I groan. Sometimes, he gets pretty new agey, and I don't know if Virago is following this, but she's nodding, puts her sword back into her scabbard effortlessly, shrugging the metal blade over her shoulder.

"That's good," she's telling him, and then she's walking in step with him toward the far altar beneath the painting of the Goddess Hestia. It's a low table covered with candles, a brass incense holder, and multiple statues of Goddesses—all his favorites. "The beast would have been repelled by any good magics," she tells him, crouching down before the altar and examining the crystal bowl that Aidan points to—the bowl that I assume held his spell ingredients. It's in two neat pieces, like this was the way it came.

Again, I feel vastly in over my head.

Aidan flops down in a chair next to Virago then, rubs at his little beard, gazing at her with wide, questioning eyes. "But I mean…" he trails off, looks up at me. "How can we really know that she's telling the truth?" he mutters to me.

I shrug, mouth dry. I *don't* know. I mean, Aidan would really be the one to know over me. He has faith in stuff, and I really…don't. I certainly don't claim to know all of the mysteries of the universe, and when I join in on Aidan's meditations, I feel something good happening in my stomach, and I relax, but how he believes in the Goddess and that spells and magic actually influence things, that rituals actually change stuff in the world…I don't know if I necessarily believe that. I certainly don't disbelieve it, and it brings him a lot of happiness. But faith has never really been something that felt like it was for me.

Virago sighs, then, and she takes up her sword.

She holds it out to us in her palms, and I don't really know what she's about to do until she nods her head to me, holding the sword out.

"A demonstration," she whispers. And then she grasps the blade with her left palm and *squeezes*.

"Oh, my God…oh, my *God*…" I whisper as scarlet blood begins to drip in a steady patter onto the dark carpeting. Virago grits her teeth together as she lowers the sword deftly, and then holds her palm out to us. The ugly wound that stretches across her open palm is mangled, raw and red, muscle and tissue visible, as well as a small shard of bone. I feel like I'm going to be sick as both Aidan and I stare at that gaping, angry wound for a spellbound moment. I don't think either of us have a single clue of what to do. I snap out of it a little, move to go grab some paper towels on pure instinct.

But Virago clears her throat, and I pause.

"Blessed mother, please help me. By your power, Lady," she whispers, and she closes her eyes.

Nothing happens for a heartbeat, but then beneath her feet, the carpet begins to…well, the best way I can describe it is that the carpeting itself is *glowing* with light. Aidan and I stare as light seems to flow up Virago's body like a reverse waterfall, twining around her limbs like a vine made of white sunshine, and pours down her arm into her hand. There's a pulse of glowing light, and then the light disappears completely, leaving black spots in my vision. I blink them away as Virago holds her hand out to us.

I feel my heart skip a beat, catch my breath.

There's no blood. No wound.

It's *gone*.

Aidan sighs out for a very long moment, then

gazes at me, his eyes wide and round.

"Oh, my God, Holly. She's real. She's *real*. She's…" He splutters, gets up, takes Virago's hand and turns it over and back again, gently pressing down on her palm a few times with his fingers. Virago stands tall, head bent to Aidan, lashes lowered, her lips twitching into a smirk as Aidan turns her hand over and over again, his mouth open. "She's *real*…" He repeats, voice wondering.

"Can you help me?" asks Virago then, searching his face. He gazes up at her, swallows, lets go of her hand.

"I…I don't know," he says. The truth. "But I can try. Hell. Maybe we *can* open a portal," he glances up at me. "The coven. With so many witches together, maybe we could raise the energy, and…and…" He's thinking fast, biting his lip. "Maybe we could open it up *on* the full moon—it would give the energy a boost for sure, at least."

"How soon is the full moon?" I ask him.

"In three days," he says distractedly, waving his hand.

"Three days?" I bite my lip, watch Virago, but she's studying my face. "Aidan, what if…I mean, the beast—it could attack in the meantime."

"I think that it's gone into hiding," says Virago, glancing over at me with her steady blue eyes. "But I must find it before the full moon and before we try to open the portal, because I believe the portal *can* and *will* be opened that day—doors between worlds are thinner during the full moon."

Of course. That makes as much sense as any of this. I run my fingers through my hair and shrug. I don't want to get my hopes up. I appreciate Aidan's enthusiasm, and his coven is full of very well-meaning people and really nice witches, but they can't agree on what type of cookies they should bake for Samhain (Halloween to us ordinary folk), and if they should do a gift exchange or raise money for charity on Yule. They're a splintered group of people with strong opinions, and them opening a portal to another world…seems like a fairy tale.

But I don't want to tell this to Virago.

This might be the only hope she has in getting the beast safely out of our world and locked away.

As I stare at her inclining her head toward my brother, I take a deep breath.

This might be her only chance to go…home.

"Okay!" Aidan cracks his knuckles. He's grinning hugely. I think this might be the greatest thing that's ever happened to him. I haven't seen him this excited in *years*. "So I'll call up all the coven members, and we can…I mean. I have no idea what I'm doing. *We* have no idea what we're doing," he tells Virago truthfully, and she nods to him, arms folded.

"To be honest, I don't know how to open a portal myself. I can do only small magics, and I had to train very hard to be able to do those," she tells us, mouth in a thin line, sighing out. "But I do know that to open a portal, the witch simply went to the space where she said the portal was, drew up energy from the ground—as I just did—and asked the portal to open. And it did. She was unable to control where the portal pointed as well as she'd hoped, but still. That was all there was to it."

"It can't possibly be so simple," says Aidan, shaking his head. "And Wiccans…I mean, we draw 'energy' up from the earth, but it doesn't glow like what just happened to you. It's very much more…metaphysical than that…" He trails off. "Um." He bites his lip. "So refresh me, here…what happens if we *can't* open this portal?"

"Oh, you know. Apparently the extinction of the human race or something," I tell him, voice small. He glances at me with a grin, thinking I'm joking, but the smile melts off his face instantly when he sees my expression, when he glances to Virago and she frowns, bites her lip.

"Not exactly *extinction*, per se," she says, trailing off. And then she sheaths her sword after wiping the remaining stain of her blood on the blade on her pants leg. "Shall I tell you both the story of this beast?" she asks then, sitting down on the edge of a plush chair. "I think it's important that you know it. You see, us knights had never faced a beast like it before. But we knew its story, and in every story there are crumbs of truth."

"Yes, please, we'd love to hear," says Aidan eagerly, sitting on the chair opposite from Virago. I fold into a loveseat, watching the strange, graceful woman across the way lean forward, her elbows on her knees, her face shadowed, her strong jaw lit by the twinkling Christmas lights wreathed around the room, casting the painted goddesses on the wall with golden light.

"My mother was a storyteller," says Virago with a soft smile. "And she told me the story this way. Once, long ago," she tell us, voice going lower, stronger, "there was a great famine. The ground would not yield crops, the beasts in the field fell ill and died, and they could not be eaten for they bloated with disease. And creeping over the mountains and valleys

of the world came a great darkness and a great fear.
And with it came the Goddess Cower…"

Chapter 7: Two Stories

In those days, the world was just beginning, and humans had only recently been molded and made by the gods and goddesses, and the humans were only now just learning how to build a life out of the land and with each other. It was the beginning times, and it was very hard, but before the famine, it had not been impossible. But now the people were dying each day, more falling, and they did not know what to do.

The Goddess Cower crept across the land, dragging her clicking wand of bones behind her. She was sister to the trickster Goddess Fox, but unlike her sister, she had no bit of balance in her, not a scrap of light to combat the darkness. Fox was a trickster, yes, but she was neither good nor evil, instead a marvelous blending of the two, as are we all.

But Cower?

Cower was all darkness.

"The people fear," she hissed into the hollows and valleys so that the desperate words echoed back to her; she whispered again and again beneath the rocks and into dripping streams. "They fear, and they are weak because of it. Now I will come to them, and I will make them believe in me and worship me."

And she rose up, with her small powers, and she came to the people as a drifting thing, made of tattered cloth and small animal bones she'd gleaned from the forest that hung in the air like a puppet. But the people were afraid, and they bowed down before her and worshiped her, because she made them fear. They built small shrines to her, and they gave her their last bread and honey and milk and meat, and they adored her because she said that she could save them. And she had not a single intention or a shred of power to do so.

And the goddess of wooded places, Fleet, heard the people whisper in the forest, heard their fear and their hope concerning their new Goddess, Cower. Fleet had been sleeping, had not heard about the famine or the fear, and when she saw how the people suffered, she rose up, went to the animals of the wood, and asked them to choose some of their kind to go and offer themselves to the humans so that the humans would survive. And the animals said, "Fleet, you are our mother, and we adore you— we would do anything for you. We will do what you ask."

But when the animals of the wood came to the humans in their villages and offered themselves to be eaten, the humans slayed the animals, and Cower said: "look what I have done for you!" claiming the animal's sacrifice as a boon she had granted the people. And the humans gave her the best of the animals as a sacrifice, and she lay back on her bed of furs, and she laughed, for she still held the dying humans fooled.

The animals did not last long, as there was not much else to eat, and the land was not yielding grain or fruit. And the goddess of sea places, Wave, heard the people whisper along the water's edges, heard their fear and their hope concerning their new Goddess, Cower. Wave had been sleeping, too, had not heard about the famine or the fear, and when she saw how the people suffered, she rose up, went to the fish of the sea, and asked them to choose some of their kind to go and offer themselves to the humans so that the humans would survive. And the fish said, "Wave, you are our mother, and we adore you—we would do anything for you. We will do what you ask."

But when the fish of the sea came to the edge of the water and offered themselves to be eaten, the humans slayed the fish, and

Cower said: *"look what I have done for you!"* claiming the fish's sacrifice as a boon she had granted the people. And the humans gave her the best of the fish as a sacrifice, and she lay back on her bed of furs, and she laughed, for she still held the dying humans fooled.

The fish did not last long, as there was still not much else to eat, and the land was still not yielding grain or fruit. Fleet and Wave came together, as they sometimes did, to discuss it.

"I fear that, as we slept, our sister Reap is sleeping, even now," said Wave, holding her hands out to Fleet. *"We must wake her."*

So Fleet stepped dry into the ocean, and Wave took her in her strong arms, and carried her down into the sea. But they could not find the Goddess Reap. And Wave stepped dripping from the ocean, and Fleet took her in her strong arms and carried her across the land. But they could not find the Goddess Reap.

They looked over the world and the water, but they did not look beneath it. And that is where Reap slept, with her seeds, waiting to rise with the greening plants, up and through the dirt, into life again.

But Cower knew where the Goddess slept, and as time went by, she grew nervous that the Goddess would wake up of her own accord and set to rights the dire mischief that Cower had begun. For Cower, of course, had released Famine out into that corner of the world, and if Reap knew what she was about, would end it quickly and severely. So Cower took some of the women and men of the village, some of the strongest women and men, for they had survived the famine thus far, and she took them with her on a trek into the mountains.

And she bade them roll a stone across the entrance to a strange cave.

"Goddess, we love and adore you," they told her, *"but why do you ask us to do this?"*

"Too many questions!" the Goddess hissed, waving her

clicking wand of bones at them. "Do as I say, or it will be bad on you!"

For in those days, no goddess or god could go against one another, and Cower herself could not trap Reap. But she could order it done. And the women and men put their shoulders against the great stone, and they heaved and they shoved and they pushed.

And Fleet and Wave came, just then, to the top of the mountain on their journey across the world to find their sister Reap. And this is what they found: a very surprised Cower, and a very surprised group of humans, and a stone half-way across the entrance to a very strange cave.

And Fleet and Wave gave a great shout, and they woke their sister Reap who crept up and out of the cave entrance, into the world, blinking against the sudden brightness of the sun.

"What have you done to the humans, Cower?" asked Fleet and Wave and Reap, then. And Cower cowered away from them, but not before sneering and spitting at their feet and saying:

"You are powerful, and I am nothing, and I am tired of being nothing. I will be remembered," she whispered.

"You have killed so many humans. So many humans," said Reap sadly, sinking to the ground and soaking up the story through the soil beneath her fingers. "But you will not again. For the cave that I have slept in? It will be your resting place. Become what you truly are, Cower."

And in the face of her brothers and sisters, Cower began to morph and change, and what she was within began to show on the outside. She grew larger, but more shadowed, she grew toothier and angrier. And she turned into a great and monstrous beast that—compelled by magic—crawled into the entrance of the cave. And the stone rolled over it, sealing her away forever.

For Reap and Fleet and Wave knew that Cower would no longer be content until all of the humans were gone. To protect them, always, they sealed Cower away.

But it is said by the few that still follow the Goddess Cower, those who wish for the destruction of the world, that she will rise again one day, and she will be more powerful than before. And she will finish what she started, now in her monstrous form.
And she will devour the world.

Virago sits with her elbows on her knees and her hands clasped before her, leaning forward and watching us both with flashing eyes. "There was a rumor in Arktos City when we began our trek up to the northern mountain range that the beast we went to fight was, in fact, Cower come back. We laughed at that idea. Surely it was just another of the wild beasts come up from the desert, come too far into civilization, easily corralled and returned to their wild home, possibly even vanquished. But *easily*. But now? I'm not so sure. I've been thinking..." she says softly, gazing past us, eyes unfocused, "that maybe the witch actually did open the correct portal to the correct in-between place. And maybe, perhaps, the beast changed the portal from leading to the in-between place to come, instead, to *this* world. If it is Cower come back, then things are much, much worse than I originally thought. Than anyone thought." She comes back to herself, gazes at the both of us, her hands spread. "So you see...I need your help, so much. I am only a lowly knight. I will do my best in the face of this, but if she rises up and vanquishes *me*, then you must carry on, try to trap her. Try to stop her."

My breath comes shallowly, and my sweaty palms are pressed to my jeans. I clear my throat. "The beast isn't going to vanquish you," I laugh, but it comes out shaky. "You're *Virago*...I mean, you just sawed into your hand with that sword, and it healed immediately..." I watch her as she gazes at me, face calm and sad.

"Everyone is eventually vanquished, Holly," she says then quietly. "What matters is if I did what I was meant to before I am gone."

Aidan is looking at the painting of his matron Goddess on the wall, his gaze distant, his thoughts somewhere else, obviously. I stand quickly, clear my throat as they both turn to me.

"All right, Aidan. We'll be back in three days. Hopefully with the...the beast. Ready to be sealed into a portal," I tell my brother, crossing my arms.

"No...no..." he blanches, shakes his head. "Why don't the two of you come back tomorrow night? For the meditation?" asks Aidan, rising. "Virago can meet the rest of the coven, we can discuss strategies, maybe try to open the portal, do a test run?"

"Okay," I tell him quietly. His brows are up, and his gaze is questioning, but I'm suddenly so tired and worried and nervous that I just want to sit down and curl up with my favorite book. "Come on, Virago..." I start to walk toward the front room.

"It was a pleasure meeting you, Aidan," she says, bowing to him, and then I'm through the beaded curtain and into the shop proper. I flip the sign on my way out, banging against the door as the tears come into my eyes, making everything blurry. "The witch is *in*" keeps turning in the breeze behind me as I practically run to the car.

Virago is slower—maybe Aidan's showing her something in the shop—so I unlock the car door sit inside and put my head against the steering wheel.

I swallow down most of my tears but two squeeze out, splashing against my jeans.

Everyone is eventually vanquished.

It's all rising in me, all of these stupid thoughts that I always try to ignore. That I fail at ignoring. I think about Mom, about how happy she was when she finally left, how the cancer never actually *changed* her. She was just Mom, and she was this really fucking happy person, and that never changed. Not ever. Because she believed that she'd done what she was supposed to do. I remember her telling me that, over and over, as I raged and grew angrier and angrier as the cancer claimed her for its own.

And after Mom was gone, I stayed with Nicole, because I was afraid to be alone. And I was afraid to end it. And it was easy, staying with her. It was so much easier to live my puppet life, to go home from work, to dream of other things and places and tell myself that I was perfectly content with not going out or doing things because it was safer, wasn't it?

Everything was safer than what my mother did, which was live like crazy.

A knock on the car window. Virago peers in, her brows furrowed, a frown deepening her features as she leans down, looks into the car. I unlock the doors, and she gets in, setting her scabbard in the back seat and folding her hands in her lap as she shuts the door quietly behind her.

"Sorry…" I mutter, rubbing at my eyes, wiping my wet fingers on my jeans again. "Sorry…something you said. I was just thinking about my mom," I tell her, then, staring down at my lap. I can already feel myself redden. I don't talk about my mother. *Not ever.* And then, somehow…

"She was this really amazing woman," I tell her, can feel the tears start to *plink* on my jeans again. I ignore them, stare down at my hands that are clasped so tightly together that my knuckles are white, my fingers red. "You would have really liked her," I manage, swallowing down a hiccup of a sob. I keep going. "She was so strong and so brave...she loved life so much, and she did all of this amazing shit. She was a painter, an artist..." I say, closing my eyes tightly. "And she painted things as they really are. That's how she always said she did it. She loved experimenting with colors, getting the exact right shade to capture something. She loved...everything, everyone. She loved life. She rode horses, and she did rock climbing, and she did it *all* while raising Aidan and me, and she loved us both so much, and she taught us so much...and then she got cancer anyway. Even though she lived the best life in the world, cancer still got her. And she died. And she was perfectly at *peace* with it all," I whisper. "And I was so *angry* at her for being at peace with it, because it was taking her away from us..." I trail off, swallow. "So I've kind of not really been living since she died. I mean. I *live*." I wipe away my tears, stare holes into the steering wheel. "I go to work, and I *love* my work. At the library. So much. I love my patrons. But then I come home. And I've stayed with Nicole because she never really has time, so it's this great, casual thing, and it's easy." God, I just came out to her. But I keep going, steel myself, keep talking. "Everything I do is just...easy..." I turn and look at her, and she's not staring into space, not watching out the window. She's looking at *me*, and looking at me intently, brow creased, eyes bright and unwavering as she gazes into the very heart of me, and so much wells up within me in that moment that I just start to cry. There are so many tears, so much grief wracking my middle, and Virago reaches out and wraps her arms around me, and she holds me. I sob against her shoulder and her tie.

"I miss her so much," I whisper, after a long moment. "Like...my gut's all empty. Like she filled it with this great joy and possibility. I don't know how Aidan believes in magic anymore. Mom took it all with her when she went."

Virago rests her chin gently on my head, squeezing her arms about me in a comforting hold. After a long moment, she whispers into my hair: "I went into training to become a knight because I lived with my mother and father in the poorest section of Arktos City. It's called the Ratter Prison. It's *very* poor," says Virago, voice clipped short and sad. "My mother and father died in the winter from a sickness when I was seven. My mother had wanted to be a knight, but hadn't started young enough. So I went into the training because she'd wanted to as soon as I was able. I understand you, Holly. I understand that grief."

I rest my cheek against her shoulder, breathe in the scent of brand new shirt, and the sweet mint that seems to be all that is Virago. "I'm sorry," I whisper, sighing out.

She shrugs, and I can feel her warm muscles ripple beneath me as she squeezes me again. "All is well," she tells me, her voice gentle. "I know that if my mother and father could see me now, I think that they would be at peace. I have done the best that I could do to become a knight. I have worked very hard, and I have poured my heart into my tasks. I think that if your mother could see you, Holly, she would feel the same.

You've done what you could do, and you have done it well. She would be very proud of you."

"But I haven't..." I tell her, pushing away from her, gazing into her intense ice-blue eyes as I try to keep the tears from coming. She returns the gaze with a quiet strength as she reaches across the space between us. She takes a wisp of red hair and then softly, slowly, like she's the lead in a romantic comedy, like theme music is playing somewhere to accompany her ridiculously romantic gesture, she tucks that wisp of hair behind my ear, her warm fingers curving against my skin.

We stay like that so long, my eyes wide, my heartbeat thundering, before Virago says, simply: "We all do what we are meant to do."

"What?" I whisper.

"We all do," she murmurs softly, and I suddenly realize how close her mouth is, the warmth of her stealing over me by degrees. If I lean forward, I could capture that mouth with my own. I breathe out with a gasp as she leans forward, crossing that small space, "what we are meant to do," she says, the words hot against me, because suddenly I want to make the distance between us dissolve.

I want, more than anything in this whole wide world, to kiss her.

Neither of us moves for a heartbeat, two, and then she sighs out, breaking the intense gaze between us. I slump a little, and then her arm is around me, drawing me down to her chest again, rubbing my shoulder gently.

For the longest moment, I want to rewind time. I want to kiss her. But instead, I close my eyes, listen to her heartbeat, feel the softest sense of peace steal over me, by degrees.

> *I understand you, Holly.*
> For the first time in…well. Forever…
> I feel seen.

Chapter 8: Fiction

Because soymilk and ketchup, the two regrettable items still deemed as edible in my refrigerator, don't exactly blend together into the most appetizing dinner, we make a trip to the grocery store and get a few frozen meals, fresh fruit and snow peas. Virago's cool visage melts at the doorway, and wonder abounds as she wanders the aisles in rapt fascination, lifting a mango to her nose and inhaling the heady aroma as she sighs in ecstasy. Looking at the grocery store through that sort of lens—that you can pretty much get any kind of food you want at whatever time you want—I have to agree with her. It is a kind of miracle. I never thought that the same aisles I grumble about rising prices and squeaky shopping cart wheels would also be where a beautiful woman shows me that there's a hell of a lot to be grateful for.

I buy a pound of Columbian coffee along with the meals and produce, holding the bag of beans up to her for inspection. I tell her the best thing she's ever experienced in her entire existence is *yet to come*. Which, you know, I realize totally *does* sound like a come on, as she inhales the rich aroma of the coffee, but she's too excited when I tell her that coffee is related to espresso, so I don't think she noticed.

Just like I don't thinks she notices the way I watch her move, how she prowls through the aisles like she's grace personified. A dancer and a warrior, all at once.

I haven't let myself think about possibilities. I guess I do believe her now. I believe she's from another world, as vastly impossible or improbable as that may be, I believe it. I believe that there's a wounded beast out there somewhere, just biding its time before it heals and then comes out to wreak havoc on the human race.

I believe that I have to break up with Nicole. But even if I break up with her now, what I want is too impossible.

So I do my absolute best to not think about what I want. Which is something I'm really good at.

We drive back to my house in relative silence, Virago fiddling with the radio dial every so often to find a new station, a new song, a new experience for her to immerse herself in. I'm too overwhelmed by everything, so the relative silence is fine by me. I have too much to think about.

And if I spoke to her just now, with all that emotion rushing through me, I might say something I'd regret.

Like: *you're beautiful. You're exquisite, really. And I'm attracted to you more than I've ever been attracted to anyone in my entire life. And you're from another world. And if this all works…then you're going back home. And you're probably not even gay. But watching you makes me think that everything I've seen that I thought was good or lovely in my lifetime was a pale shadow compared to you.*

So I stay silent.

And I say nothing.

But when we pull into my driveway, I sigh for a very long time.

Because there, ahead of my car, is Carly's. Parked.

She's sitting on my porch on the old swing, practically vibrating with excitement as she pushes the swing back and forth with her sneakers, and the second that I turn off the engine, she's dashing down the steps and is peering through the car window like a paparazzi.

"Hi, Holly!" she practically chirps, her big, goofy grin threatening to split her face in two. I open my door, and she squeezes me tightly before leaning down and peering into the car to have her first glimpse of my passenger.

"Oh, my God. *Hello*," she says then, turning her voice down about an octave and a half and purring like a Bengal tiger.

"Carly," I tell her warningly, but I'm rolling my eyes to the heavens and trying to suppress laughter. "This," I say, gesturing inside the car, "is Virago. Virago, this is my best friend Carly."

Virago exits the car smoothly, folding out of the seat like she's making a theatrical entrance into my front yard. She comes around the side of the car in a sensual, swaggering prowl, with her brow barely raised, and does a sweeping bow in front of Carly, complete with a hand at the small of her back. She then takes Carly's hand and brushes her soft lips gently over Carly's knuckles. This then makes my day because Carly actually blushes.

Carly blushes.

"Oh, my God, hello," she repeats breathlessly. She peers over Virago's graceful, bent form, mouth in an "o" as she stares at me with wide eyes, her face a combination of glee, utter shock and amazement. "What the heck?" she mouths to me.

"Let's all go on inside and get this over with," I

say then, getting out of the car and fishing the grocery bags from the back seat. "Virago, do you want to grab your sword and armor?"

"What the *heck*?" Carly breathes again as Virago picks up the bundle of her armor from the back seat and hefts her sword over her shoulder. And then, gently, takes the bags from my hand before striding toward the porch.

"She's very chivalrous," I say, hands on my hips as I follow after her with a smile.

"Did you hook up with a *knight* from the Knights of Valor Festival? Wow. Holly, I *like* this new side to you..." says Carly wonderingly as she follows after us.

"Um. No, actually." I grimace. "So, you're not going to believe this..."

She actually *does* believe this. Easily. Carly's the kind of person who, in high school, was starting a Cryptozoology club and a ghost hunters society long before ghost hunting got popular and long before they put shows about hunting Bigfoot on television. I'd known that if anyone was going to believe Virago's story and quest, it was going to be Carly, but I didn't entirely expect how enthusiastic she was going to be about it.

I should have known.

"Oh, my God, tell me what your world is like?" Carly murmurs adoringly, propping her elbows on my kitchen counter and leaning her chin in her hands. Her eyes are practically sparkling and starry as she stares at Virago.

"Well," says Virago slowly, carefully, as I spoon the coffee grounds into my coffee maker's filter. "It's very different from this world..." She trails off, considering how best to explain it.

"I mean...you have knights," prompts Carly, cocking her head.

"And it's very odd to me that you don't," says Virago with a grin. "How do you keep your cities safe from other kingdoms? How do you keep it safe from beasts?"

"Oh, my God, *you have beasts?*" Carly squeaks. "Are they bad monsters? And you have *kingdoms?* What about princesses? Do you have princesses? And queens?"

"Carly, *we* have princesses on *our* world..." I mutter, replacing the coffee pot after I rinse it out and switching the coffee maker on.

"Yeah, but not *fairy princesses.*"

"They're not fairy princesses..." Virago is starting, but Carly waves her hand, sitting bolt upright, eyes wide.

"Tell me about the *monsters.*"

"Well...I actually came through the portal with one. A beast," says Virago, eyes narrowing, clearing her throat. "Unfortunately...I seem to have lost the beast. Which is why I am here. I must find the beast and remove it from your world, or it will create great havoc among your people," Virago grimaces.

"Wait, wait, wait," whispers Carly, and then her eyes go all wide, and she's squeaking, jumping up and down for a second before she waves her hands, speaks: "Oh, my God, you're *never* going to believe this..." she tells us, dragging her laptop out of her bag and plunking it with a little more energy than I think any normal laptop could survive on the kitchen counter. "So," she begins quickly, "I work at our local public access television station—"

"She has no idea what television is," I tell her, and her bubble bursts...for about a second.

"Well! It's like...seeing magical pictures. On a magical piece of glass," says Carly brightly.

Virago nods, considering this.

"And I'm a low-paid *producer* at this television station, which basically means..." Carly thinks about this. "It means that I *make* a lot of the very *bad* magical pictures on the magical piece of glass."

"Some of them even involve puppets," I say, chuckling, and Carly shoots me a dirty look.

"*Puppet Awesomeness and the Cool Lagoon* happens to be the most high quality show I work on, missy, so let's not be sarcastic about it."

"They have a shark made out of duct tape," I tell Virago, knowing full well that she'll have no idea what duct tape is. But I needed to say it. "They don't have a big budget..." I trail off as Virago looks at me blankly. I smile, take the grocery bags from her. "...I'm just going to put the fruit away."

"No, no, stay, this is important..." says Carly, hooking my arm through hers. She turns her attentions back on the laptop. "*Anyway*, you know how I do that little local news program on Saturday mornings—this morning, actually. *Well*, last night, we got some great amateur footage, and you know how I'm into this sort of stuff...here, I'll just show you."

She brings up her video player and presses "file, open."

She clicks "monster."

"What the hell..." I whisper as the video begins.

It's clearly nighttime in the video, and it's quite difficult to make anything out, but the "exposure" setting has been turned up as high as possible, separating the shadows and objects from the darkness a little. In the video, you can see trees being thrashed around by a high wind, a ton of rain...yeah, you could assume this is from last night. And then there's a bolt of lightning, which makes the laptop screen pure white for half a beat, and then, in front of the camera lens comes a...a *thing*.

A monster.

It's gigantic. Really, that's the best word I can think of. *Gigantic* as it brushes its head against draping power lines, as tall as the trees I can hardly see silhouetted in the video. There's a crackle of electricity as the power lines fall, tugging out of their moorings on the poles by whatever this creature is. They fall, spiraling around the beast. It stalks forward, lumbering on all fours, and it has two twisting horns out of its sprawling skull, a long, wicked snout with teeth erupting at all sorts of odd angles, and slitted eyes that look reptilian as it turns and takes in the camera. It opens its mouth, and suddenly I'm clamping my hands over my ears, and Virago goes white as a sheet, because the thing is bellowing/hissing/growling/screaming, just like it did last night, and the sound is so harsh, so surreal and angry and frightening, that I can never forget it.

It awakens something primeval in me, something so ancient that my oldest ancestors must have felt it when they were being hunted.

It's then that I know fear.

"That's it..." whispers Virago, stepping forward, hands balled into fists as she grips her sword tightly. "How do I get to it? How do I—"

"I don't know," says Carly in a stage whisper,

clicking "x" on the video as it ends. "That was sent in to us by one of our faithful viewers…" She's starting to sound like a segue way on a reality television show, and I clear my throat. She flicks her gaze to mine, sighs, and tones down the drama a little. "Anyway," she continues, leaning back on the counter, "that video you just saw was sent in to us just last night. The guy who got that footage took it on his cell phone. He lives on one of the coastal streets, and he captured this just before he said that the beast dove off the pier into the ocean, and it disappeared. We aired this clip, by the way, this morning on the news, and the phone's been ringing off the hook, because a lot of people saw it but it wasn't on a regular news station or anything like that. They said we were reporting the *real* news," she says with a big, proud smile.

This coming from the woman who said her highest rated news program, to date, had been about the local babies-in-diapers 500 race that happens every fourth of July…I suppose that's pretty good. I sigh, put my chin in my hands and gaze at her with a rueful smile—but my skin is still covered in goosebumps.

I hadn't been able to see it clearly last night. Seeing the beast somewhat clearly now…I shudder. It was…terrifying. Like a sort of reptilian bull. Urgh.

…Could it really be that goddess from the story Virago's mother told her? The Goddess Cower?

"So," says Carly, spreading her hands. "I guess it went into the ocean. It's aquatic?"

Virago shakes her head. She's mulling things over now, pacing in small, tight circles, her new shoes squeaking on my kitchen's tile floor until she goes out into the living room to pace on the carpeting there. Shelley follows her loyally around and around the coffee table, her tail in a constant state of wagging-motion as she keeps her nose about a foot behind Virago, never wavering as Virago's shadow.

"It went to the ocean..." Virago muses, head tilted up, eyes gazing at the ceiling as if it holds all the answers. "Perhaps..." She turns, her hands balled into fists, gazing at me, eyes wide. "Perhaps it *did* need to heal. Ocean water can be used for healing magic. But this means that it will be able to heal much *faster* and *better*, if your oceans are anything like ours. And I have a sinking suspicion they might be."

I shrug, rub at my arms and my shoulders, sigh. "Well, I doubt your world has pollution, so our oceans might not be as great at healing as yours." I grimace. "But this means..."

"That the full moon is in three days," says Virago, gazing at me. "And the beast might rise again before three days comes."

I bite at one of my nails, my stomach turning as I close my eyes, as I consider the implications.

"Whoa, whoa..." says Carly, glancing from me to Virago back to me again. "What about this monster?"

Virago tells her. And about the story of the Goddess Cower. At the end of it, Carly's sitting on the edge of the couch, her chin in her hands, her mouth open as she stammers: "But...but...it could destroy...*everything?*"

I sit down beside her and Shelley comes over to put her pretty pointed nose in my lap, ears perked forward a little, one ear up, one ear down—classic Shelley. She's trying to cheer me up.

But that's kind of impossible.

The monster could rise in less than three days.

And then…well. I don't want to imagine what will happen then.

Virago sits across from me, mouth closed in a tight line—just watching me with those brilliant ice-blue eyes, her true gaze a million miles away as she turns inward.

I want to reach across the space between us, take her hand. Tell her this will all work out. But I don't. I sit still and stiff, with my dog pillowing her head on my lap forlornly.

We sit together in silence.

I can't sleep. Maybe it's because every single time I close my eyes, I see images of the monster from the video flickering in my line of vision, and the images of the monster keep merging with the lightning flashing and how I saw the beast last night, only as a shadow, but so enormous, so monstrous. So…huge. All of this merges together in my mind's eye, and I can't tell the images apart anymore, how the monster looked in the video, and how the monster looked in my backyard. I sigh, my hand over my eyes, and turn over one last time. The sheets are hot, and Shelley is sleeping on my legs, her dead weight pressing me into the mattress, and both of my feet are fast asleep from her weight against them. At this rate, I'm never going to get to sleep.

I need tea.

And the book that's always given me comfort when I needed it most. I need *The Knight of the Rose*.

I get up as quietly as I can, but Shelley still grumbles because her pillow of my limbs is now removed, and—crazy dog—the actual cushy mattress is apparently less comfy than sleeping on my legs. I put on my fluffy pink robe, shove my feet into my slippers, and then pad gently down the steps, avoiding the top one because it creaks.

But Virago isn't asleep on the couch, like I thought she'd be. She's not in the living room at all, or the kitchen, and the door was open to the bathroom, so she's not there either. She's not in the study, and she's not in the library. I stay very still for a long moment, holding the robe closed over my chest, my heart beating wildly against my hands as I stand in my living room, listening to the stillness of the house. Did she leave?

She wouldn't have left—would she?

And why does it matter *so much* if she did?

Yeah, right, Holly. I grimace, sigh, biting my lip. *You know the answer to that.*

As I stand in the middle of my living room, my heart pounding, a flash of light to the left makes me turn. I'd drawn the blinds over the back sliding door before we got ready for bed, but they're pulled up now, and the sliding glass door to the backyard is very slightly left ajar, maybe by a few inches. I cross over to the door, my fingers brushing against the handle as I peer out into the darkness.

It's not that dark out—after all, it's almost the full moon, and the light from my neighbors' porch lights and the street lamps out front make the backyard pretty illuminated.

So I can see that out in the center of the yard is Virago.

The flash I that drew my eyes to her was light glancing off the blade of her sword, for she stands, holding the hilt in both hands, as she crouches on the lawn, the blade hefted high and at attention over her head. The sleeves of her new shirt are rolled up, and she's not wearing her tie, her vest or her jacket, and the shirt is no longer tucked into her pants. She's unbuttoned a handful of the bottom buttons, and I can see her tanned, muscular stomach through the inverted "v" that the two sides of the shirt make, framing her skin like it's a work of art. Because it is. Virago crouches low, her thighs tight, in a sword-fighting stance. I only know that because I've seen the knights do mock sword-fighting "matches" after the jousting, because I've looked at medieval tapestries of knights, because I've read books about them and watched a ton of medieval dramas and movies. I've never actually seen this happen in real life. For…well…*real*.

I press my hands to the glass panes of the door, mouth open, as I watch her stand, statue-like, her body in perfect form, beautiful beyond description. She exudes this raw sensuality, and this great, pulsing power that renders me speechless. I am in awe as I watch her stand, head held high. Proud.

And then she bursts into motion, whipping the sword around in a seamless, circular arc as if a thousand opposing knights stand in front of her. The sword moves through the air like quicksilver, flashing and darting, jabbing and thrusting, and Virago is at the center of this maelstrom of blade, moving as effortlessly as a dancer, as graceful as one, too.

And that's exactly what it is that she's doing in that moment, I realize: she's *dancing*. It's deadly, but still beautiful, the way the sword glitters, there and then not there almost in that same instant, she moves so quickly. She's effortless in her speed so much so that it looks like she has multiple arms with multiple swords, the arcs she creates hanging suspended in the air for a heartbeat, a crescent of light, before they fade away.

It's beautiful. *She's* beautiful. I actually don't think I've ever seen something *more* beautiful.

I back away from the door, clutching at my robe, and then I turn and walk quickly back to the stairs, then run upstairs. I take the steps two at a time, actually, pausing at the bathroom because *The Knight of the Rose* is still by the tub, exactly where I left it last night. I stand, shaking, my slippered feet against the cool linoleum, soaking up the cold, even through the soles. The solidity of the cover of *my book* is now between my fingers, and then I hold it over my heart like a shield.

I close my bedroom door behind me as I enter, leaning against the wood, and folding forward and down until I'm sitting on the floor. My bedside lamp is still on from when I got up, but Shelley's ignoring me, fast asleep and dead to the world.

The first tear slides down my cheek. I'm surprised, reach up, touch the warm wetness with my finger. And then another comes. And another.

Even if I broke up with Nicole, this is never going to work. Virago and me. There are so many obvious problems. I don't know if she's like me, if she loves women. And let's not forget the ultimate and most painful clincher: she's from another world. If we're able to vanquish the beast, she's going back, and I'm going to stay here. In my world.

It's totally star-crossed is what it is. I almost laugh to myself as I cry, because it's so *ridiculous*. Why am I falling in love with a woman I can't have? Aren't I smarter than this, smart enough to realize that this was doomed from the start?

No. I don't think being "smart" has anything

to do with it.

I crack open my book, my beloved book, the book that's saved me my whole life. And there, on the page, is something that *does* make me laugh, but just a thin, faint, humorless chuckle. And then I weep again, silent tears tracing themselves down my face, *plunking* hollowly against my robe.

Miranda knelt before the Lady Seraphina, a blazing intensity to her gaze. "I have journeyed every day until the nightfall, have journeyed every night until the daystar rose," she whispered. "I have fought through the perils of the Fangheart valley and the desolation of the Shadow Mountains, have ridden on the dragon of the moon and out-witted the sirens at Briar Cove. All of this, and more, I have done to come now to your door, and kneel at your feet, beloved Seraphina. For there is no other woman in all the world for me, and I would do anything and everything in my power to prove that to you. And if your curse is not yet broken by all I have done, then will I continue to journey across this world, to every end of it, and I will fight and I will outwit and I will find more courage still, beloved lady, and I will do all of this for you. Please be kind, lady...tell me what I must do that I can free you, that I can prove to you the depth of my affections. For there is not a moment in the day in which my heartbeat does not whisper your name. All I am, all I have done, all that I would do, is for your love alone."

And Seraphina knelt down, too, her skirts billowing about her as she took the knight's face between her two soft hands, and Seraphina kissed the knight Miranda passionately, thoroughly and deeply.

For through Miranda's tireless and relentless

journey, through her courage and her love, she had lifted the curse that bound the Lady Seraphina.

And they rose together, the knight lifting the lady in her arms as easily as if she were a doll, though Seraphina was most certainly not. And Miranda carried Seraphina to the edge of the bed and set her gently down upon the coverlet.

"I have done everything for you, and I would do more still," whispered Miranda to the lady. And the lady gazed up at her with darkening eyes, pulling the knight down beside her.

"There is only one thing more I would have you do," Seraphina whispered, wrapping her fingers in Miranda's hair.

I close the book, push it away from me on the floor. I remember the first time I read that scene. I was crying then, too, in high school of course, falling in love with my best friend...Carly. It was totally star-crossed, too. Carly was very obviously straight, but we don't often want what we know we can have, do we? She'd just met David online (this is before it was super cool, and was—in fact—actually a little creepy to meet anyone online, back when there wasn't so much an internet as various chat rooms hooked up by a modem), and was gushing about him, because he loved paranormal stuff as much as she did, and he actually had the same theories for the Loch Ness monster and the Jersey Devil, and it was the most wonderful thing that had ever happened to her, meeting him, because they were obviously meant to be together, she said, and that she was falling in love with him.

And that was the very first time I wondered if I was meant to be alone my entire life.

I read that scene in the book that long ago day,

read it three times in a row, tears leaking out of the corners of my eyes as I calmed down my breathing, still felt the rush of my heartbeat. I wanted something, so desperately, like what Miranda and Seraphina had found, wanted something like that so much that, that like Miranda, I was willing to do whatever it took to find it. My passionate declaration to myself to find that kind of passionate, forever love fizzled out and disappeared as life went on, as I realized that I could never be with Carly, as I went to college and met girls who were like me and fell in love with them and had my heart broken multiple times.

I was always the one with bad luck in love. It's like my thing. And then Nicole came, and just cemented that.

I fall in love with the wrong people. With the people I can't have. It's what I do.

I'm almost famous for it.

Down below in my backyard is someone so amazing, I can't even understand it.

And I'm falling in love with her.

And we aren't meant to be.

Chapter 9: Things Left Unsaid

I wake up to Shelley, who's weaseled her way up from the foot of the bed to lay beside me on top of the coverlet, licking my face ferociously.

"Oh, my goodness, okay," I mutter, rubbing her behind the ears and sitting up. My hair is every which way, and my eyes are crusty, but those aren't *exactly* the first things I notice.

Because Virago's standing in the doorway to my bedroom, her hip leaning on the door jamb, one hand on the other side of her hip, one brow up.

"Good morrow," she says with a smile, her lips twitching to the side as I pull my sheet up to cover my incredibly sexy (hah!) pajamas that happen to have little cartoon cows jumping over deranged-looking moons in a repeating pattern. She raises her other brow, gestures behind her. "I took the liberty to make a breakfast for the both of us. If you wish to come downstairs…" She inclines her head toward the hall behind her, takes a step back, still smiling with enough raw sex appeal to make me actually melt. She does a little bow, flicking her bright blue gaze to my eyes. "Please." Then she turns and walks away, striding over the carpet in my hallway like she owns the place, her body so fluid and graceful that I can't help but watch her until she's out of sight around the corner, my eyes drawn to her like her body possesses its own gravity.

I stumble into my bathroom, gazing at my reflection. I then sigh for about five minutes at what I see staring back at me in the mirror. Great. I look *terrible*. There are dark circles under my eyes because I stayed up too late reading (and, you know, crying), my hair is all over the place (quite similar to the illustrated depictions of Medusa, actually), and my cow-and-moon covered pajamas are askew.

So, so attractive.

I drag a brush through my hair several times until it's somewhat tamed, brush my teeth, change my clothes into jeans and a blank tank top and get downstairs in enough time to open the back sliding door for a very desperate Shelley to race outside to attend to her business.

The smell hits me when I enter the kitchen, and I get a little weak in the knees. Not because Virago is standing there in one of my aprons (the one with the two giant teapots on the front over where your breasts are. A charming gift from Carly), though I do get a little weak kneed from that, admittedly. But because there are two plates on the counter, covered in carefully arranged and heavily buttered slices of perfectly-brown toast next to fresh strawberries sliced neatly in half, and a handful of the snow peas we bought last night, arranged into a fan shape around the strawberries.

"How…how did you figure out the toaster?" is what I articulately manage to get out, and Virago has such a big smile on her face that she actually ducks her head a little and clears her throat with an elegant shrug.

"You've been so hospitable to me. I wished to return the favor. Admittedly, the toasting device wasn't so difficult to understand, after you showed me how to use the television," she says, her mouth twitching at the corners as she tries to suppress her smile. She leans forward then, smoothly, and makes a lovely, sweeping bow. I stare at her as she rises again, her ice-blue eyes sparkling as she indicates the two plates. "So please…partake of breakfast, m'lady."

I stand for a long moment, wavering in indecision. Finally, I stare up at her, my heart pounding. The drama of the moment is somewhat lessened by the fact that I can't help staring at her two teapots. "That looks great on you," is what I finally get out, and she smiles again, though it's a little sad.

"Not nearly as great as the cows," she says, nodding her head toward the stairs. And the bedroom. And, I assume, my cow-covered pajamas.

"It's obvious you're from another world. No one from this planet would think those pajamas were great." I'm laughing and blushing fiercely as I take up my plate and go to sit on the edge of the couch in the living room.

My phone in my pocket rings an obnoxious version of the chicken dance. Which means that Carly is calling me.

"Hey," I mutter into the phone, propping the plate on my lap. Shelley is running around gleefully in the backyard in tight circles, sniffing and peeing on pretty much every blade of grass. I watch her thoughtfully as static interferes with the reception of the call for a second.

"…oh, my God, Holly?" Carly squeaks, the roar of a very busy television station behind her voice. "Oh, my God, *turn on the TV…*"

My blood goes cold. I almost drop the plate as I jerk upright, but I manage to fumble with it and set it down on the coffee table, grab the remote and almost drop it, too. I do manage to turn the TV on, and I switch it immediately to the public access television station.

"…reports are pouring in from the streets beside the bay that something large has been moving beneath the water," says the news anchor in her pale beige business suit, eyes wide as she presses her earpiece to her ear, staring at the camera. Behind her against the blue backdrop in the news room is a picture suspended over her left shoulder of a dark, shadowed hump in several waves of water, not entirely unlike the famous doctored photos of the Loch Ness monster. But this is not the Loch Ness monster.

This is *our* monster.

Our beast.

Virago stands to the side of the television, her lips pressed together, fiddling with the back tie of the apron as she carefully draws out the bow she'd tied behind her waist, takes the apron off over her head, folds it neatly and sets it aside on the counter. Virago now looks almost out of place in her tie and shirt and jacket, like she doesn't belong in them. Like she doesn't belong here.

I have to keep reminding myself…she *doesn't*.

"This is not a whale, folks," says the reporter, glancing down at her desk as a piece of paper is handed to her from off camera. The wrist attached to the hand holding the paper has a gigantic poppy tattooed on it. Carly.

"Listen, can you get down here?" hisses Carly into the phone. I almost forgot I was holding it to my ear. I blink.

"What?"

"We're getting a lot of different footage that

we're not showing right now. And my station manager would like to talk to Virago."

"Carly, you didn't *tell* her— " I practically squeak into the receiver. She sighs the longest and most long-suffering of sighs.

"No, no, c'mon, you know me better than that," she tells me in hushed tones. "But I told her that there *might* be someone who had a bit more info on the monster, and right now she's desperate for that. Right this *minute* more people are tuning into our station than pretty much all the other days of this month *combined*, Holly. It's our highest rating in *all of time*. So can you both get down here pretty quickly? And anyway, I think it's important for Virago to see this stuff. Maybe we can figure out where the monster is with enough cobbled together footage—maybe we can go find it…"

Go find it. Panic seizes me, and suddenly breathing is a little harder. But…if Virago finds the beast, she might die during the ensuing battle. And, at the very least, if all goes well, finding the beast means that Virago will leave.

Oh, my God, Holly, did you *really* just think that? (Yes.) This beast could leave the water, could begin hurting people pretty much at any time, and I'm worried about losing…

Well. Let me be honest here: losing one of the most amazing people I've ever met. I glance up at Virago who has her arms folded, who is watching the television intensely, her eyes searching, her jaw clenched, her feet spread, like she's about to head into battle.

It was only a momentary thought, accompanied by everlasting heartache and pain, of course. Of *course* we're going to go down to the public access station, of *course* we're going to find out where the beast is, try to locate it, fight it. We need to, technically I guess, save the world.

"Yeah, we'll be right there," I mutter into the phone, end the call.

Virago flicks her piercing blue gaze to me, and I'm swallowed deep into that perfect blue of her eyes.

God, I knew this wouldn't last forever.

I just didn't think it'd end this soon.

I need a latte.

The minute we get in the car, I should be turning my wheel toward the public access television station—it's actually not that far from my house, as the crow flies. I buckle myself in, wait for Virago to buckle her seat belt, try not to watch how a stray wisp of her ink-black hair falls into her eyes, as she bites her lip a little, sitting back in the seat, rolling her shoulders back like she's preparing for something.

At the very least, I need a little caffeine for whatever's about to happen next. I mean, I don't know…what if we head out to go after the beast right away? After the night I had, if I don't have some caffeine in my system, I'll probably be dead in less than ten seconds. Not the greatest strategy.

"We're going to go get some coffee," I tell Virago, which is met with a small, tight sideways smile and a brief nod.

"Sure," she says. "I still haven't had any."

"To be honest, I'm not sure if it'll make you explode," I mutter, backing out into the street. "You're already capable of a lot of amazing things, and well...general awesomeness. What if you just...can move so fast, you vibrate out of existence?"

She cocks her head as she considers my words, as she gazes at me. She shakes her head, then, as I start off down the street, as she adjusts the strap of the seatbelt over her chest.

There is a long pause. A moment in which there is only the background noise of my car, and the silence of nothing to say.

But then:

"Holly..." The single word she murmurs is so soft, the two syllables like velvet as she speaks them. Like she's tasting them, savoring them. Savoring my name on her tongue.

"Yes?" I try to tell her, but it comes out as a sort of half-cough. Because Virago is reaching out between us, and she grasps the hand that was curled in my lap, my right hand. She gently curves her long fingers over it, bending them to conform to my palm, squeezes...

And then she just holds my hand gently, softly, warmly.

My heart is beating too quickly. I breathe out, try to pay attention to the road. I can't be having all of these feelings—the same feelings from last night—right now. I'm fairly certain that Virago holds my hand and arm because people are more affectionate on her planet, not because she's attracted to me. That, right this moment in particular, she's trying to comfort me.

And, anyway, *I can't be having these feelings right now*. Not today. Because Virago's going to be leaving in a short amount of time, and I have Nicole...

Oh, Nicole. Nicole who hasn't contacted me since I saw her at the Knights of Valor Festival. Nicole who would never contact me if I didn't contact her first. Nicole who forgets that she has a girlfriend most of the time. Forgets that I, perhaps, even exist.

I'm starting to feel incredibly sorry for myself, and that's where a latte will come in handy. We can't feel sorry for ourselves when espresso is coursing through the blood, making you feel confidence and overwhelming energy in equal doses.

"Hey, Henry," I practically shout to the speaker when we get to the drive-through. "Can I have two triple vanilla soy lattes?"

"Aren't we in a feisty mood this morning?" asks the barista companionably over the crackling speaker. "Pull up, darlin'."

"Triple?" asks Virago, a slight hint of trepidation hanging in the air between us.

"Triple shots of espresso. You'll like it," I tell her, nodding, as I pull out my wallet.

I pay for the drinks, and then pull out of the Starbucks parking lot, heading eastbound toward the TV station. "Here," I tell her, handing the hot cup over. "Be very careful, it's *very* hot," I tell her as she doesn't hesitate, but tips her head back and takes a gigantic swig out of the paper cup that was too hot to even *hold*.

To her credit, that gulp of latte doesn't end up all over my windshield in a spit take, but after she swallows it, she makes a little sigh. "Yes, very hot," she manages, voice a bit gravelly, and then she chuckles a little.

"Oh, my God, you really are a knight, aren't you?" I mutter in wonder, tightening my hands on the steering wheel "That would probably have killed a random person. Or at least inspire a lot of lawsuits," I tell her after I take a careful, tiny sip from my drink.

"Well," says Virago softly, her rich, deep voice curling toward me like a beckoning finger. I chance a look at her. Her eyes are hooded, her gaze so intense it sends a delighted shiver down my spine in spite of myself. "Knights can bear much more than others," is what she whispers then.

I swallow, feel my skin grow cold. Bear? What is she bearing? Is she talking about the beast, having to find it and fight it? I don't know what to say, so I keep silent, my heart thundering in me until we're turning into the parking lot of the news station. I pull into an empty spot, throw the car into park, turn off the ignition, fiddling with my key chain as I gaze down at my lap and then out of the front window, not really seeing anything.

I should...I should tell her, I realize, the clarity of that thought dawning on me as bright as the sunshine outside. I should tell Virago that I find her attractive, and then it'll be out in the open, and then it would exist, that statement. And she'll know. She can do whatever she wants with that information, but I absolutely, positively have to tell her.

I gather courage, but I don't really have a lot of courage to gather, and then I'm turning to her, my mouth open, everything I am the biggest ball of nerves that ever existed...

But whatever I was going to say is completely interrupted, because Carly is there, then, knocking loudly on my car window.

I jump out of my skin, my courage and resolve evaporating instantly.

"*Holly, come on,*" hisses Carly through the closed window, hefting a clipboard and about five pounds of printed paper in her right hand. She jerks her thumb inside, takes another pull on her cigarette before stomping it beneath her high-heeled shoe. "There's lots of stuff, *looooots* of stuff going on," she mutters as I open the car door, get out stiffly, jaw clenched.

The moment is gone. Whatever I was about to say...it'll have to wait.

If I can find the courage to try and say it again.

"Lots of stuff, Carly?" I ask wearily, and then she's shoving the clipboard into my hands while she presses the headphones harder against her ears, cupping out the outside sound with her hands as she mutters into the microphone attached to her headset.

"You just don't even know—read that, okay?" she mutters, and then she's jerking her thumb inside, with an obvious indication that we're to follow her. She's trotting back toward the building, tossing the cigarette onto the pavement before I have a single second to respond.

Instead, I simply follow after her and crush the smoking butt beneath my flip-flop, grinding the butt into the ground before we push through the door, too, and into the station. Virago is a warm and strong presence beside me, her long fingers curling around my elbow in a quick, smooth motion, squeezing once before she lets go.

For comfort. She's doing that for comfort.

I swallow.

The secretary of the station is not at her desk. That's the first thing I notice. Cheryl's been at her desk every moment of every time I've come in since Carly got the job. That damn secretary is as dependable (and probably as immovable) as Mount Everest, and she's *not there*? I didn't think the woman ever even peed. But as we head into the crowded main hallway of the station, I understand why she's not at her post.

Everyone's running *everywhere* in a controlled sort of chaos. The televisions hanging overhead are playing the same news anchor—she's a new one, probably won't last long, they never do at public access TV—who's nervously (and obviously) reading from a teleprompter.

"…we have confirmed sightings of the unidentified animal on multiple streets in the North End as of *this* hour," she says, her voice shaking. I wander toward the recording studio, almost running into Carly as she dashes back across the hallway.

"Come on…we're going to talk with Deb," she says, inserting her arm through mine and all but dragging me down the rest of the hallway as Virago follows along behind us. "C'mon, Virago—she wants to talk to you, too," shoots Carly over her shoulder.

Deb Oliver, the station manager, is currently slumped in her chair in her office, running her hands through her hair and tugging her gray curls at odd moments as she watches the live feed on the television propped up on the folding table across the tiny, closet-sized room from her desk. That dilapidated folding table holds not only the blaring television, but several reams of paper, a very dead aloe vera plant, and a framed picture of her husband brandishing a small, stuffed crocodile. I've never asked how they came in possession of a small, stuffed crocodile—I probably don't want to know.

"Holly," mutters Deb with a sigh, leaning forward, breathing out and tapping the desk with a chewed-on pencil. She's not looking at me, though—she's staring right past me at Virago. "Who's this?"

"Virago," says Carly, jerking her thumb to Virago, who's folding her arms, inclining her head to Deb genteelly. "This is the woman I was telling you about—"

"Do you know *anything* about this monster?" asks Deb, grabbing a pen from behind her ear, and a sheet of scrap paper from her messy desk. She's poised to start writing, but Virago clears her throat.

"I honestly don't know much about it," she says then, head cocked. "I know that this beast is not from this world."

"*What?*" asks Deb, and the pen's flying out of her hands, across the desk as she starts to hyperventilate, waving her hand, trying to take deep breaths and failing. Then she slumps backward in her chair, defeat making her expression turn gloomy. She drinks too much espresso, which is why she can change so dramatically from one heartbeat to the next.

She stares up in disgust at Carly, shaking her head. "Carly, why the hell did you bring me this chick? Another world?" she mutters, waving her arms around, opening the top drawer of her desk and taking out a pill bottle. "I need to fucking retire," is what she says, taking two of the little pink pills out of the bottle and swallowing them dry.

"Deb, seriously, get a hold of yourself. Take a couple of deep, cleansing breaths, okay?" says Carly, rocking back on her heels as she waves her arms in front of her like a yoga instructor, sweeping them out and in like she's about to start a meditation session. "You got this!" she follows up cheerfully before she presses the headphones to her ears again. "Oh shit, Mandy's taking calls—"

"I *told* her not to take calls on the air. It's what

you do on talk shows, not on *news* shows," Deb groans, peering at the television screen. "Go yell at her, okay?"

Carly salutes in reply and races out of the room.

"Look," says Deb then, leaning forward, tapping her blunt finger on her desktop. "I need this shit straight. Holly, who the hell is this jokester?" She waves her hand toward Virago.

That's just how Deb talks, but it still rubs me the wrong way as I stare down at her, seated in her swivel chair, and frown.

"Deb, I'm not certain how to break this to you, but it's not exactly the Loch Ness monster out there," I tell her sharply, folding my arms in front of my chest. "This isn't something that can be *explained*. It's a *monster* out there, *literally*, and Virago is here to…to kill it. Because it's very dangerous," I tell her, summarizing the reasons that Virago needs to find the beast succinctly, and—I hope—drawing no further questions about other worldly origins for the beast. And for Virago.

"Wait…*kill* it?" says Deb, scribbling something furiously on a piece of scrap paper with another pen that she fumbles out of her desk drawer. She glances up, just then, narrows her eyes shrewdly at Virago. "Why are you gonna *kill* it? Are you some big game hunter or something? What exactly *is* it that you're trying to kill?" Deb has worked in news long enough that she thinks that if she asks the question in enough different ways, eventually she'll get the answer she wants to hear.

"I don't know exactly what it is," repeats Virago, crossing her arms, too, as she shakes her head. She raises her chin, her eyes glittering dangerously. "I do know that it will put many people's lives in danger, so I do what I must do in order to keep that from happening."

"*Danger?* Oh, God, this is seriously too good to be true," mutters Deb, drawing a big circle around whatever it is that she scribbled down. She's rolling her eyes, too, which means that she obviously doesn't believe that last part. Deb flicks her gaze up to the television, and then groans out loud. "That damn kid is still taking phone calls, I have my phones ringing off the hook and hundreds of email messages are pouring in from everywhere because we are the *only* news station in all of *Boston* who's saying anything about this right now." She places her hands flat on the desk and glances up at us with her sharp gaze. She shrugs. "So, okay, here's what we're going to do, kids. I'm going to send a cameraman with you for the day to shadow you, see you meet this monster head on." She's already picking up her phone to page the secretary as she rattles off quickly, like something in very fine print: "I mean, if you're okay with that."

"Are you kidding? Absolutely not," I tell her instantly, mouth open in shock, at the exact same moment that Carly—dashing into the room—shouts "sure!"

"*Carly,*" I hiss, rounding on her, but she's already giving Deb a big thumbs up and turning to me as she grabs her headset off and tosses it onto Deb's desk, running her hands through her frizzy hair.

"I'll do it—I'll be the camerawoman," she tells the room at large. "I know how to work the camera, and besides, I can get you the footage quicker. But I'll just shadow her for a few hours, okay?" She's already tugging on my arm, practically trying to drag me toward the open door out of Deb's office. "*Surely* you'd agree to just a few hours, Holly."

"Shadow?" says Virago, perplexed, as I sigh.

"Carly's going to follow us around with a big old camera perched on her shoulder to take constant video of us," I say with a single brow raised.

"It's for posterity's sake," Deb tells us, already turning away from us, and typing much too hard on a beat-up looking laptop. "Be back by seven, Aisley," she snaps at Carly, and Carly gives me a great, big smile as she pushes me by the small of my back right out of Deb's office and down the corridor, Virago following along at a more sedate pace, shutting the door behind us.

"Carly, what the hell were you thinking? Virago can't be found out. If people hear that she thinks she's from another world...I mean..." I trail off, hissing into her ear as we round another corner, heading toward the equipment rooms. Carly fishes a set of keys out of her pocket, unlocks the creaking metal door, pushing it open and flicking on the light with another eye roll.

"God, I *know*, why do you think *I'm* the one shadowing you?"

"Why are you shadowing us at all? This just complicates things," I mutter, following her into the dank, musty-smelling equipment room. The public access station has always been a little low on funding, but the way that most of the cords to various pieces of electronic equipment are stored are by elaborate knots, and there are used coffee cups sitting on top of old computer monitors, and about a foot of solid dust on the top of every single thing. To make matters worse, most of the cameras the public access station uses were manufactured a couple of decades ago, and are so out of date that getting film for them is more difficult than it's worth.

Not that this ever phases the employees of LEM Public Access Television, a hardy bunch of people who work extra hard because they believe in the station and public television devoutly. Carly—one of LEM's biggest supporters—picks up a choice piece of vintage camera equipment right now, hefting it onto her shoulder. At least this camera doesn't have coffee rings on top of it (and who knows how much liquid has been spilled *on* them) like most of the other equipment, so will probably work. She fiddles with it, peering inside the VHS component.

"Hey, I want in on this, too, you know," she tells me, glancing up with a bright smile. "I mean, think about it. I'm the one who most of this information has been funneling through, so I know right whereabouts the monster was just sighted. We can work together," she says, encouragingly. "We'll put our three heads together, and we'll find that beast in no time at all, you'll see."

My trepidation starts to clear. Carly's right, of course. After all, she's been getting all of the reports, the information moving directly through her, and if we can get to the beast, not only will we have a chance at cornering it and keeping it from hurting other people, but she'll also get a pretty spectacular news clip that will make the television station the highest rated in our city. That'd be pretty awesome for her, *and* for the station, Deb and her grouchiness notwithstanding.

And, honestly, if Carly comes along, I won't be able to do any passionate declarations of love, infatuation or attraction to Virago. And perhaps that's just as well right now.

We've got to get our heads in the game. Right now, somewhere in Boston, there's a massive beast who could hurt anyone at any time.

That's got to be stopped.

I glance at Virago, feel my heart sinking in me as she smiles fetchingly at Carly, steps forward and offers to carry the camera out to the car for her with a genteel nod of her head. Carly actually blushes a little at this kind offer, and then hands Virago the camera without a second thought. Of course Virago hefts it up and places it lightly on her shoulder like it weighs about as much as a butterfly. Because to Virago, the woman who picks up swords like they're matchsticks, it probably *does* weigh as much as a butterfly.

Carly and I exit the storeroom, and she fiddles with the key in the lock, making certain the door is locked behind us. She glances up at me, and then turns back to the lock with a sideways smile as she mutters, "Damn, you've got it bad."

I round on her, feeling my cheeks burn instantaneously. Virago is already a ways down the hallway, striding confidently back the way we came, the camera easily balanced on her shoulder. God, I hope she's out of earshot.

"What the hell?" I hiss to her, but Carly's got one eyebrow raised, and her tongue in her cheek as she stares at me imperiously.

"You think I can't see that you've got the hots for Virago?" she whispers back to me, removing the key from the lock and trying the door handle. It doesn't budge, and she deposits the key ring back into her jeans pocket. "I mean, seriously, Holly, satellites can see you drooling from *space*."

"First off, that's disgusting," I mutter, following after her as she saunters down the hallway. I glance up at Virago, but I still think she might be out of earshot.

I lower my voice to a tiny whisper anyway. *"Second off—"*

"Second off, you've got it *bad*, and that's *completely obvious,"* Carly repeats, grinning at Virago who turns to look back at us down the hallway. "Two seconds!" she calls out, practically singing. "Holly and I have to powder our noses!" Then she grabs my shoulders and all but shoves me through a swinging door and into the lady's bathroom we were passing. The last thing I see is Virago's perplexed face before the door slams shut behind us.

"She doesn't know what 'powdering our noses' means, Carly," I sigh and shake my head as Carly turns to the mirror, starting to rearrange her ponytail this way and that, drawing it up to the top of her head with a few specific tugs as she glances at my reflection with brows raised.

"She'll figure it out. But, this is serious conversation time right now, Holly. What the *hell* is going on?" Carly rounds on me, her expression stern, her mouth turning down at the corners. "You have the hots for her, that much is totally and appallingly obvious. So have you broken up with Nicole yet?"

I'm spluttering. How do you explain to your best friend that you don't (as she so eloquently put it) "have the hots" for someone when you totally do? There's no use in lying to her, but it's hard admitting it to *myself* that I find Virago ridiculously attractive.

That I think I'm falling in love with her.

I lean back against the cold tile of the bathroom wall as the truth of that statement moves through me. I mean, maybe I'm not falling in love with her. To be honest, would I even know what it feels like? I don't think I've ever fallen in love with *anyone*. I don't think I fell in love with Nicole when we first started going out. I knew that I liked her, so I pursued her. That was it. There weren't any deeper feelings than physical attraction, and I thought that was good enough in the beginning of a relationship. I thought that was good enough to inspire me to start something with her if I thought she was attractive, and she thought I was attractive. I thought that things could grow from there.

And when I look at Virago, yeah, there's a hell of a lot of physical attraction. But it's not just that. There's so much *more*. When I gaze at that woman, that woman from another world, I see this entire sort of package, because she's kind, she has this great sense of humor, she's incredibly thoughtful and good and a *knight* for heaven's sake. And she likes my dog. There are so many little things that I never thought about before, that it never occurred to me really mattered until I didn't have them with the woman I'd been intending on spending the rest of my life with.

Honestly, and I know this sounds terrible, but I thought you were *supposed* to settle in a romantic relationship. No one's perfect, and I thought if you were too picky, and had too long of a list of qualifications for a romantic partner it would mean that you'd spend your entire life alone.

And now I find out that all of the things that were on my list (that I'd, admittedly, never even thought about *putting* on a list until I met Virago) are realized in this one amazing woman.

The gut-wrenching, painful-as-hell part is that she's from another world. And we are absolutely, positively not meant to be together because of that.

I think about Nicole. About how she hates Shelley, how she doesn't have time for me anymore.

How she still wants to be my girlfriend, the kind of girlfriend who doesn't make commitments like moving in together, the kind of girlfriend you can call up on the weekend if you need someone to go to a party with or you'd like some time in bed. The kind of girlfriend that's, honestly, almost meaningless. I've become that to Nicole when all I ever wanted was something romantic, something love-filled.

Maybe I wanted too much.

So much sadness fills me that I answer Carly with what makes the most logical sense. Because it's the only thing I can cling to in that moment of realization that Virago and I are not meant to be.

"No," I whisper to Carly, feeling my heart sink inside of me. "I haven't broken up with Nicole yet. I don't…" I swallow, let it spill out of me, the one idea I haven't even wanted to think about yet. "I don't honestly know if I will."

She stares at me, her eyes narrowing, her hands placed on her hips.

"Just…just think about it, Carly," I tell her quietly. My heart has sunk so low in me now that I can feel it starting to break along the edges. "Nicole and me? We're all right together. I've put so much time into the relationship. Four years. Maybe this is as good as it gets for me."

"What are you *talking* about?" Carly reaches forward, grabs my shoulders, shakes me gently. "Holly, seriously, you're starting to scare me. I know you, okay? I know how you over-think shit. And I can tell you right now that this is actually much, *much* simpler than you're making it." She takes a deep breath, searches my eyes. "You like Virago, it's obvious. So just admit it."

"Of *course* I like Virago," I whisper, letting the truth come out of my mouth. Now it's real. Now I can't take those words back.

"So here's the most obvious and simplest resolution in this whole damn universe: why don't you just *tell* her?" asks Carly, drawing out the words in frustration. It's obvious, of course. I *should* tell Virago how I feel about her.

But I *can't*.

"You don't understand," I manage, swallowing. "I…I have Nicole," I tell my best friend, feeling my insides begin to crumble as she stares at me, her mouth open in consternation.

"Holly," she whispers, her face full of emotion as she tries to find the right words. She opens and shuts her mouth, and then clears her throat. "Holly," she repeats, words soft. "This is your *life*."

The bathroom door is pushed open, and one of the producers comes in, eyes wide and pausing when she sees us, Carly's hands gripping my shoulders, obviously very emotional. "Sorry," she mutters, walking quickly past us to get to the bathroom stalls, her gaze ducked down.

"You and me…we'll talk about this later," Carly mutters to me, shaking her head and straightening with a frown, tugging on the edges of her shirt as she turns angrily back to the mirror and yanks on her ponytail. I take a deep breath, and then we're back out in the corridor where Virago stands patiently waiting for us, camera on her shoulder, other hand on her hip, her head to the side as she stares easily down the hallway, eyes unfocused, like she's thinking about something very important.

"Ready to catch us a monster?" asks Carly

brightly.

"No," I whisper at the exact same moment that Virago's eyes narrow, that she nods emphatically.

"*Yes*," she tell us, her voice ringing out with strength.

We set off down the corridor together, the oddest pairing of the Three Musketeers that ever existed: a knight from another world, a public access television station producer...

And a woman who wants something she can never have.

Honestly, that sounds much more dramatic than it needs to be. I can be realistic sometimes, and this is just the way it is. I'm already in a relationship with Nicole. Virago is from another world, destined to return there as soon as possible. I would have probably continued on with my relationship with Nicole if Virago had shown up, Nicole and I acting like nothing had ever happened. I wouldn't have known that there was someone out there who was perfect for me. I would never have known how much I was missing.

But now I do know.

And it's the simple truth to say that it breaks my heart.

Chapter 10: The Red Herring

"What, exactly, are we looking for again?"

Casting an amused glance at Carly, Virago shakes her head almost ruefully as she rolls her shoulders back.

"An enormous beast," mutters Virago, glancing up at the bright sun.

The three of us stand together in a small cluster down by the commercial fishing vessels at the docks. It's a powerful scent of fish that's surrounding us currently, and I'm trying to take small breaths through my mouth because the odor from the boats, the warehouses and the crates, rising in steady waves from the heat baking us, is pretty horrific. Virago is currently staring out at the water, Carly's staring at Virago (and pointing her camera at Virago unwaveringly as it balances on her shoulder), and I'm standing beside both of them as we watch the undulating surface of the bright blue bay and look for...

Well. I don't really know what we're looking for either, to be honest.

"Different patterns in the water," Virago explains quietly, as if she heard my unspoken question. "We're looking for currents underneath the surface that might show us that there's something large moving under the water."

"But couldn't a random current be a big fish or

a shark or something?" I ask her, staring hard at the blue ocean. Nothing much moves save for the rhythmic surface.

"Granted, that may be the case…but this is where it was last sighted. So a random current *may* be other creatures. Or we may just get lucky, and it could be the beast," says Virago quietly, narrowing her eyes at the water.

She's right: according to the tweet that someone directed at Carly's public access news Twitter account, the beast *was* just sighted here about ten minutes ago. Carly had gotten an alert on her phone as we were loading the camera into my car, and then we'd taken off quickly from the LEM public television station, speeding through the relatively quiet streets of Boston, thankfully a little less busy than usual because it was a Sunday.

We arrived here at the docks, and there was, of course, no beast in sight.

The tweet had been mostly ambiguous about detail—if the beast was out of the water or in the water, it hadn't said. But since the tweet was the most recent eyewitness account, we'd had to follow it. The other eyewitness sightings had also placed the beast in this general area, though the most recent ones had said that it was hiding out between warehouses, not in the water. But when we walked around, we saw nothing really out of place, and I assumed that a gigantic monster-type thing would probably knock over some crates at the very least, or leave a trail of water behind it. But there was nothing.

Maybe people were getting spooked? Eyewitness accounts, police usually say, are almost always less than reliable.

But I still thought it'd be pretty hard to mistake seeing a monster out and about on dry land.

"How long do you want us to stare at the water, Virago?" Carly quips, but Virago shrugs her shoulders easily, sighing out.

"It's difficult to judge. You do not have to wait with me, my friends." Her jaw clenches and flexes as she swallows, taking a deep breath. "I'm sorry that I may have brought you on a merry goose chase. I just need to find the beast," she whispers now. "Before he hurts a single soul. I will not let that happen. Not on my watch."

There were hundreds of eyewitness accounts of the beast today. Most of them saw something out in the water, which is causing a flurry of "Loch Ness Monster?" questioning on social media web sites like Twitter and Facebook, and just as much speculation on the public access news station's comment threads. Three or four people (the most recent before the tweet that Carly received) supposedly "saw" him out of the water, and even then, they couldn't corroborate their story with anything specific, only thought that they saw a shadow moving between buildings down here by the docks.

So, all clues considered, the beast is probably still in the water. Which is like trying to find a needle in a haystack.

And still, Virago feels responsible that we're not finding it.

"It's all right," I tell her soothingly, reaching out to touch her arm with gentle fingers. She glances sidelong at me with a relieved expression. "We'll find it," I tell her adamantly.

I mean, of *course* we'll find it. There's never

been a part of me that thought we wouldn't. She glances out at the water with grim resolve and a nod, and for a moment—just a moment—I let my eyes trace the curve of her chin, her jaw, her cheek. I watch her unabashedly, gaze at her like I'm memorizing her.

And maybe I am.

"Oh, shit, I've got to take this," mutters Carly, almost dropping the camera in the ocean as she drags her smart phone out of her back pocket and glances down at it with a frown. "It's Deb. Be right back." She sets the camera down on the concrete we're standing on and sprints away, holding the phone up to her ear, pressing her palm to her other ear, and already muttering a greeting into it.

God, what terrible timing.

Virago and I are alone. And my heart's already beating too quickly, my palms are already too sweaty, and my mouth is as dry as a desert.

The wind off the bay sweeps over us, bringing the fresh, salt scent of the ocean with it, pushing away the overpowering smell of fish from the docks. The soft wind moves through Virago's hair, her high ponytail that—while it no longer sports a wolf's tail—is still soft and fine and ink-black, looking velvety enough that I want to reach up and touch it, run my fingers through her hair just to see what it would feel like against my skin.

Virago, glancing out at sea still, clenches her jaw, sighs out quietly as she shakes her head and rocks back on her heels. She murmurs quietly: "You know, my lover would call me foolish."

I feel the world fall away from beneath my feet. There is such a deep, sharp pain that pierces me at that moment that I'm utterly speechless. But I grapple with it for a long moment, take a few deep breaths, try to sound normal: "Oh?" I reply, coughing a little.

"Well," says Virago, rolling back her shoulders, shaking her head a little as she widens her stance, crosses her arms, continues to rake the bay's blue surface with her equally blue eyes. "My former lover, truly. We've not been together for six moons or so, since we parted ways." Her gaze flicks to me now, one brow up as she searches my eyes. "She would tell me that I am foolish to sit here, watching the water for a beast I do not know is even there."

I stare at her, my breath coming far too quickly in me to explain away, my mouth open. I probably look dazed, as I stand there trying to calm my racing heart, but I don't even care as I shake my head, clear my throat again, the purest joy I've ever known washing through me.

Oh, my God.

She said "she."

That's it. That's *it*. Virago loves ladies.

Thoughts, emotions, vibrant feeling begins to spill through every part of me, and I'm grappling with all of it, but a specific thought comes to the forefront: Does that mean that all of the times I thought she was coming on to me...she *actually was?*

Okay, now's not the best time to go over all of that, Holly. *Think.* I lick my lips, don't have a clue what I'm supposed to reply with, so I go with my gut: "that's not the nicest thing to say to your girlfriend," I tell her, one brow up while inside I do an elaborate dance of joy complete with metaphorical tambourines.

Virago shrugs elegantly, her mouth narrowing to a hard line. "Elladin was always very...pragmatic. She thought that my being a knight was foolish. Too dangerous, she thought, but also a childish dream. She saw that I had a good head for ciphers and urged me to become a bookkeeper in her father's tavern as it was steady, constant, safe work." Virago spreads her hands, shakes her head. "I had no stomach for bookkeeping, though. I knew what I must be, knew it from the earliest of ages, knew it was in my blood and my bones to become a knight. I had to follow my heart. And Elladin did not agree with this, thought it was too fanciful to follow one's heart. So we parted ways."

I stand there, my nose wrinkling, as I try to imagine Virago as a bookkeeper. I fail utterly. I mean, it'd be admittedly sexy to imagine her in a poet's white shirt, elegantly dipping a feathered quill into a pot of ink, but she's just...not really the type. She wields a sword. She wants to slay a beast. She's not a "sit there" kind of lady.

"Well," I whisper, feeling my cheeks become hot, but pushing through the words anyway: "from where I'm standing you're not foolish. You're here because you want to help people. And that's the best thing in the world..." I trail off, take a deep breath, flounder. I don't know what else to say. "In my opinion, anyway," I finish stupidly, my voice soft.

She's casting a sidelong glance in my direction, and the corners of her mouth are pulled upwards, her full lips curving into the most beautiful smile, just for me. "That's very kind of you, Holly," she tells me, then.

And she reaches across the space between us, takes my hand in her own warm one, and squeezes it once, twice, gently, her long fingers folding into my palm like they fit there effortlessly. She stands, holding my hand for a long moment, a too-long moment, perhaps. Then she lets it go, and my warm, tingling hand drifts down to my side, my heart racing inside of me as she looks back out to sea, the cold ocean breezes washing over me, making me shiver, the wind playing with her ink-black ponytail and passing over her beautiful face...

"All right—I've got some bad news, ladies," Carly mutters, trotting over to us with a grimace, shoving her phone back into her pocket. She shrugs, rocks back on her heels. "Unfortunately, I think we've been given a bad lead. There are now reports coming in that some sailing vessels a few miles out at sea are seeing a massive creature under the water. Big as a whale, they're saying, but it can't be a whale because it has *spikes* along its *spine*, so I'm kind of thinking that's our little monster guy. Anyway," she sighs, wrinkling her nose, talking fast, "Deb's calling me in, so I've got to head back. I can keep you updated, but—for right now—beastie seems to be out of our hands until it decides to swing back to shore."

Virago inclines her head to Carly. "Thank you, Carly. You will keep us posted?"

Carly salutes, then smiles at the both of us. When Virago turns to look back over the ocean again, Carly gives me the cheesiest grin imaginable, and two thumbs up signs. Then she's lifting up the camera and all but sprinting back to our car with the ancient piece of equipment on her shoulder.

"I doubt that the beast will hunt fishing vessels if it is still wounded. And even if it is not, it is not stupid," says Virago, her blue eyes flashing. She turns to me, folds her arms carefully in front of her. "We just have to bide our time. Wait. But what of the ritual? I must think of a way to lure the beast back toward shore if only for the ritual. And it is so soon..." Worry tightens her features.

The ritual. Oh, crap. Aidan's ritual by the coven to try and trap the creature.

Aidan. I glance at my watch and groan. "Oh, crud—we're supposed to stop by Aidan's shop tonight for the weekly meditation circle," I tell Virago, jerking my thumb back to the car. "Who knows," I tell her, uncertainty making my words soft, "maybe he can track the beast with some witchy magic or something?"

Virago's lips twitch up at the corners, and then she glances down at the chipped concrete beneath our feet as a smile takes over her entire face. She tries to hide it but fails as she glances back up at me, her blue eyes smoldering.

"Or something," she agrees companionably, taking my arm in a gentle hand and threading it through hers as we make our way back to the car.

From the back seat, Carly watches our interactions, barely keeping her glee to herself as she pretends to fiddle with the camera, but is not-so-secretly grinning widely and trying to hide it with her hand.

But no matter what, I've got to keep my head in the game. We have the beast to find. There's Nicole and a host of other problems looming.

But still.

This moment. This moment right here is good. No matter what happens next, I've had this moment and all the ones leading up to it.

That has to be enough.

Right?

Chapter 11: Open Doors

"Now, everyone, take hold of the hand of the person next to you. Together, we create this never-ending circle of energy that keeps us safe in this place. Safe to explore the deepest parts of ourselves—safe to explore our own inner depths."

I open one of my tightly closed eyes and peek at my brother. The rest of the people in the meditation circle are calmly seated on the brightly-painted wooden folding chairs in the circle, each holding the hands of the people on either side of them tightly, eyes closed, chins up, deeply breathing as they began to sink into a light meditative state.

My brother's in rare form tonight.

I mean, he's usually pretty theatrical about these kinds of things. He's always told me that you need rituals and meditations to have a certain kind of production about them, full of the mystery and good energy that's made the idea of magic survive the entire time that people have existed. He's intoning the words now in his deep voice, softening them so that his words are light enough to follow, but still something you can let go of once you get into a deep meditative state, following your own intuition and the messages that the universe supposedly sends you.

Virago's seated to my right, and she's gripping

my hand tightly. Much tighter than the guy to my left, the one with the short beard, whose name I can never remember. Virago's fingers in mine make me think about things I shouldn't be thinking about. Mainly about her reveal today that she used to have a girlfriend. A lover. A *woman*. Her grip is so strong, her hand warm and sure around mine that I can't *help* but think about these things.

I *should* be trying to imagine world peace or something. But all I can think about is this gorgeous woman, holding my hand.

But the truth is that this weekly meditation circle isn't gathered for world peace tonight. We've met together to try and open the portal to her world just to see if we can do it. We're *not* gathered here so that I can sit and stare at her out of slitted eyes that should actually be closed so that I can start to meditate.

I cast one last, tiny glance at her, at her raised chin, at her serene profile, and then I close my own eyes again, let out the tiniest of sighs.

"I want you all, tonight, to relax," my brother says quietly, his voice drifting in a soothing lull over us. "And I want you to imagine, in the very center of our circle tonight, a bright white circle of light. I want you to imagine a door."

There's a very good chance that this won't work, my brother warned Virago. Aidan had looked so worried when he'd brought it up to her earlier, biting at his lip and trying to be as frank as possible with her as he could. But she assured him that it was wonderful for him to even try to help. That she appreciated his efforts. That she couldn't do this alone and any help we could give her would be mightily appreciated, no matter the outcome.

And then she'd sat down in the circle with the rest of us. And Aidan, who'd already briefed his coven-members of the task at hand, had sat down at the other end of the circle and begun.

He'd begun, in fact, just like this was a regular meditation. The kind of meditation where we visualize sending good energy (usually in the form of white light we raise together) to people in hospitals or the Middle East.

But this isn't a regular night or meditation. We've never, for example, concentrated on the center of the floor in front of us, visualizing a door to *another world*.

My heart begins to beat more quickly. There'll be no relaxation achieved tonight.

Virago grips my hand tightly, her wide, strong palm pressed against my own, the solidity of her skin, her warmth, drawing me in, so that I'm mostly concentrating on where we connect.

No, no. I take a deep breath, try to clear my head.

I imagine a circle of white light on the center of the floor in front of us. I imagine it glowing brightly. I imagine it so bright that, even though my eyes are closed, the darkness of the room—lit by a single candle on the goddess altar behind Aidan—becomes so light, light as day in fact, that I have to open my eyes so that I can see what's going on.

That's strange. The room is actually a whole lot brighter than I remember it being behind my eyelids. I open my eyes just a little, now, just to take another peek.

In the center of the floor in front of us, exactly like I'd imagined it in my mind's eye, is a circle comprised entirely of white light.

"Oh, my God," the guy in the beard next to me whispers.

"Keep concentrating, everyone," my brother intones, but you can tell by his enormous grin that he's ecstatic.

I can't believe it myself.

We did this. This isn't some airy fairy new age imagining of sending good energy to someone who may, or may not, ever feel that good energy or have something good happen to them because of it.

This is real. This is physical. There is actual *white light* in the center of the floor in a circle.

It's…*real.*

Virago is rising smoothly, her hand gently unclasping a little from mine, but not letting it go. She straightens gracefully and takes two firm steps across the floor between her seat and the white light. She peers down and into the circle.

Because she hasn't let go of my hand, I follow her rising unsteadily to my feet and wobbling over to peer down into the circle, too, and beard guy follows me. Everyone's actually standing and coming closer now, to peer down into the white light…

But when you peer down into it, you realize that it's not white light anymore.

It's a portal. A portal to Virago's world.

The portal in the floor looks a little like I'm staring down into a manhole, but I'm not…I'm staring down into another world that's about ten feet below us. It's night down there, just like it is here. And it also appears to be summer. There's tall grass on the ground, and the air is rich with the heady scent of unfamiliar flowers. It's a meadow, what we're looking down on. There are trees ringing it, I can see a little, off to the right—pines, by the looks of them.

But that's really not the most interesting part. Because in the center of the portal, straight down, standing on that meadow and among those flowers, are four knights.

The only reason that I know they're knights is because they're wearing identical armor to what Virago was wearing when she came with the beast onto my lawn. All four of them are women, and all of them have their equally long hair pulled up into a tight ponytail, with wolf's tails hanging from each one, blending in with their regular hair. The knights wear fur capelets, and have broadswords in worn leather scabbards hanging on their backs.

And they're all staring up at us in consternation, their mouths open in shock, eyes wide as they stare up through the portal into *our* world...which probably does look pretty strange to them.

"Magel?" says Virago in a hushed whisper. Then she's shouting it: "Magel!"

"Virago!" thunders the tallest woman back. She has bright red hair that falls in waves down her back from her ponytail, and even though it's night and quite dark wherever this is, I can still see her eyes flashing in that darkness as she raises her arm toward us. She reaches out her hand to Virago as she shouts: "have you slain the beast, sister?"

Virago lets out a small sigh beside me, but then she's shaking her head, grimacing. "No. Not yet. There were...complications. But there is hope that within two days, the beast will be vanquished and plague us and no living creature evermore."

"Do you have what you need to complete this

task?" asks the woman—Magel, I suppose her name is. Her jaw clenches as she stares up at us. She no longer looks as happy as she did a moment ago. "Are you being assisted by knights?"

"No," says Virago clearly, "but those who help me are just as brave and good. I will prevail, sister. I will return soon, triumphant."

"May the goddess go with you..." Magel is saying, but her voice seems to be getting smaller—more distant—and then the white light ringing the portal begins to fade. As the light flickers, what we see before us in the portal begins to flicker as the white light dies. In an instant, the scent of summer meadow is abruptly gone, and so is the portal in front of us, the white light flickering and dying completely now, leaving an afterimage of a circle when we close our eyes.

Like the light of the portal, the small candle on the altar flickers and goes out, too, plunging us into utter darkness.

Everyone's silent for a long moment. Until: "Did we just...did we really just experience that?" a woman in the darkness whispers in hushed tones.

I can hear someone fumbling around in the dark, and then Aidan flicks the lights back on. The paintings on the walls look so fluorescent under the Christmas tree lights around the edges of the ceiling, and we all look sallow, pale, and more than a little in shock as we all stare at one another.

"Yes," says Aidan, sounding more surprised than me. "That actually *did* just happen."

We're all looking to Virago now.

"Thank you so much for your help, my friends," she tells us, inclining her head to us and pressing her fist over her heart as she breathes out. "It was good to see my fellow knights again. That they have stayed, waiting for me—that they have not forsaken me. That I know, now, that you can open a portal…this is all great news. We *can* trap the beast. I know it now." Her low voice ends on a growl. She turns her attentions to Aidan, her bright blue eyes flashing. "Next time, the portal must open to a place between worlds, if you can muster it. That will keep everyone safe."

Aidan shrugs his shoulders, still grinning hugely. "I mean, I don't even know how I just did that. We just opened a *portal*, I mean that's some seriously intense shit right there." He shrugs, shoves his hands deep into his jeans pockets. "Honestly, I think it had something to do with you, Virago—that you helped steer the energy into creating the portal or something. I mean, I don't know how else to explain it." He shrugs again, turns his smile onto his coven members. "All right, time for tea and cookies, everyone! Let's ground ourselves after that out of this world meditative experience!"

I hang back as the coven members gather along the folding table pushed up against the far wall, practically groaning under the weight of canisters of hot water and Styrofoam plates covered in store-bought cookies.

Virago remains with me.

"Holly?" she whispers questioningly, reaching out across the space between us to gently, softly, trace her finger over my cheek. My heart begins to beat wildly in me, and I'm too tired to try and quell it this time.

Virago pulls her hand back from my face, and there's a tear brightly etched on her finger.

I sniffle, feel inordinately stupid, and scrub at my cheeks with the back of my hand. "Oh my goodness, will you look at me?" I manage, chuckling a little, though it comes out as a harsh sound between us. "Don't mind me," I whisper to her, breathing out.

"What is the matter?" she asks me, her brow furrowed.

I glance up at her then. I stare up at this impossible woman, this woman who's so beautiful and good and kind and wonderful and *sexy as hell* and everything you could ever imagine wanting in someone you'd give your soul to spend the rest of your life with.

"You'll be going home, soon," I tell her, shrugging a little as I wrap my arms around my middle. The AC in Aidan's back room of his shop is kicked up to the highest power, and it's actually a little chilly back here, in contrast to the hot summer night I dressed for in my tank top and shorts. I shiver a little, run my hand through my hair as I shake my head. "It was...it was amazing to see the other knights, see a glimpse of your world," I tell her. Because it was.

It was amazing and magical and it's absolutely the place that's meant for her. Because *she's* amazing and magical. I know she's meant to be there.

She belongs there.

Virago reaches out again between us, and again, her warm, caressing finger is tracing a pattern over my cheek, down to my jaw. But now she softly, but with a gentle strength, tilts my chin up so that my gaze must meet hers.

"Right now," she tells me, her calm, certain gaze pinning me to the spot, "I am exactly where I want to be."

I stare at her, my heart racing in me.

The spell is broken, ironically, by a witch.

My brother clears his throat beside us, and we both turn to glance at him.

"Cookie?" he asks, grimacing when he realizes that there was a moment happening between us. At least, I really, really, *really* think it was a moment.

I am exactly where I want to be, she'd said. Virago scoops up a cookie, smiles at my brother, laughs at one of his jokes as he holds the plate of cookies out to me.

I take a sugar cookie in wonder, let the sweetness melt on my tongue as I take a small bite.

Where I want to be.

Virago walks over to the gathered coven members, the sound of her voice drifting over me as I turn her words over and over again in my heart.

My heart that, if it skips anymore beats, I'm probably dead.

I eat the entire cookie, grinning like a fool.

When we get home, it's almost ten o'clock. And I have work in the morning.

Work! Regular life, with all of its obligations and responsibilities, is going on around me while extraordinary, magical things are happening at the same time, and it's hard for me to put that together in my head.

I have to go to work at the library tomorrow. We're having children's story hour at four PM, and while I don't work in the children's department, my friend Alice, who's the head of the department, always needs a little extra help, so I'll have to find time in my schedule to help her corral some kids and get them interested in the story.

While Virago is here. On our world. Looking for the beast that could destroy everything.

I sigh and sit down on the couch the minute we come in. Shelley launches herself onto my stomach and proceeds to worm around on the couch and on top of me, ecstatically kicking her legs and feet into the air while I watch her, a smile turning up the corners of my mouth while I shake my head and chuckle at my ridiculous dog.

"I'm going to let her out," I tell Virago, rising and crossing the living room to open the sliding glass door for Shelley. The dog tears past us and launches herself out into the night. "Will you let her back in if she comes back to the door?" I ask Virago, yawning. "I'm going to get dressed for bed, and then I'm going to make both of us a nice, strong cup of chamomile tea."

Virago's mouth twitches at the corners, too, as she tries to suppress a smile. "Yes, m'lady."

I cast her a sidelong glance, but Virago's brows are up innocently, and she's sitting down in my favorite chair, placing one ankle on her knee gracefully and leaning back like she owns the place. I try not to stare at her smoldering form relaxing in my favorite chair, and instead go up the stairs and close the bathroom door behind me.

Well. Today has been...eye-opening.

I wash my face, run a brush through my hair, brush my teeth (absentmindedly, since I'll have to brush them again after I drink my tea, or, hell—I may live on the wild side and *not* brush them after my final cup of tea. I'm a rebel like that), and then slip into my bedroom and out of my shirt and jeans and into my least hilarious pajamas, which are still somewhat joke-y since they're covered in little wizard hats and wands.

A gift from my brother.

How do I have a funny pajama collection, you ask? Well, it was certainly never *my* idea. I shake my head ruefully and tug at the top buttons of the pajama top, smiling at myself in the mirror.

I'm trying not to think about the fact that Virago told me she once had a girlfriend. That she placed her hand against my cheek and promised me that she was exactly where she wanted to be.

I pull my phone out of my purse and check the screen.

Still nothing from Nicole.

I replace the phone with almost shaking hands, setting my purse down on the trunk at the foot of my bed as I nibble at my lip.

God, what do I do?

Every single atom in me wants to make a move on Virago. I want to tell her that I'm attracted to her. I want to sweep her off her feet (no small feat considering that she's taller and much more muscular than me). All of my old patterns are starting to flare up. I want to pursue her. I want to kiss her.

But doing so would open up such an immense can of worms...

I stare at my reflection in the mirror above my dresser. I look wild-eyed. I take a deep breath. I can't stall anymore. I'll just...play it by ear.

I head down the stairs to the living room lost in my thoughts, but I pause on the landing, because there's a sight greeting me that I really couldn't have expected.

Shelley is lying down like a Sphinx on my living

room floor, her paws placed neatly in front of her, her fluffy tail thumping hard against the wood floor. The coffee table and my favorite chair have been pushed out of the way to make room for Shelley…

And for Virago.

Who is also lying down on my living room floor.

She's lying on her stomach, propped up on her elbows. And she's practically nose to nose with Shelley. "You do it like this, good beast," says Virago gently, and then she's turning slowly until she's lying on her side, and she continues to make the rotation onto her back and then again onto her side as she makes a full circle of rolling on the floor.

Rolling *over*, I realize.

She's trying to teach Shelley how to roll over.

Shelley makes a low, guttural "woof" sound in the back of her throat, reaching her nose out toward Virago with her silly little grin that she always gives me when *I* try to teach her anything. I always imagine that she's thinking "what are you doing, you silly human?" But she's also staring with rapt fascination at Virago, who doesn't seem to mind that she's lying on a floor in front of a dog, her shirt's immaculate white sleeves rolled up to her elbows, the shirt unbuttoned at the collar, I realize, and untucked from her pants.

God, she's beautiful.

I stare at her as she smiles at my dog, her full lips curling up so beautifully that it takes my breath away, as she nods to Shelley. "All right," says Virago, rolling back the other way slowly, keeping her eyes trained on Shelley as she says commandingly: "roll over. There's a good beast!"

Because for the first time in her entire life, Shelley's

actually paying attention as Virago rolls over. Shelley angles her neck and lays her head down on the ground, and then slowly, carefully, as Virago repeats another rotation, my goofy dog is actually on her side, rolling over, too. But just a little.

And then Shelley, wagging her long, fluffy tail the entire time, makes a single rotation, rolling completely over. She bounces up onto her feet at the end of it, wagging her tail so hard that it's in danger of knocking the tea cup off of the coffee table.

I clear my throat and take the final step down and into the living room. Virago, chucking a little, rises up to one knee, and then is standing as she brushes off her knees and her bottom, shaking her head ruefully.

"Sorry," she tells me, glancing at me with one brow raised. "Shelley's undersides had gotten muddy, and she wouldn't sit still for me to dry her off." She jerks her thumb to indicate the clean paper towels crumpled on the floor by the sliding glass door. "I thought," says Virago with a sly smile, "that she could learn the trick on command."

"Frankly, she doesn't know how to do *anything* on command," I tell her laughing. "She's such a good dog, but it's mostly because she's so damn nice. She doesn't know a single trick—she doesn't even know how to sit!" I shrug, make my way around the counter and take the kettle over to the sink, running the cold tap. "How did you do it?" I gesture with the tea kettle lid at my (usually) incredibly disobedient dog who's sitting at attention at Virago's feet. "I mean, even *dog trainers* find her impossible. She's just so cheerful and kind of flighty that she doesn't pay attention to a single word that anyone says. A trainer once said she was unteachable, actually," I snort.

"Oh, that's not true," says Virago, shaking her head as she leans on the counter, running a long-fingered hand through her hair that I try, very, very hard not to watch. She pulls out her ponytail, and then around her shoulders comes this glistening, shiny wave of ink-black hair. Virago carefully gathers it into a ponytail again, fastening the tail higher on her head as she smiles at me.

God, she caught me watching.

"While the water boils," she says slowly, carefully, one brow raised, "do you want me to show you?"

"Show me what?" I ask, almost dropping my kettle as I realize it's overflowing with water. I switch off the tap, set the kettle onto the burner and turn the burner onto high as Virago watches me, smiling in amusement.

"I'll show you how to teach her," she tells me gently, her velvet voice drifting over me, even as she raises her hand to me. I take her hand, placing my fingers into her warm palm, and she grips it tightly as she leads me around the edge of the counter, my heart beating approximately a million times a minute. She kneels down in front of Shelley, still holding onto my hand. I follow suit, trying to pay close attention to my dog and not the fact that Virago's warm hand is still in my own. She hasn't let me go.

"All right," says Virago, inclining her head toward my rug with a smile. "Lie down."

I take a deep breath, can feel the blush start to redden my cheeks. For a moment I hesitate, but then I do exactly as she says. I kneel down, and then I'm lying down on my living room rug next to this gorgeous woman, our hips next to each other, *almost* but not quite touching.

Shelley, of course, thinks this is the Most! Fun! Ever! And proceeds to bark at us, her tail wagging so hard that the television remote, positioned on the edge of the coffee table that Virago dragged out of the way, goes flying to the floor.

"Good beast," says Virago soothingly, and then she lies down fully on her stomach beside me, propping her chin in one hand. She holds out her other hand, her pointer finger extended, to Shelley.

"Lie down," she says, her low voice strong and commanding as she points down to the ground.

Shelley, to my utter and complete shock, lies down instantaneously, like she's a perfect well-trained stunt dog. Which, I promise, she absolutely is not.

"Good beast," Virago murmurs, smiling encouragingly. "All right. Now watch your mistress and I!" Virago turns to me, and I realize how close she is. That we're lying down on my living room floor right next to each other. The heat from her body radiates to me, and all I can see is her beautiful face, close enough to kiss.

"Now," says Virago, her mouth turned up at the corners. She practically whispers, the words rolling out of her beautiful mouth softly and slowly: "Roll over, Holly."

I stifle a laugh, because this situation I'm in? It's practically ridiculous. But then I'm rolling over, my arms tucked next to my torso, my feet kicking against the floor as I try to control the roll. God, I *feel* practically ridiculous, but when I'm fully rolled over all the way, I see that Virago was rolling over beside me, mirroring my motions. To my completely surprise, when I glance up at my dog, Shelley is rolling over, too, as if she's mesmerized by Virago's command.

Virago's still rolling, though, coming toward me in a slow curve. And I know she's much too controlled, much too graceful for what happens next.

She bumps gently into me. Virago has rolled into me. And to steady herself, she places one arm, elbow down, on the carpet on the other side of me.

She's practically on top of me, now.

My breathing is coming much too fast as I stare up at her, at her piercingly blue eyes that seem to pin me to the spot. Her body is so warm in all of the places that it touches mine, her arm curving around my waist to hold herself up is almost hot to the touch, heat that I can feel radiating through the fabric of my pajamas. I *want* so much in that moment. I want her to reach down and brush that beautiful, full mouth over mine. I want to taste her, want to kiss her so passionately that all of my longings will be concentrated into that one single moment when we meet together, skin against skin, mouth to mouth, heart to heart.

Virago is gazing down at me, searching my eyes with her own piercing blue ones as we stare at one another for a long moment. I think she's going to say something just then. She swallows, begins to frown, her full mouth downturning at the corners as she begins to say...

A whistle sounds. The tea kettle—the water must already be boiling.

I'm so flustered that I practically jump at the sound. I groan and struggle up onto my elbows as Virago grimaces, too, and sits up, no part of her touching me now. She stands, and then she's offering a hand down to me. She won't meet my eyes as she helps me stand, pulling me up effortlessly. I head into the kitchen, get the chamomile tea bags out of the cupboard with shaking hands and place them into two mugs, letting the boiling water wash over the tea.

In the living room, Virago gently ruffles the fur behind Shelley's ears, just like I do, as she talks in low tones to the dog, telling her what a good girl she is.

My heart still pounding inside of me, I bring the too-hot tea into the living room, setting the mugs onto the coffee table pushed to the side.

"Virago," I say, clearing my throat. Virago rises from her position, kneeling next to Shelley, stretching overhead. When she does that, her shirt rises enough so that I can see about an inch of her tanned, toned middle, and I wonder what it would feel like…

"Yes, Holly?" asks Virago, her tone almost amused. I can feel myself redden, and I don't look at her as I hand up a cup of the tea.

"Well, I have work tomorrow," I finish stupidly, which is *not at all* what I was going to say, but it seemed that the moment of a declaration of love and attraction had probably already come and gone. "And you need to try and find the beast, but I don't think you should do it alone. I mean…our world is pretty…" I falter on the word "dangerous" as I stare up at this amazing knight, her sword carefully lying on the couch. She could probably take on anyone, but that doesn't mean she should wander around the city of Boston by herself. "I mean, our world is pretty *complicated*," I finish, chewing on my lower lip. "Do you just want to…" I trail off, uncertain. "You could come to work. With me. If you wanted. I work at a library," I continue quickly when her brows furrow together. "It's full of books—"

"We have libraries on my world," she says with

a small smile. "And I did love them there. I'm sure I would find them just as enjoyable on your world."

"So then it's settled!" I'm utterly relieved. "You can come in with me tomorrow, and then we can try to locate the beast." I rise too quickly, a little of my tea sloshing out and hitting the carpet where, moments before, Virago and I were rolling around together. Albeit not exactly the way I wanted. But it had happened.

"Holly," says Virago. And she's rising too, setting her mug of tea down easily on the coffee table as she crosses the space between us and takes my elbow gently in her hand.

"Yes?" I say, feeling my heart pounding in me.

And then, upstairs, I can hear the stupid, incessant beeping of my phone. It's a specific rhythm, that pattern of beeps, though.

Nicole.

Nicole is calling me.

Are you *kidding* me? How bad can my luck *possibly* get?

"I'm sorry...I've got to take that," I stammer miserably as I take a step backward, and then I'm bolting up the stairs. When I enter my bedroom, I carefully shut the door behind me, and then my heart is in my throat as I pick up the phone from my purse, start the call and press it to my ear.

"Nicole?" I say, a little breathless.

"Hello," she says woodenly.

I slump a little, setting my mug of tea on the table beside my bed, sitting down on the edge of my bed as I toe at the carpet with my slipper. I try to make my breath come slower, take a deep breath in, feel the awkwardness press down on me like a lead blanket.

The silence stretches on for a full moment before I make any sort of effort at a conversation.

"How are you?" I say then, trying to keep my tone even.

"I think that the time for pleasantries has come and gone," says Nicole with a practiced snarl. "Are you going to apologize for what happened at that asinine festival or not?"

Her tone cuts me like a knife. And after the wave of pain comes another equally sized wave.

Of anger.

I'm so tired of all of this. I felt *guilty* downstairs that I was having these thoughts about Virago. But Nicole doesn't want me, hasn't wanted me for a long time.

This needs to be over. We're not right for each other.

That much is fairly obvious.

"Asinine?" I whisper into the phone, feeling my hand shaking as it holds the phone to my ear, but feeling firm resolve curl like a fist in my stomach. "Nicole, I admit, Carly stepped over the line. But you could have—"

"I should never have even been there in the first place. I only went to *appease* you." She spits out the word like it's poisonous. "You're always so *precious* about that festival, and I assumed that if I didn't go, I'd never hear the end of it. You'd sulk about it for weeks, and frankly, I have no energy to deal with your petty needs right now."

"*My* needs?" I whisper.

"Look," she says then, her tone hard and sharp, "I want to see you tomorrow."

For a long, full moment, I am utterly speechless. She

wants to "see" me for one reason and one reason only, and you know what? I'm not in the mood. I'm not in the mood to be cast off and away like I'm meaningless to her. I'm not in the mood for someone who no longer cares about me to tell me what to do.

"No, Nicole," I say, my voice not in the least bit shaking, to my surprise. "I want to see *you* tomorrow. I'll meet you at your place. We...we really need to talk."

"Finally. I have about an hour between four and five. We can, perhaps, get in some intercourse, clear this up. You can apologize to me in person."

I'm fuming so hard that if I were a cartoon character, flames would be coming out of my ears. Thankfully, I am *not* a cartoon character.

"Fine. I'll see you then." And then I hang up.

But the anger that had fueled me so powerfully while I was speaking with her is gone in an instant. Because I think about how she spoke to me. The sharpness, the demanding cruelty in her voice. And I remember that when Nicole and I first got together, she used to speak to me so softly, so gently. She used to make time for me and my "asinine" needs. She was thoughtful and brought me flowers and take-out. And I didn't exist solely for her. I was my own person, and we loved each other equally.

And it's not that way anymore. And it's never going to be that way again.

I feel so deflated as I sink down deeper into the edge of the bed, let the phone fall into my lap as I realize exactly what I have to do.

We've dragged this out for far too long.

Tomorrow afternoon, I'm going to break up with her.

I was supposed to for a very long time, now.
I can, at least, finally make this right.

Chapter 12: Books and Breakups

Virago insists on taking her sword with us to the library.

"I cannot leave Wolfslayer here," she says firmly when we're ready to go, standing by the door with my purse, my thermos of coffee, and Virago decked out in all of her jacket and button-down shirt glory...with her scabbard belted tightly—and unmovingly—onto her back.

"Wolfslayer?" I ask her perplexed, and then nod. "Oh, right, right...your sword. You killed wolves with that?" I frown. The animal lover in me says that this is Not Okay, no matter how much I'm falling in love with this gorgeous creature. (And yes, I *am* falling in love with Virago, but at this point in time, I've decided not to do anything about it. I think. Not yet anyway.)

"Well, not exactly *wolves*," she says with a grimace and a wave of her hand, "but the name 'Wolfslayer' worked better as a sword name, and was a bit more concise. My wolf tail," she points up to her ponytail, even though the wolf tail no longer resides there, "was cut off from a murderous werewolf. There are groups of them in the country who terrorize entire villages, killing everyone they encounter. My band of knights and I followed the wolves back to their lair. There were many people the werewolves had held captive, ready to cannibalize and eat. We killed the wolves and set them free. It was my very first quest, so I named my sword after it."

I'm staring at her with my mouth open, but I shut it and swallow. Cannibalistic werewolves. Of course. Why did I think she'd randomly hurt an innocent animal?

Also…cannibalistic werewolves?

I probably shouldn't poke further into that.

"Well, be that as it may," I start, but Virago's folding her arms in front of her, her feet hip-width apart, a single brow raised as she shakes her head slowly.

"M'lady Holly," she says formally, inclining her head to me. "If you would have me leave my weapon here…"

I watch her carefully, brows up, my own arms folded.

"Then I will do as m'lady asks of me," she says softly, her piercing, blue gaze searching my eyes as— *holding* my gaze—she slowly, carefully, starts to unbuckle the sword from over her shoulder.

The buckle, of course, lies right on top of her chest.

She's slow and methodical as she runs the leather through her hands, unhitching the buckle with long, nimble fingers. I swallow, can feel my cheeks start to turn a very unflattering shade of red. She takes the buckle off, and it's over then, the sword lying, sprawled on my couch, its pommel glinting in the early morning light.

"There," Virago says with a slow, sensuous smirk as she gazes at me. "Better?"

"You're being cheeky," I admonish, but my

voice is a little high-pitched when I say it, and it's obvious that I'm more than a little flustered. Did I *really* just call Virago *cheeky?*

Well. I guess it was better than letting "sexy as hell" slip out.

"Thank you, Virago," I manage, and then I hold open the door for her to stride out of my house and into my car and then into my workplace that I have a feeling will *never* be the same again after Virago has been there.

But Virago, of course, doesn't let me hold the door open for her. She reaches over my head and touches the frame of the door lightly with her warm hand, brushing it lightly against my fingers.

"After you," she whispers, her mouth turning up at the corners, "m'lady," she finishes lazily, causing my already flushed cheeks to deepen in color.

"*Definitely* cheeky," I mutter, stumbling out the door and down the walkway to my car parked on the street. I somehow manage to get the car doors open, and then after grappling with the seatbelt because I'm so damn flustered, we're on our way to work.

Well, actually, with a brief detour to the coffee shop first.

"Hi, Henry!" I tell the drive-through microphone when we pull up. "I need two large coffees with soy milk, two sugars a piece, and an extra shot of espresso in each?"

"All business this morning!" the barista practically purrs through the microphone. "Is your new girlfriend with you?"

"She's not my girlfriend, Henry," I mutter between clenched teeth, stealing a glance at Virago over my shoulder. She's looking out her window and not paying attention, I think. But then, if she's not paying attention, why is she smiling a little as she tugs on the seatbelt positioned over her chest?

I pay for the coffees (trying to ignore Henry's knowing grin), and then it's just a few blocks more to the library. Virago doesn't say very much as she takes a few sips from the to-go coffee cup, but when we pull into the parking lot at the library her eyes light up at old brick building nestled comfortably in front of us in the middle of the parking lot.

It's not the main library of Boston, but the Thorn Branch Library has its own history. The stained glass windows along the front edge of the parking lot— all depicting flowers in full bloom—were made by Tiffany over a century ago, and though the library itself is on the smallish side, it has one of the most robust communities behind it. This was one of the buildings that was *almost* hit by the great Boston molasses flood (if you're not from around here, you might never have heard of this. No joke, this actually happened—a molasses storage tank burst and flooded the streets in the early twentieth century. People died, buildings were destroyed...all from molasses!), so it has historical significance because it was spared, too.

No matter what though, history and pretty stained glass windows aside...there's a feeling I get, deep in my heart, when I pull into the parking lot of Thorn Branch Library.

Because, no matter what, this place has been here for me. My co-workers evolved into some of my closest friends.

In a library? I'm at home.

I'm so excited to share this with Virago. Even if it's just for a day. Even just for a little while...I want to show her the place that makes me the happiest in the world. I don't know why I think she'd understand that, but as I sneak a glance at her, I know she does. She recognizes that this is a good place, too, as she gazes at the building with a soft smile brightening her features.

"This is where you work?" she asks, gesturing to the library. I turn off the car, take the keys out of the ignition and smile at her.

"Yeah," I say, taking my coffee cup out of the holder.

"It's a castle," she breathes.

I glance at the building, my head to the side. I guess it sort of *is* a castle. It has three brick towers and turrets (though they're only two stories high), and with the stained glass windows colorfully marching along the side of the building...sure, I can see a castle. After all, I thought it looked like a castle, too, when I came for the job interview here many years ago now.

"Thank you," I tell her, and we both get out of the car. "So," I tell her, chewing on my lower lip. I'm not exactly certain how to break it to her that Mondays are always Kid Days, and on Kid Days you're liable to get a migraine if you're not a big fan of kids.

One of the first school buses is pulling up now.

"There's going to be a lot of children," I begin to tell her, but the school bus doors are swinging open, and a tidal wave of kids pours out of the bus onto the pavement of the parking lot. Shouting, screaming, laughing, ecstatic kids. Alice, the head of the children's department and a good friend of mine, is unlocking the library doors from the inside, opening the doors wide to accommodate the press of children. Her long blonde hair is piled on top of her head in a sweeping curve, and her cat glasses twinkle from their beaded chain around her neck. Today she's wearing skinny jeans and a vanilla blouse, impeccable as always—I have no idea how it stays that impeccable around the kids, but that just happens to be one of her super powers.

"Hey, Alice!" I wave to her and trot across the sea of children and pavement to give her a big hug. Alice peers over my shoulder, her brows rising over the cat glasses as she picks them up and perches them on top of her little nose. She's staring at Virago.

"Well," is all she says, grinning at me as I instantly begin to shake my head.

"It's really not what you think—" I begin, but she waves her hand, chuckles, lets the children flow into the library around the three of us, like a dam that's burst, water flooding everything.

The day's already begun, and I haven't gotten a chance to explain that Virago is not, in fact, my girlfriend. That I have not, in fact, broken up with Nicole.

As I walk behind the circulation desk, my stomach clenches at that thought.

No, I haven't broken up with Nicole. Not yet.

That's tonight.

I take a deep breath and turn on my computer as the kids' happy chatter becomes background noise. I turn to Virago who's followed me quietly to my desk.

"Do you want me to tell you where any particular books are? You should be entertained for hours…we have everything you could think of…probably…" I trail off, clear my throat. "Do you want more coffee?" I ask, indicating her already empty to-go cup. "Do you *need* anything?" I fret.

"No," she says with a soft smile. "I am perfectly content, Holly. Please do not trouble yourself on my account."

"Okay," I say, poking at my keyboard as my old computer begins to make the whirring noise that indicates that it's *thinking* about starting up. I mean to say something else to her, but this little girl (I'm thinking maybe she's five or six) that I've never seen before runs up to me with a stricken look on her face, brunette curls bouncing.

"Miss, I have to tell you something," she says, tugging on my shirtsleeve.

"Yes, sweetie?" I ask with a wide smile as I lean down toward her.

"I *really* have to go," she tells me in a stage whisper, her face contorted in a dramatic grimace.

"Oh, okay…uh…" I straighten and look wildly around for the teacher.

The rest of the day erupts into similar chaos.

One of the children goes missing (not really— she showed up in the basement where we keep the old research files, though how she got down there beyond the locked "employees only" door is somewhat beyond me), a little boy tinkles on the carpeting (but just a little, and our long-suffering janitor happened to be in today) and my coffee gets spilled onto my keyboard (not a huge tragedy, thankfully we have an extra keyboard in the storage room and I'm not electrocuted on the spot). By the time lunch rolls around, I'm utterly exhausted in that good, bone-deep way that you get when you've done something that you love for too many hours in a row.

"You look like you need more coffee, missy," says Alice, setting a cup down next to my mouse. She poured the coffee into one of my favorite mugs: it has two small chips out of the rim, and a well-worn slogan on the side: "I'd rather be reading," printed next to a little bookworm holding a big hardcover. I take up the mug gratefully, blow on the billowing steam from the coffee's surface and take a single, thankful sip. Alice's brows are up over her cat glasses as she watches me, her head to the side, as if she's considering telling me something.

The most recent bus of kids just left, which means that we have a ten-minute break until the next bus shows up. I stifle a yawn behind my wrist and blink up at my friend expectantly. She clears her throat. "Have you seen..." Alice drifts off, glances at me meaningfully as she considers how to put whatever she's going to say next. She settles on: "Have you seen where that woman you brought in got to?"

Virago. Oh, my God, I was so busy and this morning was so crazy that, somehow, I forgot about *Virago*. Alice chuckles at my expression and pats my arm with a wry shake of her head. "I wouldn't be too worried—she looks perfectly content. I just want you to catch a glimpse...it's pretty cute." She jerks her thumb toward the non-fiction history section and puts a finger over her lips in the universal gesture of "sh."

I get up from my chair, move quietly around the corner and peek down the aisle.

Virago is seated on the floor, her back against a shelf of books, her legs folded in front of her gracefully, a book propped up on her lap, and her elbows propped on her knees as she carefully curves her body over the book, utterly intent on devouring it. Her brows are furrowed in concentration, and she traces a few lines from the page with a long finger, entranced by what she's reading.

My heart skips a beat as I watch her read that

book. She's so obviously engrossed and delighted by what she's finding between the covers. If I'm not mistaken she's reading one of our medieval histories right now—I know the shape of the book (it's a big, clunky hardcover), even when it's seated in her lap. She seems to be devouring information on our world's version of knights and castles and all the chivalry that went along with that, because there's a small stack of other hardcovers and one paperback book beside her, all medieval histories.

I realize, as I watch her, an odd little fact, something I didn't think about until this very moment. Nicole? She doesn't like to read books. I've never seen her reading anything but her phone or the paperwork that she's brought home from the office. I mean, it's not a bad thing. That's just Nicole—she's not a reader, and there's nothing wrong with not being a reader.

But I didn't know what it would do to me, seeing someone I find so incredibly attractive...seeing her *reading*. Virago is *beautiful*, sitting there, reading that book, turning the pages with tapered fingers, her full lips pursed in concentration....

So much emotion floods through me at that moment that it takes my breath away.

God, I want her so badly in that moment, I don't know what to do.

I snap out of it, try to stomp down on all that emotion. I cough a little into my hand and Virago, a million miles away, raises her head and looks at me.

The moment our eyes connect, she smiles so widely that the entire aisle seems instantly brighter, like someone turned on a second set of lights.

My heart skips a beat as Virago rises, dusting off the bottom of her pants, holding the book elegantly in one hand as she strides toward me, prowling like a great cat.

"Time ran away from me," she says almost breathlessly as she leans against the shelf beside me. She stares down into my eyes, a mischievous smile tugging at the corners of her mouth. "What did I miss?"

"Nothing," I tell her, reaching out between us and taking her hand. One of her brows rises, and she glances at me questioningly. I let go of her, feeling suddenly very self conscious.

"Do you...do you want more coffee?" I manage to ask her.

She smiles down at me, then, her smile deepening. "Yes, surely. That would be lovely."

"Keep...keep reading," I tell her, patting the book in her hands. "We have comfortable chairs, if you want something nicer to sit on than the ground..." I gesture over to the wall of couches alongside the biography section.

She shrugs, gazes down at me, her eyes flashing with a blue fire. "I'm fine here, Holly. Thank you. Don't trouble yourself on my account." She reaches out and grabs my hand at that moment, squeezing it gently before she lets it go.

I turn away from her, practically holding my breath as I try to quell my heartbeat. I stumble, unseeingly, toward the coffee nook to make her a cup.

I know what I'm going to do now. I just can't fight against it anymore.

I mean, yes, of course, tonight I'm going to break up with Nicole. It terrifies me, the thought of that painful conversation, but it needs to happen.

Because after I do the right thing, after I end

things with Nicole...

I'm going to tell Virago how I feel.

I spill a little of the hot coffee on my hand as I try to pour it into one of the old mugs by the coffee maker. It brings me back to reality, and I pour in a little cream and sugar into the mug, too. I can't ignore how I feel about Virago anymore. To ignore it, I think, would be unnecessarily painful to me. So she's heading home probably tomorrow. That's all right. At least I can tell her.

I turn and almost drop the mug of coffee because Virago's there, just then. She reaches out and takes the mug from my hand, her brows furrowed.

"What happened here?" she asks, turning my hand over gently to show the bright red welt I got from the hot coffee.

"It's nothing," I tell her, shaking my head, but Virago doesn't stop staring down at it. She sets the mug on the counter, and then smoothly, she's down on one knee in front of me. I stare down at her, dumbstruck, as she closes her eyes, brings the back of my hand up to her mouth.

She kisses me gently on the back of my hand, her warm lips so soft and tender that I shiver beneath that touch.

For a moment, there's a soft blue hue to the light in the coffee nook, and then the blue tinge is gone.

And the red welt on the back of my hand is gone, too.

Virago stares up at me. I stare down at her.

Her beautiful, full lips tug into another smile, and Virago gets up gracefully, taking up the mug of coffee from the counter and taking a very slow, calculated sip.

"It's very good," she tells me with a casual wink. "Thank you."

I watch her prowl back to her aisle and her book before I realize that my mouth is open.

God, I can't take much more of this.

I have to tell her how I feel.

Tonight.

I don't really remember the first moment that I realized my relationship was going south. I wish that I could pinpoint the exact moment that I knew things weren't working out as well as I'd hoped between Nicole and I, but it didn't really happen like that. It was more of a gradual decline, what this relationship turned into. I didn't wake up one morning and realize that she didn't love me anymore. That, perhaps, I didn't love her anymore, too. It just slowly and painfully turned that way, our relationship transforming from something healthy and good to something that neither of us should have been in. Until we arrived here.

I take a deep breath, and I knock on Nicole's door.

I drove Virago home after work. Things were strangely quiet in the car. I'd checked out the medieval history book on my library account for her, and she was flipping through its pages as she leaned back in the passenger seat, not saying much until we got home.

"You go to do something important this evening, don't you?" she asked me quietly. I nodded to her at that, uncertain of how to tell her exactly what I was up to. But she didn't ask anything else. She only reached out, touched my cheek with a beautiful, warm finger and traced a curve over it as she studied my face.

"Goddess go with you," was all she said then, and she'd turned slowly and gone into my house to let Shelley—who was much more excited to see Virago than me—out for a bathroom break.

Which left me in my car to drive to Nicole's.

Nicole lives in a super expensive condo building right in the heart of Boston, which I'd always thought was a beautiful place to live. I love my city—if I could afford it, I would live right in the heart of Boston, too, but I'd never choose to live in her building. For one thing, the condos there are way too expensive for a librarian's salary, and for another, the people in her building just aren't really my kind of people. They're all the thirty-something executive types at start-ups, all worked to the bone and too exhausted and stressed out to ever even tell me "hi" when I meet them on the elevator up to her twelfth floor condo.

I take a deep breath as I stand outside of Nicole's door, waiting. I square my shoulders, rehearse (for the millionth time) what I thought I might say to Nicole.

But that all leaves my head when the door opens, and it's not Nicole who greets me, but her assistant, Mikaylah. Mikaylah happens to be about twenty-one, model-like and utterly perfect (if you're into that sort of thing), with long, straight black hair, and an unwavering smile.

She stands there with that unwavering smile as she clutches an iPad to her chest and waves me in. "Miss Holly, you're right on time," she tells me with her best soothing voice that I know she's used on Nicole's problem clients. "Right this way. Nicole has exactly one hour free, so this is just perfect."

"One hour?" I reply, my brow up, but her smile deepens, and she nods enthusiastically.

"She made me check and double check her appointments so you could be assured that much time. This way, please..." She continues to clack over Nicole's expensive tile with her high-heeled shoes.

"I think I know my way around Nicole's place, Mikaylah," I tell her gently.

"Of course, of course," she says with another nod. "Do you need anything? An espresso perhaps?"

I'm boggled that Nicole's condo has apparently also been transformed into Nicole's office, or at least Nicole's second office. That Nicole's assistant is here means that Nicole has been working even more non-stop since the Renaissance Festival, and...

"Holly."

I turn, sigh out.

"Hello, Nicole," I tell her.

Nicole is dressed in another blue business suit, a frown already transforming her pretty face into an unhappy mask as she folds her arms and stares at me with an unhappy expression.

"You're late," she tells me, and then she turns without another word and walks into her bedroom as if she expects me to follow her. Mikaylah stares at me helplessly with a shrug, and then trots off toward the kitchen, leaving me alone.

I follow Nicole into the bedroom and shut the door.

"I was here right on time," I tell her with a sigh. "Your assistant was asking me if I wanted coffee—"

Nicole has her back to me, and she's paging through something on her laptop, which is set up on a desk right across from the sumptuous king size bed.

The bed that Nicole and I have spent a lot of time in. But not recently, these last few months. Hardly at all, actually.

Nicole turns, again not looking directly at me. Her jaw is clenched as she stares at a spot a little above my shoulder. "I have something to say to you, Holly," she growls.

I stand there straight and tall, holding my purse. She's not told me to get comfortable, and at this point, I don't feel enough at home to take the liberty to do so myself.

I watch her, and I wait, my heart beating fast.

"Mikaylah and I have been sleeping together," says Nicole, clipping the words out like she's reciting by-laws at a meeting. "For over a year now."

I stare at her.

I don't really feel anything when she tells me that, which is strange. I probably should. I know I will later.

But now it's in the moment, and this isn't going how I thought it'd go. Everything's unraveling. I feel like I'm struggling to catch up when it shouldn't have been this way. I should have been the one to start it.

But it's already started.

"I...I don't think we should see each other anymore, Nicole," I tell her softly. The words are choked out with emotion, which surprises me. I didn't think I was feeling anything yet...

That's when it all comes crashing down on me.

I'm filled with so much intense emotion that moment, that this is all I am: hurt, betrayal, anger, and an intense sadness that fill and consumes me at the same time, like a fire ripping through me.

"I agree with you completely," says Nicole,

crossing her arms in front of her. She holds my gaze now, and, God, how stony her eyes are. "I've taken the liberty to pack up the few things that you had here." She gestures to a paper box with a snug-fitting lid beside her on the desk. "So you can be on your way."

I stop at that, tears filling my eyes. I take a single step forward, take a deep breath. "That's…it?"

She's already clicking at things on her laptop, already turned away from me. "I don't have time for much else," she says with a tight, controlled sigh. "Mikaylah can see you out."

"No," I tell her, rolling my shoulders back, blinking back the tears. "You owe me more than that. You've been sleeping with her for a year—"

"I should have ended things with you a long time ago," says Nicole, glancing at me then with sharp eyes. "But I didn't have the time for this relationship. You and I. Mikaylah has been open and accommodating with the type of relationship that *we* have had, and it's been very helpful to me."

Frustration claws at my insides. She's treating this—and me—like it's a year end review. Not the end of a relationship that had existed for *four years*.
"You cheated on me," I tell her angrily.

She shrugs. And she says nothing else, only goes back to looking at her laptop.

Like I'm not worth the time.

Like I'm not worth an explanation.

And I *know* I'm worth both.

"Nicole," I tell her, stepping forward as I grip my hands into fists. "You cheated on me with your *assistant*. You were always so…so selfish. And I never saw it because I was trying to see the best in you—" I'm spluttering. I want to hurt her, in that moment, as

220

much as she's hurt me, but I'm already deflating. And I don't *really* want to hurt her. I stare at her for a very long moment, at this woman who I thought I had feelings for, this woman who I've spent years of my life with. *Wasted* years of my life with.

Nicole is shallow. And selfish. And unkind. And maybe I did discover all of that too late. Or maybe I refused to see it from the start. Maybe I was blind.

And maybe I should have never been with her from the start.

But I *was*. I was with Nicole, and I've got to own that fact. I've got to own the fact that we should have broken up a long, long time ago, but I kept nursing the relationship so that it could limp along because it was the easiest of all the options. It was easier than admitting that I'd failed when I'd tried to find a girlfriend who was right for me. I'd failed our relationship.

And yes, Nicole should never have cheated on me. She should never have been so distant and unkind and selfish. But perhaps to someone else she wouldn't be.

Perhaps to Mikaylah she's perfectly wonderful.

"Goodbye, Nicole," I tell her, because there's absolutely nothing left to say. I turn on my heel and I open the bedroom door, tears standing bright in my eyes as I move through her condo, toward the front door.

"Wait," Nicole calls from behind me.

I stop. I don't turn. I hear her high-heeled shoes clicking on the tile, and then Nicole's beside me. Sometimes she used to wrap her arms around me from behind, kiss the top of my head, draw me close and hold me close. I always liked that. And it would be wonderful for her to do that again, for her to tell me that she wished me well. But she doesn't do that. She hands over the box of my things, carefully training her gaze on the far wall, and not looking at me.

Mikaylah, frozen in spot like a rabbit sighted by a hunter, stares at me with wide eyes and an open mouth.

But I walk away from both of them, closing the door behind me on the way out.

It's over. It was messy and it was painful and hard and hurtful, but it's over.

I don't really start crying until I get to my car with my small, paltry box of possessions. The only few pieces of my life that had remained at Nicole's place. I'm pretty certain there's nothing of Nicole's at my house for her to take.

God, no, we weren't right for each other. But I'd cared so much for her, and I'd wanted her to care for me, too. But it's over, now. Nicole has Mikaylah, and I know that in a few days, I'm going to hope that they're happy together. I'm not exactly at that point right now.

And me?

Well, I don't have anyone.

I know I'm feeling very sorry for myself right now, but it's the truth. I'm going to go home, and I don't have the strength to tell Virago how I feel about her tonight. I'm going to make myself a cup of tea, I'm going to crawl into bed, and I'm going to have myself a very good cry.

And I'm going to fall asleep alone.

I feel a little stupid. Maybe I should have told Virago sooner, maybe I should have flirted with her, or maybe I should have kissed her when I wanted to. I didn't because of Nicole, but now I feel like I've been naive. An entire year Nicole and Mikaylah were sleeping together, and I didn't even notice anything between them? A couple of months ago, I went down to Nicole's office to see her, and Mikaylah greeted me as brightly and nicely as she always does…as she did today.

There was nothing out of the ordinary. Nothing that told me that Nicole and I were much, much worse off than I'd imagined at that point.

But we *were* much worse off. And we'd been worse off for so long, that maybe I just thought that's how relationships *should* be.

God, how did I make such a mess of things? How did it come to this? I feel so used and sad and small. I start the engine to my car, take a tissue out of my purse and dab at my eyes, crumpling the soaked thing into a ball.

Somehow, miraculously, I make it back home in one piece, even with my blurred-from-tears vision.

I park the car, get out of it, stop when I shut the door, because Virago is sitting on the porch, on the swing, rocking it back and forth with the tips of her toes as she reads her book, her head bent, her brow smooth, but her eyes narrowed in concentration. She glances up only as I start up the walkway from the sidewalk and she hears my feet on the concrete. Virago glances up at the sound and she smiles at me, but that smile vanishes almost instantly as she rises to her feet, as her brows narrow when she sees my expression.

"What happened?" she asks, moving toward the steps as I ascend them. I shake my head, sniffle as I jingle my keys, aiming for my front door, but Virago stops me, puts her warm hand over mine.

Tears begin to fall down my face quickly, one after the other, tracing hot, wet patterns down my cheeks as I glance up at her.

"Oh, God, Virago, I've made a terrible mistake," I tell her, then.

Virago says nothing, only wraps an arm around me and my shoulders, and gently urges me to come sit beside her on the swing. The swing shifts out from beneath us as we sit down, but then I'm pushing with my feet flat on the floor, and the swing moves back and forth, back and forth, the soothing rocking motion that I love as I shift my weight on the seat with a long sigh.

Virago, I note somewhere in the back of my head, still has her arm around my shoulders as she sits down next to me. Her arm is warm against me, *she* is warm against me.

"Virago," I tell her, taking a deep breath. "I had a girlfriend, too. Or I did. Until tonight."

She doesn't say anything, and my eyes are too tear-filled to see her very clearly, so I just keep going.

"I knew I was supposed to break up with her for a very long time, but I just…didn't. And I found out tonight that she's been sleeping with her *assistant* for over a year. A *year.* And I never saw it, never thought she was capable of it…" I trail off, because the tears are coming too thickly now, and my heart hurts so much, twisting inside of me.

Virago breathes out softly, slowly, squeezing her arm around my shoulders. "Did you love this woman?"

I don't even think before I answer, and my answer is this: "No," I tell her, and my voice is soft, but certain. "I mean, I thought I did. But I didn't really know what that meant, and I just…didn't. And she didn't love me." I breathe out, gaze down at my hands clutching my car keys and another damp tissue. "I've wasted four years of my life because I wanted what I didn't have but I should have broken up with her years ago, and I…I've been really stupid," I say, taking a deep breath.

Virago shakes her head, and then with a gentle strength, she's drawing me close to her, so that my head is resting on her shoulder. I stiffen in this position, because it's so intimate, the most intimate action that Virago has ever done. But surely she doesn't mean it that way.

"Holly, of all people I have ever known, you are one of the smartest," Virago tells me quietly. "You are not stupid. I read today a book in the library. And it said something that I think is very good. It said 'the heart has its reasons which reason knows nothing of.'"

"Blaise Pascal said that," I tell her quietly.

"Well, it's very true," she says gently. "Do not worry yourself so much. You cared for this woman, and that is important. That is good. And it is over now. But it was important that it happened. It was not wasted time."

"Are you sure, Virago?" I ask her, sitting up as the tears run down my face. "Because what if I'm never…" I choke on my words, swallow them. *What if I'm never going to be brave enough to tell you how I feel? You'll leave, and this will all be over, and you will never have known that I cared about you.*

Virago shakes her head again, smiles gently at me. "Holly, all will be well," she tells me with such surety and conviction that it *must* be true.

I sit back heavily against the swing, and then, as if drawn by a gravity, I drift down until I'm softly pillowing my head on Virago's shoulder again.

I concentrate on taking deep breaths, on trying not to think about wasted time. I try to concentrate on the muscle of Virago's shoulder, how her body conforms to hold mine so gently and thoughtfully.

I try to memorize this moment.

Out on my lawn, a firefly drifts gently along the shorn grass, glowing brightly every few heartbeats as it tries to find a mate.

But there are no other fireflies on my lawn, and I sit there wondering if, like me, that firefly is meant to be alone forever.

Chapter 13: The Joust

I wake up to the fine, pungent aroma of espresso right under my nose.

I open my eyes, blink at the scene greeting me.

"Howdy," says Carly, shoving the to-go coffee cup even more under my nose, waggling it back and forth. "Wake up!"

I sit up groggily, stare at my best friend who's sitting on the edge of my bed with a latte in her hand like it's the most normal thing in the world on a weekday morning. "Carly?" I manage, taking the coffee cup from her and taking a sip from it. It's filled with my favorite vanilla latte, complete with two extra shots of espresso. I take another sip, frown at her. "Not that I'm not happy to see you, but...what the hell are you doing here?"

"Good morning to you, too," she says with a brow up as she gets up off my bed with a shrug. "I came by because I took the day off, and Virago let me in. I figured you'd need some help finding the beast before tonight, and I thought maybe we could rent a tour boat or something this afternoon, go out on the big blue sea, or—"

"Sure," I tell her tiredly, taking another sip of latte. "Hey, thanks for getting this for me...it's just what I needed." I rub at my grimy eyes, stuck shut at the corners from the excess tears I cried last night.

God, last night. What a train wreck last night was, complete with Nicole telling me she'd been sleeping with *Mikaylah*, who's probably not even twenty-one yet, a baby, and Nicole had been sleeping with her for one *year*. *God...*

"Oh, I didn't get that latte for you," says Carly with wide eyes. "Virago did."

I stare at my best friend, my mouth open. I swear I hear a distant record-scratch as my eyes widen. "*What?*"

"Virago walked up to the drive-through. It's only a couple of blocks," she admonishes me and my stricken face. "She found a five-dollar bill on the sidewalk, and she took Shelley for a walk this morning and wanted to get you something, and I quote 'after the night you had,' which, of course, made me think you guys had slept together, but you look like hell, so I'm guessing you probably didn't, and—"

I set the latte on my bedside table, push the covers off me. "Virago walked to the drive-through to get me a latte," I repeat.

"*Did* you guys sleep together?" asks Carly suspiciously.

I sort of deflate at that. "No," I tell her quietly. "I broke up with Nicole last night. That's what Virago was talking about when she said I had a rough night."

Carly stares at me with her mouth open for a full minute. I actually made her speechless—what I thought was an impossible feat. "You...you actually did it," she whispers.

"Yeah," I tell her, flopping back on my elbows on the bed with a sigh. "I guess I really did."

"But that's *amazing*! Oh, my God, Holly, you *actually did it!*" Carly claps her hands over her mouth as she realizes the volume of decibels her voice is at. "But that means," she says, lowering her voice to a whisper again, "that you're perfectly free to move forward with Virago—"

"No," I tell Carly, shaking my head as I feel the sadness begin to descend again. "Virago's going back to her world today. Why would I tell her? It would just complicate..." I take a deep breath. "Well, it would complicate everything."

Carly reaches forward, takes my shoulders again and gives them a little shake, her brows furrowed. "Holly," she whispers, her eyes round and very, very serious. "This is your *life*. If you don't tell her, you're going to regret it for the rest of your *life*. Please—"

"Good morrow!" says Virago, who happens to be leaning on my door frame again, her hip pressed against the wooden frame, and her arms folded in front of her. Her shirt sleeves (freshly laundered last night while she took a long shower, and I tried not to think about her taking a shower, and failed utterly, even though I was perfectly miserable) are rolled up to the elbows, and her shirt is unbuttoned on the bottom until it's half-way up her navel. She looks comfortable and happy, the smile spreading across her face so bright that, inside, I can feel my heart melting.

"Good morrow...I mean morning," I tell her, and then I pick up the coffee cup, point to it. "Did you get me a latte?"

"But of course," she says, her lips twitching at the corners as she tries to suppress her mischievous smirk. "You have been very kind to me, m'lady Holly, and I wanted to do some small kindness for you. I hope it meets your expectations?"

God, yes, you do, I think, but I nod, try not to

think about that. "Yes, thank you," I tell her in a small voice, and Virago pushes off from the door frame. For half a heartbeat, I think she'll saunter into the bedroom, continue the conversation, but she turns away (did I imagine that she turns regretfully?), and shuts the door behind her.

Carly looks at me with very wide eyes. "Are you guys *sure* you didn't sleep together last night?"

"Oh, my God, get your mind out of the gutter," I tell her, trying not to smile myself as I crawl out of bed. My eyes may be gritty from tears, but hell, Virago walked through a drive-through and got me a latte. I stand up, stretch a little. "I asked my supervisor if I could take today off yesterday because I knew we'd need all day for the beast, and—"

For a moment, Carly looks stricken, and it's odd enough that I falter mid-sentence. "What's wrong?" I ask her.

"No, it's nothing," she says quickly, sitting down on the edge of my bed again. "It's just that…I thought you were going to work today?"

I stare at her for a long moment. "I mean, normally I would, since it's a weekday," I say slowly. "But, you know, there's that tiny matter of a magical beast running amok somewhere, who we really need to find. But, seriously, Carly, what's up?"

"Nothing, nothing," she says in such a way that I know, absolutely, that's not true, that there is very much *something* going on that she's not telling me. Carly's always been a crappy liar.

"Okay, I'm going to use the bathroom, and then I'm going to ask you what's up again, okay?" I tell her. She grimaces at me a little and waves me on to the bathroom. I gather up my robe, a change of clothes from my chair by the door, and then go into the bathroom and shut the door.

I run the shower very, very hot and try to be quick about it—we have a beast to catch!—but end up taking a little longer than I would have liked because my shower head runs on the slower side. When I'm finally done rinsing out all the conditioner, I step out, towel myself off and vigorously rub the towel on my head.

Oddly enough, I hear the front door open and shut.

Huh. Probably Carly getting something out of her car or something. I don't really think anything of it until I'm in my jeans and t-shirt, having combed through my hair and given up on the thought of makeup for the day. I step out of the bathroom, letting out a cloud of steam with me from my extra-hot shower...

And Carly's right at the door.

"Hi," I tell her, placing my hands on my hips. "Okay, seriously, there's something up. What's going on?"

"Absolutely nothing," she says, but the corners of her mouth are twitching something fierce, and when she actually places her hand over her mouth to hide her smile, I frown at her.

"What," I say as sternly as I'm capable, "is going on?"

"I told her!" she blurts out then with a wail. "I told her you'd never go for it! I know you, I told her, but—"

I raise a single eyebrow, cross my arms in front of me.

"Virago?" I call out.

There's no answer.

"Virago's gone," says Carly quietly.

I feel my world fall away from me. I feel such pain rend my heart in two that I can't breathe.

"What?" I whisper, pressing my hand to my heart, willing the pain to stop. "Where? Why?"

Carly bites her lip, shakes her head. "She made me promise not to tell you."

"Carly—"

"Hey," says Carly gently, stepping forward and gripping my elbows with fierce fingers. "It's okay. I promise it's okay, all right?" Her eyes are flashing with happiness, so maybe it's not really all that bad. "She wanted me to take you somewhere. It'll all make sense, soon, but don't be upset, okay?"

"I don't understand," I begin, but she shakes her head.

"Get dressed. We have to go," she says, smiling as she presses her hands to the small of my back and all but shoves me into my bedroom.

"Carly, I *am* dressed," I tell her testily. My level of patience is beginning to wane.

"Well," says Carly carefully, glancing me up and down. "Where *we're* going? You're a little under-dressed, my dear."

Mystified, I take what she hands me, and she closes the bedroom door behind her as she all but waltzes out of my bedroom.

I stare down at the bundle of clothes in my hands.

It's the dress I always wear to the Renaissance Festival.

"I feel like I'm being kidnapped," I tell Carly when we're in her car, driving to an undisclosed destination. I thought we were headed to the Knights of Valor Festival, but we're not taking the usual way, so I guess not?

I have no idea what's going on, and it's got me more than a little flustered.

"Drink your latte. Do kidnap victims have lattes? I highly doubt it," Carly answers confidently, making a right hand turn onto a road I've never been on leading more toward the heart of Boston.

"Carly, if you could just tell me—"

"I," she says with a sniff, "have been sworn to the utmost of secrecies. So shush and drink your latte."

"Carly," I tell her patiently, drawing out the syllables of her name, "we don't have *time* for whatever…well, whatever *this* is. We have to find the beast, and—"

"Don't worry about the beast," says Carly with conviction, her eyebrows up.

I blink at her, splutter: "Don't *worry* about it? Are you *crazy*? This is the fate of the *world* in our hands, and you—"

"There's no reason to worry about it—we know where the beast is," she says quietly, gripping the steering wheel a little tighter.

I stare at her.

She casts me a sidelong glance as she makes a left hand turn and shrugs. "I was going to tell you about it, but this morning has been a little…well, I've been distracted," she mutters vaguely. "Anyway, the beast hasn't moved from the same spot for about twelve hours, and we know exactly where it is, and it's not moving, so—"

"And where," I say, gritting my teeth as I take a deep breath, "is it exactly?"

"About a mile off-shore. It's in an underwater cave, and it's not leaving," says Carly with another shrug. "Virago thinks she may have hurt the beast a little more than she thought, and it's taking longer for the creature to heal or something, and it needs a little time out to regroup. I don't know. I just know that it hasn't moved, so we're good."

"But—but…" I splutter, trying to piece everything together in my head. "That's great! But how are we going to get the beast from there to Aidan's store?"

"Well," says Carly carefully, "Virago had an idea that maybe we should take the whole coven on a night boat ride. It makes a lot of sense, you know. If we can get everyone out there, then we won't have to attract the beast toward land, get innocent people involved, and we can banish it from out on the water. It makes more sense that way anyway."

I stare at my best friend for a long moment, opening and shutting my mouth. "But…but why didn't Virago talk over any of this with *me*?" is what I finally settle on. I know it seems silly, but I wanted to be at least a small part of this. I wanted to help her, if even in the smallest of ways. But I didn't. I was fast asleep, probably snoring, while she came up with this brilliant plan by herself, because she *is* brilliant.

"Virago was occupied," is Carly's maddeningly vague response to that.

"Carly," I mutter warningly, but she turns a bright-as-the-sun smile on me.

"Almost there!"

I blink and look out the passenger side window,

noting my surroundings. "But…"

We pull into the "parking lot" of the outskirts of the dog park where the Knights of Valor Festival is still set up.

"You *were* taking me here," I whisper mystified to Carly, who grins hugely as she shuts off her car. For it being so early on a Tuesday, there's still a lot of cars and people here, but she still managed to find a good parking spot, close to the entrance.

"Yeah, I took a long way so it'd confuse you," she says with barely concealed zeal. "Clever, right?" She winks at me.

"Carly," I say, my heart pounding in me as I hear from somewhere not very distant, a hearty chorus of "huzzah!" "What's going on?" I ask her point blank.

"Just a few more minutes of humoring me, and you'll find out," says Carly, all but leaping out of her driver's seat, and stretching. She turns to me as I get out of the passenger side: "I *promise*, okay?" She smiles encouragingly. "Just a *wee* bit more humoring."

I stare longingly at the front ticket turret. The last time I was here—just a few days ago now, I can hardly believe it (it seems so long ago now, so much has happened!)—it was such a sad, miserable day that contained so much hurt and pain for me. But those darker memories seem to leave me now, the tension evaporating from my shoulders as I stare at that brightly painted turret. These last few days…God, there have been a lot of ups and downs. But I'm here now. The beast has been found. Perhaps we have a solution.

I don't know what's going on, but I'm at one of my favorite places in the entire world. It can't be bad, whatever is about to happen.

I walk with Carly toward the turret. She's grinning at me and keeps glancing away when I glance over at her, as if I couldn't notice that gigantic smile on her face. She shoves her hands into her jeans pockets, tries to act casual, but I totally know better.

What could possibly be going on?

When we reach the turret, the woman at the counter leans forward. "Are you Holly?" she asks me. I recognize her from when we came to the festival a few days ago, but I don't remember telling her my name.

I glance sidelong at Carly, who is the pure picture of innocence (hah!), and nod. "Yes, I am?" I tell her uncertainly.

"Wonderful!" she says, leaning forward a little more with a wide smile. She taps her money box and shakes her head. "No charge! I've been told to let you through," she says decisively. "Please go on quickly, the show's about to start!"

"What show—" I begin, but Carly hooks her arm through mine and all but hauls me through the line and into the festival itself.

"Thank you very much!" She shouts back to the woman in the turret, then she glances down at her wristwatch. "Oh, my *God*, I didn't realize what time it was!" she moans, shaking her head. "Oh, my God, seriously, they absolutely can*not* start without us!" She breaks into a trot, dragging me along.

Utterly mystified, I allow myself to be dragged across the entirety of the Knights of Valor Festival.

Until we come to the jousting arena.

Okay, so "arena" is kind of a generous term. The Knights of Valor Festival *does* set up in a dog park, and they do the best they can, but the "arena" is really just a cordoned off section of the park, delineated by a waist-high picket fence on well-mowed grass. I'm always surprised that they let horses gallop around in the enclosure, because they always divot up the grass, but the owners of the dog park are really good people, and never seem to mind.

Speaking of horses, there are four tethered to posts at the edge of the arena where a crowd is gathering, "ooh-ing" and "aah-ing" over them. They're all the big, heavy horses that were once used in jousting, long ago, and they're wearing brightly colored saddles and raiment so that it's easy for you to pick a color side and cheer for them. There's red, green, yellow and blue.

And, standing next to the blue-covered horse…

I blink, stop, transfixed to the spot.

It's Virago.

She's wearing her knight's armor, the same armor she wore when we first met, the curved and curling breastplate over her leather pants and shirt, the metal twinkling in the bright sunshine. Her hair is swept up high in her signature ponytail, and the silver wolf's tail drapes easily over one shoulder. She's not wearing her fur capelet—it's lashed behind the saddle—but she's definitely wearing the hell out of her boots.

Virago stands at complete ease, talking in low tones with one of the knights (a guy, because almost always all of the knights at Renaissance Festivals are guys), while she buckles her sword in its worn scabbard and sheath over her shoulder.

I'm struck speechless for a long moment, but then somehow I find my voice. "Virago?" I whisper, and then I'm taking a few steps forward. "Virago?" I say louder.

Virago turns in my direction, but before I can see her face, Carly's grabbing my arm and practically dragging me over to where the crowds have gathered to watch the jousting. "Not yet, not yet!" she mutters to me, but I'm twisting around, trying to see Virago. She's disappeared, though, seemingly swallowed by the crowd.

"Carly, what—" I begin, but I'm drowned out by the din of the loudspeaker.

"Lords and ladies, welcome to the morning joust!" says a man loudly, his voice crackling over the bad sound system. "We have a *very* special treat for you today, so if you weren't planning on watching the joust until the afternoon, I implore you to change your mind and come on over to the arena! This is going to be a big one!"

I glance at Carly, but she makes a little shrug and smiles at me, then turns her attentions onto the arena. I follow suit, brows up.

Virago, in her armor, talking to a knight…my heart's starting to beat quickly in me. What the hell is going on? What the hell is about to happen?

I have an inkling…

On the side of the arena, Virago mounts the massive black horse bearing the blue colors easily, one foot in the stirrup, and then rising into the air like she vaults up and onto an enormous horse all the time (which, I realize, she probably does). The horse has arching blue pennants on its reins, and blue flags draping down on either side of him, beneath his saddle, a bright white star standing prominently on his forehead, and three white socks. Virago masterfully sits on top of him, urging him forward and directing him to stand in the center of the arena with no visible cues that

I can see. Beside her, the knight she was speaking with has mounted the red-color horse, a big bay who's snorting and tossing his head unhappily, chomping on his bit and shaking his head over and over, the pennants from his reins flapping back and forth. The male knight is dressed in the more typical medieval armor, and is holding his helmet in his arm as he looks out over the crowd with a scowl.

Virago is looking out over the crowd, too, but when she sees me, her eyes stop raking the assembled audience.

The smile that stretches across her face is brighter than the sun, her eyes flashing so brightly that I'm speechless.

"Here ye, here ye!" says the announcer over the sound system. "Silence! For the lady speaks!"

The crowd immediately falls silent, a complete sort of silence that makes the jangling of the horse's bridles sounds very loud in the quiet. The audience stands and waits. My guess is they've probably never seen a woman in the jousting arena before, too. It's probably rarer than seeing a bald eagle.

"Good people," Virago calls out clearly, her voice echoing with power through the assembled crowd as she raises a hand to us, her other gripping the reins of her mount. "I have come here this day in a quest of honor, and of love." She tilts her chin and her unwavering, piercing gaze to me, as the world falls away from beneath my feet. "My heart belongs to a woman who is as fair as the sky on the first morning of spring," she says clearly, though her voice becomes a little choked with emotion. "This woman is as good as all the saints and as beautiful as a thousand dreams. Though I have but known her for only a short while, I have found my heart and my being utterly enchanted by her. She has bewitched me. I am but her humble servant, and I have come here, this day, to profess that I do love her. And I would do an act of service so that she may, hopefully, give me the courtesy to woo her."

Virago's impassioned speech has silenced the crowd utterly. You can hear a pin drop.

She's staring at me as she says every word with such total conviction and open passion, her blue gaze pinning me to the spot.

I stand there, my heart pounding in me.

I can't believe this.

But it's real.

This incredible woman, this woman I've wished for with my entire soul, is astride a massive horse in the middle of a make-shift jousting arena, making a speech in front of all of these people...

Declaring that she loves me.

And she wants to show me how much.

She wants to *joust* for me. Or, really, in a much more feminist fashion, because she's jousting for the *courtesy* of wooing me.

Oh, my God.

"I challenge you, then, sir!" says Virago with a wry grin as she urges her horse forward, her mount trotting in a very pretty circle around the male knight astride of his bay gelding. "I challenge you to a joust to prove my devotion to my lady!"

"And I accept!" says the knight, playing along and placing his helmet smoothly on his head. "It won't be much of a challenge, though!" he shouts, brandishing his fist in the air. "After all, what place does a *lady* have in the jousting arena?"

This earns him a very vivid "boo" from the

crowd. All of the knights always trash-talk each other (usually in ye olde speech), but Virago seems to have managed to get the entire crowd on her side—no small feat in the jousting arena. When Virago raises her fist in the air, everyone applauds and cheers her. When Mr. Knight Guy raises his fist in the air...he's greeted by silence.

I don't know what to think in this moment. It kind of feels like I'm in the middle of a really wonderful dream, and that I might wake up. But as Carly wraps her arms around me and gives me a big hug with a laugh, as I realize that Carly helped Virago out to get me here, that Virago must have gone to great measures to get the Knights of Valor Festival people to let some random woman ride their jousting horses and actually *joust*...when I consider all the trouble she must have gone to in order to orchestrate this...

I cover my heart with my hand as I watch her wheel the horse around gracefully as she begins to warm him up. She's rolling her shoulders, and when one of the squires hands her up the jousting pike, I know this is real.

She is, *literally*, jousting for my hand.

"Now," says the announcer over the loudspeaker. "Knights, prepare for the joust!"

Virago wheels her gelding around in a nice, controlled trot, and vaults off his back when she reaches our side of the arena. She strides up to me, and in one smooth motion, she's bowing low in front of me, a hand behind her back, and her other arm sweeping in front of her.

"M'lady Holly," she says in a soft stage whisper that carries across the hushed and listening crowd. "Would you give me your blessing to joust for your hand?" Her eyes are twinkling and bright, and she holds out her hand to me as I stand there, heart pounding, mouth open, trying to believe that this moment is real.

"Yes," I whisper, and she smiles so brightly, it eclipses the sun. She rises and straightens, the wolf tail and her ink-black hair pooling over her shoulder as she smiles down at me. I want to reach up, wrap my arms around her neck, kiss her so desperately...but she nods to me, holds out her hand again. "M'lady Holly, may I have some token of yours, to carry with me into battle?" she says strongly for the crowd.

Carly presses something into my hand, and I'm staring down at it, perplexed.

It's a lace handkerchief. Oh, that's right. Ladies used to have their knights carry a token into battle to give them strength (supposedly), but really to remind them of what they were fighting for.

I reach out with my handkerchief, hold it out to Virago.

Virago takes it gently, bending her head low again as she brushes her full lips over the back of my hand with a flourish.

A shiver goes through me as the crowd "ooh's" and "aah's" again, and then Virago mounts her gelding in an easy leap, tying the handkerchief with one hand around her right upper arm.

"For you," she says softly, nodding to me, and then she wheels her gelding around, and the male knight on the opposite end of the arena wheels his mount around, too. I hadn't realized it, but he was getting a handkerchief from a woman on the other side of the arena—probably his girlfriend? She waves at him as he ties his handkerchief around his arm, too.

"Honor be with you!" announces the loudspeaker.

And then the two knights are urging their horses forward. The mounts move from a trot to an all-out run as they hurdle toward each other, pikes aimed down. Virago's not wearing a helmet, only leaning forward over her horse's muscular neck as she narrows her eyes in concentration, aiming her pike at the male knight's shield. The knights in Renaissance Festival jousts always aim at shields, because to aim at the opposite knight would be unthinkable—this isn't to-the-death fighting. As soon as I think of that, I'm staring at Virago, my heart in my throat...because Virago isn't carrying a shield...

But it doesn't matter. Because Virago hits the knight squarely in the shield, and—spectacularly—he somersaults off his horse onto the ground with a metallic clang and a very loud "oof."

The crowd goes wild. They're jumping and cheering as Virago brings her horse down to a walk and dismounts from him smoothly, standing tall on the ground and raising her arms to the crowd. She begins to stride toward the knight who gets up onto his knees, then onto one, staggering into a standing position.

"Stand and face me!" he bellows. A squire boy is running up to him from behind with a sword in a scabbard. The knight takes the scabbard roughly from the boy's hands and unsheathes the sword, swinging it through the air in an impressive arc.

Virago stops, her eyes flashing as she unsheathes her own sword from the scabbard on her back.

They face each other, these two knights, poised and ready for combat, their handkerchiefs tied onto their arms fluttering in the small wind that moves through the arena.

There is absolute dead silence as the woman and the man face each other, swords poised.

Everyone's eyes are glued onto the two knights, but all I can watch is Virago. She moves so dancer-like, yet with such power as she circles this knight slowly, placing each boot surely on the ground, her sword arched easily over her head, as if she's ready to strike.

And she is.

She moves lightning-fast as she darts forward, clanging her sword against the knight's. The knight swings around and down toward Virago, but she sidesteps the swipe and brings her sword up again.

The male knight's sword goes flying from the blow and thuds dully onto the grass.

Again, the crowd erupts as Virago steps forward and takes the handkerchief from the knight's arm. She holds it aloft as the deafening cheers rise around us.

Virago strides, then, across the rest of the arena toward me, her chin high, her eyes glittering and bright blue as she reaches me. With a flourish, she sinks down on one knee, holding out the handkerchief from the knight to me.

"M'lady," she says, boldly and clearly, "I have won. May I please have the distinct honor to woo you?"

My heart is in severe danger of bursting out of my chest, something I never thought the word "woo" would inspire in me. I take up Virago's hand, and then I'm pulling her into a standing position, throwing my arms around her neck.

And then, finally (*finally!*), I'm kissing her.

I have to stand up a little on my toes to do it,

but my body conforms and presses against hers now like we fit together. And even though she has a metal breast plate, even though it's cold and I can feel it through my dress, I press myself against her. My mouth finds hers like we each possess a gravity that calls to the other. Her lips are full and soft, like velvet, as my mouth meets hers, as I inhale and breathe in all that is Virago. The scent of sandalwood is all around me, of a musky spiciness, and leather, as she wraps her arms around my waist, as I wrap my arms tightly around her neck, like I'll never, ever let go. And maybe I won't.

Her kiss is magic. It's more than I could have imagined (and did imagine), as she drinks me in deeply, her tongue against my tongue, her warmth consuming me. Her hands are tight at the small of my back, but then she's lifting me up, and she's spinning me around and I laugh against her as I stop kissing her for just one small moment. But then I'm back on earth again, and I'm holding tighter to her, because I'll never let go this time.

All of those moments where I thought she was flirting with me, all of those moments where I wanted to tell her, and so desperately, how I felt about her...and all this time, she's been feeling the exact same way about me. I take a deep breath as, again, Virago picks me up gently around my waist. She lifts me up, her arms tight around my ribs as she holds me to her, and then I'm back on the ground, Virago's smiling mouth captured in my own.

"Virago," I whisper, when we stop for a moment, when Virago's forehead is pressed to my own, and I realize that she's panting against me. From the exertion of jousting and sword-fighting, or from something else, I'm not exactly certain. Not until her eyes open and she pins me to the spot with her gaze that has darkened with want and need do I realize my want is reflected in her, too.

She wants me as much as I want her.

"Holly," she whispers, the word low and guttural. A thrill races through me, a shiver I can't contain, and I stare up at her, all of the want that I've pushed down or repressed in me whenever I looked at her coming to the surface now with such an intensity that it takes my breath away.

She takes my breath away.

"You crazy kids!" says Carly brightly next to us. "Hate to interrupt you, but the Queen of the festival wants a word with you!"

Most every Renaissance Festival has a queen (usually some version or variation of ye olde Queen Elizabeth), and now, coming toward us across the jousting arena, is a woman in a complete costume (and very good rendition) of Queen Elizabeth, complete with bright red hair under a bright gold crown, a sumptuous and enormous dress dragging across the festival grass.

"For today," says the queen, raising her bejeweled scepter to the two of us, "you are the ladies of this festival. Bravo to you, lady knight! And bravo to you, lady Holly, for having such a brave knight champion!"

"Hip-hip-hurrah!" chants the crowd as Virago bows low before the queen, then turns to me with shining eyes, gripping my hands tightly, with love.

Carly mutters about having something to do (as she saunters away with a mischievous smile), which leaves Virago and me at the festival practically alone (well, with a ton of people coming up to congratulate Virago on being the "coolest knight ever!" we're not really alone, but it's so sweet and supportive of the festival goers, it's kind of wonderful, really).

So together, Virago and I enjoy the festival: I buy her a gigantic turkey leg on a stick, she bests the arm-wrestling guy at arm wrestling. We both try on corsets (she declares that she could never wear one, and I completely agree with her—as much as I love the look of them, I can never breathe in one!), and toward the middle of the afternoon, Carly drives us back to my house for us to get ready for the boat ride. But since we're not casting off for a few more hours yet we still have a little time to ourselves...

And, honestly? I have the feeling that Carly drove us back early so that we could get lucky.

Trust me, I know Carly, and her mind is perpetually in the gutter. Also, when she drops us off, she gives me a big wink and mouths "good luck!" at me as I shut the car door behind me. I roll my eyes, but chuckle a little as Carly drives away, and Virago and I—arm in arm—walk slowly up the sidewalk toward my house.

Suddenly, I'm very self-conscious. Yes, I've imagined this possibility, this *intimate* possibility before, but now that the possibility is, well, possible...I'm really nervous.

The thing is, I'm usually not a move-fast kind of lady when it comes to this stuff. For the right woman I am, and Virago is very much the right woman, but it's still unlike me that I'm thinking about how to broach the subject of possibly sleeping together with Virago.

Because I want to. And we need to. Because if we don't do it now, it's not going to happen.

Something that we haven't spoken of, that we've carefully not brought up, is the fact that Virago might very well be going back to her world tonight.

And I'll be staying here.

We'll be separated...forever.

When I unlock the door and move through the living room soundlessly to let Shelley out, I grip the sliding glass door handle tightly as I shut it. Virago moves into the living room, unbuckling her scabbard and resting the sword gently down onto the couch.

She doesn't say a word as she moves slowly up behind me. She says nothing as she presses her full mouth to the bare skin of my neck.

We don't speak as we move slowly, sensuously up the stairs, her hands on my back, my thighs, as we ascend together, not exactly the most graceful creatures as we become tangled together, our mouths on each other as she traces a kiss down my neck and on the skin of my belly as she lifts up my shirt. I'm a few stairs higher up than she is, and I lace my fingers through her ponytail, through her wolf's tail, and I press her mouth against me. Finally, finally, we get up to my bedroom, to my sanctuary piled with books and warm quilts, and I push Virago gently down onto the bed.

There are no words as I carefully untie the leather laces along her armor that connects it together. The thongs fall away, and then the armor clunks gently against my hardwood floor. Virago is in leather pants now, and she chuckles at my appreciation, weaves her fingers through *my* hair as I lean down and brush my mouth over hers, over her neck and down into the dip between her breasts. I tease my fingers up under the hem of her leather shirt, and then I'm peeling the leather up and over her head, breathing in the perfumed scent of her flesh that the leather bares. She is so soft, so warm, beneath my hands, but she doesn't remain beneath me long. She rolls me over deftly, smiling down at me with a wicked smirk as she lifts my blouse up and over my head, tugs my skirt down, looping my panties with the skirt's waistband.

I'm suddenly naked beneath her. She crouches over me like a beautiful predator, all muscled arms and taut stomach as she bends her head to me, grazing my mouth with hers as she begins to trace a delicious, electrifying kiss down my neck, over my breastbone…

God, how she takes my right breast in her mouth, how the heat of her travels to the very core of me. Her velvet mouth impresses warmth against me, impresses a strong tongue that flicks my nipple to almost-painful, delicious attention. I squirm beneath her, whimper, as one strong hand presses the mattress down beside my head, the other inching slowly, slowly, slowly, up my thigh.

I spread my legs to her, asking, begging, as I pant, as I rise up to meet her, grinding my hips against her leather-clad legs. She shifts her weight, presses a knee between my legs, and then I'm gasping as she presses weight against my center, as my wetness connects with the leather. She angles her body, shimmies out of the pants, and then it's her own hot center against my own as she rises up and over me like a goddess, her bright blue eyes flashing as she stares down at me for a long moment, pressed on top of me.

"What have you done to me, Holly?" she whispers, lowering herself so that her breasts press against mine, her hips against mine as I cry out, as she begins to rhythmically, hypnotically, pulse her hips against my own. "I am undone by you," she growls into my ear, and then she captures my mouth with her own again as I open myself to her, to her hand that inches its way over my belly and into the deepness of me. I cry out against her, arch myself against her, as she holds me tightly, as she curves her fingers inside of me, as she presses her mouth to my mouth, to my heart, to my skin and over every inch of my body. We move together seamlessly, like we have always moved this way, and time outside of us stands still.

When I come, she is kissing me fiercely, and I am open to her utterly, to this beautiful warrior woman I could never have dreamed up, but who holds me close, tenderly, as I ride through the waves of bliss she caused in me.

"Love," she whispers to me, holding my gaze with impossibly blue eyes.

"Love," I whisper weakly, brushing my lips against her own as I shiver beneath her, held in the sanctuary of her arms.

It is in that moment that I know, no matter what happens after now, this heartbeat, I know that I have been utterly happy. Utterly loved.

I hold her gaze as I trace my fingers over her hard, muscular shoulders. It's my turn, now. I hold her gaze as her eyes roll back, as she moans lowly as my hand finds her wetness.

I touch her bravely, daring in these moments, to show her all that I've felt, all that I've been unable to express until now.

Chapter 14: Hunter and Hunted

I wake up to the sound of my cell phone ringing somewhere downstairs inside my purse. I sigh out, open my eyes, and then I'm acutely aware of the fact that Virago has her arms wrapped around me tightly, that she's fast asleep, breathing softly and evenly, her taut stomach rising up and down. That we're naked, tangled together.

Oh, my God…it happened. It actually *happened*.

I stare at her for a long moment before I glance at the clock. It's only five. We agreed with Carly and Aidan—and, by proxy, Aidan's coven—to meet together at six down on the pier, which means we should be leaving in half an hour. But still, I can't bring myself to wake her. Not yet.

In sleep, Virago's features are softened. She's gorgeous, commanding, passionate in real life, but when she's asleep, the harder edges are filed away, and she just looks beautiful. Perhaps even vulnerable as her face softens gently. I trace the contour of her high cheekbones with my gaze, of her full mouth, and the pulse that beats rhythmically upon her neck. I take in the wonder of this perfect creature, and I would maintain my gaze, memorize every inch of her…if my damn cell phone didn't keep beeping insistently downstairs.

With a sigh, I extricate myself as gently as I can

from her embrace. She continues to sleep, though her eyelids flutter. I know for a fact that she's a very light sleeper, and my heart beats a little faster to realize how comfortable she must feel with me to not wake up.

It's heartbreaking in that moment, as I stare down at her and wonder if I'll ever have this opportunity again to watch her sleep, to wake up after making love to the wonder that is Virago.

I swallow, take a deep breath, force myself to get up. I grab my robe from the foot of my bed and slip into it, gazing back at her one last time.

I tell myself: no matter what, you've had this. You've had this moment. But it doesn't help the pain.

My heart is breaking as I slowly descend the staircase. As I reach my purse and pull out my phone.

Five missed calls from Carly. I sigh, hit "send" on her most recent call. I glance up, surprised that Shelley isn't begging to be fed, when I glance at the shut sliding glass door with wide eyes. Oh, my goodness, I forgot to let Shelley in before we headed upstairs. She's still outside. I cross the living room and open the back door, whistle out for her.

There are dark clouds encroaching along the horizon, and what was once clear blue sky about an hour ago has turned ominous and black above our neighborhood. I frown and stare up at it as I whistle for Shelley again.

"You've reached Carly's cell! Leave a message, I'll get back to you," chirps out from my cell phone.

"Hey, Carly, it's me…sorry I missed your calls." I smile into the phone as I head out down the back steps. "Uh. Call me back, okay?" I end the call, slip my cell phone into my pocket, glance up.

Around the corner of the pile of what *used* to be

my shed looks like Shelley. It's her white-gold fur anyway. "Shelley, honey!" I call to her, whistle again. That's not like her. The shape moves away, around the corner of that big patch of shrubs out back. The gate to my neighbor's yard is behind the shrubs, and I worry for a moment, wonder if my neighbor Clark left it open between our yards, but then my cell phone is buzzing in my pocket. I make my way across the lawn, grumbling to myself as I fish the phone out, accept the call and press it to my ear.

"Holly? Oh, my God, Holly?"

My heart's in my throat. It's Carly, and she sounds panicked. I've *never* heard her sound like this before. There's terror in her voice.

"Carly, what's wrong, are you all right?" I yell into the phone.

I hear a *creak* from behind the shrubs. Dammit, the gate must have been left open.

"Holly!" There's static on the line, the call drops for a moment, but then I hear: "...it's there!"

"What?" I say into the phone, walk around the shrubs.

"Holly!" says Carly, shouting every syllable: "the beast left the water! It made its way through the neighborhood! It was just spotted on your *street!*"

I feel all of the air leave me as I stare at the shape on the ground behind the shrubs.

It's Shelley. She has a gash in her side. My precious dog's blood is leaking out onto the ground.

"Holly, can you hear me? The beast is coming for Virago!"

The line goes dead. The line goes dead because the phone is falling out of my hand. Because I rush to my dog's side, lift her beautiful little head into my lap as a sob chokes itself out of me. Her eyelids flutter, and then close, Shelley's head falling limply into my lap.

A shadow falls over me. Even though the sky is dark enough for me to wonder if it's still day, a shadow still falls over me from behind my neighbor's fence.

I look up…and up…and up…into the face of a monster.

It's enormous. Taller than a house, taller than my neighbor's house, I realize in the back of my mind as it towers over me. It has spikes along its leathery spine, and it's standing on its back legs as wide as tree trunks. It looks a little like Godzilla, if all of his features were larger and much more threatening and pointy, and as it opens its mouth, as its razor sharp teeth, longer than my arm, I think dully in the back of my head, it lets out a sound that no low-budget Godzilla movie could ever duplicate.

This is a scream and a moan and a growl and a screech, all rolled into one. It hisses at me, and the spines along its back flatten as it narrows its eyes and bares its teeth down at me.

I stare up at this beast, this monster, as I hold my dying dog in my arms. I hate that beast so much in that instant that white, hot rage burns me through stronger than the fear. This *thing* hurt my dog. It's going to hurt me, but before it hurts me, it hurt this beautiful, innocent dog that I've loved with my whole heart ever since the day I met her as this ridiculous little puppy who wagged her tail at me the second she saw me, and has never stopped wagging it since.

The creature opens its mouth and lets out a scream again, and I realize that my body is shaking as I hold Shelley tightly.

I realize I'm going to die. It's going to lunge at

me, sink its teeth in me, and it's going to hurt so much. God, I don't want to die. I don't want it to hurt like this.

I stare up at that monster, and fear fills me like water, rushing into every part of me as I hold tightly to my dog.

"Stand and face me, beast!"

I and the beast turn at that, and striding across the lawn toward us is Virago. She's holding her sword aloft with cold, clear anger etched hard on her face. As I stare at her, I realize that she's only wearing her leather shirt and her leather pants. Her armor is on the floor of my bedroom.

Panic consumes me as Virago lengthens her stride, as she trains her piercing blue gaze onto the beast. "Virago, don't!" I scream, but then Virago is in front of me, shielding me and Shelley from the beast.

She's an amazing warrior. I know this. But her armor is on the floor of my bedroom.

Virago could die.

"Please don't," I tell her, lifting Shelley up with some difficulty. The beast hasn't moved, is simply standing there, narrowed eyes calculating as it stares at us. "Please don't," I tell her again, a sob making the words come out small, but Virago's arm is around me tightly as she pushes me behind her, as she stands straight and tall, holding the sword in a challenge up to the beast.

Shelley wiggles a little in my arms, glancing up at me then with actually open eyes. I stare down at my dog, then back up at the beast, shock and terror making everything seem extra sharp and more real, somehow.

The claws that come out of the sky are attached to a massive paw, a paw that's as wide as Virago is tall.

It swipes at Virago and me and Shelley, but misses somehow, because Virago's arm around me tightens, and then she's lifting me and Shelley in one arm, and moving us across the lawn.

I stumble a little when she sets me down as gently as possible, turning and swinging the sword up at the last possible moment to block the attack. There are sparks where the claws and the blade meet, and then Virago is pushed backward, toppling backward, rolling across the lawn as the beast swipes at her again.

It wasn't supposed to be like this. We were all supposed to rent a boat and do a calm, peaceful meditation out on the water and open the portal and send the beast to a place between worlds and send Virago home. It was supposed to be practically *serene*. No one was supposed to get hurt.

It's not supposed to happen like this.

But it is.

I scream. I find my voice, and I'm shrieking as the beast turns suddenly, moving too quickly for sight as it swipes its barbed and deadly tail at Virago. Virago rolls out of the way, falling heavily on her shoulder, just in time, but she's slower getting up this time as she rises, holding the sword tightly in front of her and panting. The beast grapples forward, lunging and crawling on all fours over my neighbor's fence (flattening it in the process with a shriek of broken wood). The beast swings again with its barbed tail, and Virago rolls to the right...

Under the beast's claws.

Virago makes no sound as the claws rip through the leather of her shirt, piercing up and into her ribs.

The beast lifts up its paw and its claws, Virago dangling on the end of them, her stomach pierced through.

I'm screaming as the beast throws Virago to the ground, as it makes its own triumphant sounds, turning its gaze now on me. But I don't even see it. I run over to Virago with Shelley in my arms, set my dog onto the ground as gently as I can as I cradle Virago to me. Virago's eyelashes flutter, and her eyes close, blood pulsing and pumping out of the wounds in her stomach out and onto the ground.

Overhead, lightning arches, brightening up everything like a strobe light.

The beast makes a terrible sound, part scream of defiance, part roar.

The sword lies in the grass beside Virago's limp hand. She's unconscious. Perhaps she's dying. I don't know. But the woman I love with my whole heart saved me, and now she's giving her life for it.

It wasn't supposed to be like this.

I stare up at the monster, tears making everything blurry as I set Virago's head gently down onto the grass. I grasp the hilt of the sword with two hands, but even holding it in two hands, it's practically impossible for me to lift it up, it's so heavy. But there's adrenaline pulsing through me now, and I lift it up, manage to hold it level with my heart as I point it at the beast.

If I didn't know better, I would think it's laughing at me as it throws its head back, as it shrieks again.

I'm going to die. But I'm not going to die like this, with my lover bleeding at my feet, my dog dying in my backyard.

I'm going to die causing this beast at least a shred of the pain it caused me.

I don't even go to the gym, but adrenaline is still moving through me with every pulse, and that's what gives me the courage to move forward now. And I do. I lunge forward as quickly as I'm able, swinging the sword around.

I don't think the beast was expecting anything from me. Because it didn't move when I moved. It stays perfectly still as I slam into it.

I bury the sword in its stomach. I bury the sword all the way up to the hilt. It felt like I was stabbing into something soft and pillowy...the beast had scales, I realize, staring at where the sword pierced through. And the sword pierced it in the softest place possible.

Its weak spot.

Overhead, lightning arches across the sky again as the beast tilts back its head, screaming in agony as it begins to writhe in front of me.

I hold onto the sword for all I'm worth as the beast scrabbles with its claws, but its writhing is growing weaker.

I hold onto the sword, panting, until the beast doesn't move anymore, as its head slumps down onto the ground, and it twitches beneath the sword.

And then something even stranger happens.

I'm still clinging to the sword, but it begins to fall out of the beast. Because the beast simply isn't there anymore.

For a single moment, there's a glowing light that's so bright, I can't see anything at all. But then I can make out the fact that there's a woman lying on the ground in front of me, the sword sticking out of her side.

She has long black hair that's matted and

tangled, and she appears to be wearing animal skins stitched into a crude dress. She has the palest skin I've ever seen, and when she opens her eyes to look at me, I take a step backward.

They're jet black, those eyes. There aren't any pupils or irises...her entire eye is as black as the night sky.

She opens her thin lips and moans. I keep holding onto the sword because I don't know what else to do.

"Be merciful," says the woman in a sibilant hiss, then. "Kill me."

"Who are you?" I say, my voice shaking but my grip on the sword still strong.

The woman casts me an almost disgusted glance. "I am Cower," she whispers, drawing out the word with a half-snarl. "And I was once a Goddess. But I have been a beast for so long, and now this...I have been defeated by a mewling woman. Kill me. I cannot bear the shame."

Anger rakes its way through me, but I continue to grip onto the hilt of the sword, cast a glance back at Virago. I can see her chest rising and falling weakly. She's still alive. But she's losing so much blood. Shelley is breathing, too. They're both still alive.

I don't know what to do.

"Why are you in...uh...human form now?" I hazard to Cower. The woman gives me another disgusted look.

"I become what I truly am when I am vanquished," she says, like she's reciting rules from some rulebook. "Finish me off, mortal. I can't bear this."

I stare down at her for a long moment. Virago

might die. The woman I love with my whole heart is bleeding in front of me. I should kill this creature...this woman, I guess. This beast. She's done so much harm.

But I'm no killer. I did what I had to do to save Virago. I'm not going to have anyone's blood on my hands.

"No," I tell her. And then I jerk the sword out of her stomach. Cower makes a gurgling sound as I toss the sword into the middle of my backyard. I move away from her, crouch down next to Virago, tears beginning to leak out of my eyes.

"Virago," I whisper, cradling her head into my arms, pressing my lips to her cold forehead. Virago's *never* cold. Something is terribly wrong. "Virago..." I say, but then I'm weeping, choking out the syllables of her name over and over again as I hold her to me as tightly as I can.

She's dying. I can feel her dying in my arms, can feel all of her strength, all of her *life* leaving her.

"Virago, just use the magic..." I whisper to her, taking a deep breath. "Please use the magic to make yourself better. You can make yourself better. *Please*."

From somewhere far away, I can hear voices. Yelling. People running across the lawn toward us.

Carly skids to a stop next to me. And Aidan, too, my brother paling immediately upon seeing the sight of so much blood, blood that continues to stream out of Virago's middle, soaking the lawn beneath her.

Suddenly, I know what to do. It's the slightest chance, but it's the only possible thing I can think of. The only thing I can think of that might save her.

"Aidan," I tell him, gritting my teeth as I choke down another sob. "Can you make the circle appear? Can you make the portal?"

He stares at me, eyes wide, already shaking his head. "I don't know, Holly...God, maybe? The rest of the coven members are going to get here soon, and I don't know if I can do it without them...anyway, why do you want the circle? Where's the beast?"

I shake my head. "The beast is a woman now. Like in the story Virago told us," I tell him when he stares at me blankly. I jerk my chin toward the woman lying in the grass, paling as blood pools out of *her* side, too. "Listen, this isn't about her," I tell him quickly. "Virago's dying. She won't wake up. She healed herself before, right? If we can get her to her knights, they can probably heal her." He stares at me with confusion, and I shake my head again. "Aidan, it's the only way. She's dying. I can feel her *dying*," I whisper. "She needs help."

He rubs his face, takes a deep breath. "Okay. I mean, *maybe* I can make the portal appear. I don't know. But you'll have to help me, you need to concentrate, too. Carly, concentrate. Imagine a big white circle on the grass, okay?"

"Like, white light, or just a white circle?" asks Carly, her voice strained.

"Don't be so literal about it," Aidan mutters. "Just imagine a glowing white circle on the grass, okay?"

I close my eyes and imagine the glowing portal we saw before. It might not work. God, it might not work at all. There might not be a portal, and even if there *is* a portal, why would the knights still be waiting in the field for her, and even if the knights *are* waiting in the field for her, what makes me think that they can heal her?

I think about Virago. I think about her

standing tall and strong in front of me. I think of kissing Virago. I think of her smile and her laughter. I think of her kindness and her grace.

She is the most amazing person I've ever met in my entire life.

She can't die. Not like this. She deserves a beautiful, quiet death at an extremely old age, after having a million adventures. I want to have a million adventures by her side. I want to be with her for my entire life, I want to spend all my days with her.

She deserves a full life.

She deserves to *live*.

Behind my tightly closed eyes, I begin to see a light…

I open my eyes with a gasp. There's the portal in the middle of my lawn, a circling, glowing door of light. Aidan crawls over to the edge of it and stares down and in.

"Oh, hello," he says, with a grimace. "Um…you're friends of Virago's, right?"

"We are," comes the commanding voice from one of the female knights. I recognize that voice. Was her name Magel? "Where is Virago?" she asks firmly. "Where is the beast?"

"Well, uh," says Aidan with a shrug. I can tell he's desperately nervous. "Um, Virago's hurt," he says, speaking too quickly, that nervousness making his words short. "She needs your help. And, uh, apparently the beast is now a woman?"

"Virago's hurt? How so?" snarls the woman.

Carly helps me move Virago gently, or, really, as gently as we can. She takes up Virago's boots, and I try to pull Virago by her shoulders. We get her over to the edge of the portal.

There, about six feet down, is the other world. The scent of meadow assaults me, but the scent of sweet grass and bright flowers is stronger now because oddly enough, it's day there now, not night, and the sunshine is so bright, it's almost blinding. Magel stands with her feet planted wide, hands on her hips as she stares up in trepidation, until she sees Virago.

"Oh, Goddess," she murmurs, breathing out, her face stricken.

"Can you help her?" I ask, tears streaming over my cheeks, falling gently onto Virago's face. She doesn't move. She doesn't stir. She's hardly breathing anymore.

The woman glances to me, then back to Virago again. "I do not know. But we will try." She holds up her arms.

As gently as we can, we push Virago down and into the waiting arms of her fellow knight. As we do so, though, the pulsing white of the circle begins to falter around us.

"Quickly!" Magel shouts. "The beast! Send down the beast!"

We gather up Cower, though—admittedly—a bit less delicately, and throw her down onto the ground, where she staggers up to her hands and knees, coughing up blood.

"This one will be well," says Magel with a shake of her head and a sneer as she turns away from Cower. "And Virago—"

The portal falters again, the scene before us fading in and out.

"Please concentrate, Aidan," I mutter to him, and he's nodding.

But, from one instant to the next, the light goes

out. And in that instant, the circle is gone. It's just...gone. It's as if there was never a circle on my lawn to begin with.

"What?" I ask, shock making my body shake. I crawl forward, I thrust my fingers into the grass, press down against the earth, tears streaming down my face. "Oh, my God, no...Virago...Aidan, please, can you bring it back?"

"I'm really trying, Holly," murmurs Aidan, eyes wide as sweat begins to appear on his brow. "I'm trying *really* hard. But I just...I can't, nothing's happening. What if I can't make the portal appear without Virago?"

Panic begins to consume me. "No, no, no...she could be dead. I have to see her," I tell him, shaking his shoulders. "She could be *dead*," I whisper.

Aidan grips my arms tightly, shaking his head again as a single tear leaks out of his eye and makes its way down his cheek.

"Holly, I'm so sorry," he whispers, searching my face, his eyes wide. "I'm *so* sorry. I don't think I can open the portal again."

He's right. Even when the coven members arrive, even when they concentrate, sitting in my backyard for an entire half hour, hands linked and joined together, absolutely nothing happens. Nothing appears. There is no circle of light, no doorway to another world, no meadow and flowers and knights.

No Virago. And there is no portal.

Aidan and Carly give me a tight embrace and hold me close as I sob.

Virago could be dead. She could be alive.

But I'll never know.

Because she's gone.

Chapter 15: Remember Me

That night I spend in the waiting room of the emergency vet as they operate on Shelley. I cry in the waiting room, cry and don't care who sees me, Carly holding tightly to my hand and watching me with a pained expression as I weep into box after box of tissues.

Shelley lives. It's a miracle, the vet tells me. They send her home with a cone, antibiotics and pain pills. I lift her into my bed at eight o'clock in the morning, and curling around my dog, we both fall into an exhausted, dreamless sleep.

I wake up, halfway through the day. I give Shelley her pills, don't even have to give them to her in peanut butter. She takes them obediently from my hand, flopping her tail weakly on my bed as she stares up at me with soft brown eyes. I'll have to wash the blankets from her wound dressing, but I don't really care.

My dog is alive. It's really the only thing I care about at this point.

Honestly, I don't care about much else. Because everything else is too painful to think about.

There are messages from Carly on my phone. A few messages from Aidan. He's called another emergency meeting of the coven, trying to get them to open the portal again. He apologizes over and over again in his texts. It's not his fault. I tell him that in a text back, put my phone back into my purse, stare out at my destroyed backyard.

Weeks pass. Time goes on, caring little for the pain I feel, caring little for my broken heart.

Did Virago live? Is she alive somewhere, somewhere impossibly far away?

Then, as more weeks pass, I half wonder if all of this was a dream.

But it wasn't. I know it wasn't. Because Wolfslayer remained in my backyard, that beautiful sword that Virago loved so much. I dragged it in. I washed it off, polished it. I set it gently on the couch.

Every time I wonder if it was a dream, I wonder if Virago ever even existed…I go and I sit down next to that sword. And then I curl my hand over the hilt, holding it as tightly as I can.

It's real.

Virago was real.

Please, please, please let Virago be alive.

That's what my life is now. I go to work. I walk Shelley. I read books, and I slip into the stories, because it's the only escape I have from the heartbreak that is my life. And I think, over and over again: *Please, please, please let Virago be alive.*

That's what my life is now…until one night. One late July night.

A night to remember…

"Honestly, I don't care, Carly," I tell her gently, cradling the phone between my chin and shoulder—no small feat with a slim smart phone.

"I really wish you *would* care," my best friend grumbles. I proceed to chop the carrots against the cutting board, sigh as I swipe them off into the boiling pot on the stove.

"You and David can show up whenever you want. You could come over now. Whenever you want is fine," I assure her, giving a quick stir with the wooden spoon.

"I'm sorry I invited us over—" Carly begins, but I clear my throat.

"Hey, I appreciate that you did," I tell her quietly, stir the boiling water again. "I mean, I know I'm kind of a homebody these days. I just..." I trail off, hold the spoon poised over the water as I gaze out the window at my backyard. The divots that the beast made out of the earth were carefully pressed back into the grass by Carly and her boyfriend, David. The broken boards of the shed were taken away on David's flatbed truck. My neighbor Clark repaired the fence between our properties.

Honestly, my backyard looks like nothing ever happened in it.

But I know better.

"It'll get better, honey," says Carly quietly. "I promise it'll get better."

"Yeah," I say, the word coming out a little strangled as emotion chokes me. "Just...whenever you get here is fine," I tell her with false brightness. "I have to finish making the soup base, okay?"

"Soup in July?" asks Carly, mystified.

"You know my love for chopping vegetables," I tell her, and she actually chuckles at that.

"We'll be there in a half hour," she tells me, and she hangs up.

Shelley lies patiently in the center of the kitchen, waiting for her third meal of the day with a forlorn nose on crossed paws. I pat her head absent-mindedly as I cross the kitchen to throw the leftover carrots into their bag in the crisper in the fridge. I straighten, holding a heart of celery, consider the rest of my fridge. I think about what else I have to put into this soup base. Maybe some thyme. Yes, a pinch of thyme would be really good, it'd go well with the flavors, I think.

Out in the backyard there's an odd flash of light, like a spark.

I stare out the window into the backyard.

For a moment, a long moment, I know that what I'm seeing can't possibly be real. It can't possibly be real because I've wanted it so much and so badly. I've dreamed of this moment every night, I've thought about this moment every heartbeat of each day that's gone by...

It can't possibly be real.

I grip the edge of the counter, feel the solidity beneath the palm of my hand, feel the water from the carrots that pooled on the counter, feel the floor beneath my feet.

It's real. This is real.

The celery falls from my hands to the floor.

It's impossible, what I'm seeing. But it's true.

She's here.

Virago.

I'm running out of the kitchen, through my living room, and out my sliding glass door. My knight strides across my backyard, clad in new armor, a new leather shirt and pants and boots, but the only thing I really see, the only thing I have eyes for, is her eyes, her bright, flashing eyes that consume me utterly.

Her smile is so brilliant, it eclipses the sun.

We collide, she and I, her arms wrapped tightly around me, spinning me around and around as her mouth finds mine. We kiss together, my arms around her neck, holding her close like I don't really believe she's here, as if I don't really believe this is happening, as if I'll never, ever let her go again. The warmth of her mouth on my own—it's real. The softness of her mouth, her tongue...all of this is real. I don't really believe this is happening...

But it is. The scent of sandalwood and leather rises all around me, her ink-black hair pools over my hands, and her full, warm mouth covers my own.

Virago is *alive*.

My entire body sings where it presses against her. Shelley is barking joyfully, bouncing around us when I disengage from the kiss, not because I want to, but because I need to look her in her eyes, just...just to make certain that this moment is actually happening, I suppose. I need to be grounded in this moment, in this moment I imagined over and over but could never dare hope for. I press my forehead against hers, feel a sob begin to tear through me, but I shake my head, hold her tighter.

"You're alive," I whisper, the words coming out in a hush. I'm almost afraid to speak them, as if speaking will destroy the magic between us.

But nothing can destroy the magic of this moment. "I'm alive," she whispers back, "thanks to you." My toes curl in pleasure at the sound of that perfect voice, her words low and gravelly and full of velvet as she practically purrs, lifting me up again so that my mouth meets hers, her arms wrapped strongly about my waist, holding me tenderly but with such strength that my feet leave the ground.

"How did you find me?" I whisper breathlessly, then, when she sets me down gently, when her mouth moves down, down to my cheek and my chin and my neck. She straightens, looking down earnestly into my face, searching my gaze, her bright blue eyes piercing me deeply as she gazes into the very heart of me.

"You call to me," she says, lifting my hands to her mouth so that she can press a kiss to the back of each of them, her warm lips brushing over my skin and making me shiver in delight. Her low tone is a growl as she breathes the words against my skin: "And my heart answered you."

Overhead, the very first star edges its way out of a purple sky, drowsy and swinging low to the west. A waning moon, bright and beautiful, dips toward the horizon.

And far, far down below, on a planet I always thought was perfectly normal, my dog barks and makes crazy circles around us, bounding joyfully around her two favorite humans.

And my knight in shining armor literally sweeps me off my feet.

I honestly don't know what the future holds or what lies ahead of us. But I do know that there will be more adventures than I can even imagine.

And we'll build our story together.

The End

The sequel to *A Knight to Remember* is out now!

Date Knight continues Holly and Virago's adventures—are you ready to follow along with them? Just search for "Date Knight, Bridget Essex" wherever you buy your books!

Acknowledgements

A Knight to Remember has been with me for a very long time. I wrote the rough draft of the novel many years ago, and then simply held on to it. I write mostly paranormal stories, and *A Knight to Remember,* while being firmly entrenched in this world, was more fantastical than paranormal. I loved writing it so much, but I held onto it.

One night, while having dinner with one of my dearest friends, author P.J. Bryce, P.J. and my wife, Natalie, were talking. "Hey, whatever happened with that knight book you wrote?" asked P.J.

I told her that I'd done nothing with it. She was scandalized by that. "It's good!" she said. "You should publish it!"

"But it's so unlike anything else I've written," I told her worriedly. Natalie and P.J. both shook their heads. "Publish it," they said. And because they thought I should, I did. I trust their opinions deeply, and—without them—this book would still be collecting dust. You two are the most wonderful women I've ever been blessed to know. Thank you for encouraging me to put out this story. :) And for the wonderful dinner!

Honestly, being a writer is a very lonely endeavor. I spend so much time in my head that the encouragement and support that I've been given by the people who love my stories is humbling and wonderful. I could *not* do what I do without the emails, the Facebook posts and the incredibly supportive community I've found. You are wonderful people, and I'm so utterly grateful for you! Thank you for loving my stories, my ladies and my words. :)

As always, Terri inspires me every day to keep telling the best stories I'm able. Thank you so much for your support and encouragement, friend. I'm grateful for you! Marian and Ruby are precious to me—I love you ladies so much!

And to the one I cherish most: Natalie, you make my life beautiful. I love you, I love you, I love you. Thank you for sharing this journey with me. Every day, we build our story together. Je t'aime, chérie.